THE VAMPIRE QUEEN

K.M.

CONTENT WARNING
THIS BOOK CONTAINS A LOT
OF ADULT THEMES, VIOLENCE,
AND SEXUAL ACTS.

To my friends,

You are not forgotten.
I must come to terms with my own
mistakes to tell your story full.
While the story within these pages will be
lost, you would know these events well.
The best death is written with a truth
laden with the trauma of the fallen.
Rest easy my friends, for your story will
be told.
First I must learn not to see you in my
dreams.
I must learn to not think of your families
who looked to me as I departed.
I must learn to let go.
I must learn to forgive myself.
I just need to know you forgive me as
well.
Though you may look down upon me
from your new home, please know I have
not forgotten you.

-    K.M.

SPC KNIGHT
SFC BANNERMAN
SGT ALVIS
SGT LUTZ
SPC BENTER
SSG CONNER
PFC LADD
PFC MARQUIS
PFC CHILDERS
SPC LANE
SPC CASTRO
PFC RICA
SFC SIGLOCK
PFC ZOUNEK
SPC KNOPP
SPC WILSON
SPC JOHNSON
SPC BROWN
PFC AUGUSTINE
SSG BEUNING
PFC COGDAL
PFC NELSON
SGT ANDERSON
SPC MOUNTAIN
SSG RICKY
SPC FOULKE
PFC GUERRERO
SGT MICHAELIS
SPC SMITH
LT SATERLINO
PFC KEETER
SGT HILL

PFC SHEPHERD
SPC BOHANNON
SGT BALDUFF
SGT JASSO
SGT MADDOCK

TABLE OF CONTENTS

CHAPTER 1 – A VAMPIRE, A THIEF AND A JESTER WALK INTO A BAR

The copper smell of blood lingered on Alaric's fingers as he dropped the two pairs of human ears onto the wooden table with a wet slap. The village councilmen recoiled, chairs scraping against the stone floor as they pushed back from the grisly trophies.

"The Blackwood Brothers send their regards," Alaric said, his deep voice filling the small chamber. "Or they would, if they still had mouths to speak with."

The head councilman, a portly man named Giles with a gray-streaked beard, leaned forward cautiously to examine the evidence. His nose wrinkled in disgust, but there was relief in his eyes.

"You're certain these belonged to the Blackwood Brothers? Both of them?"

Alaric's hand rested on the obsidian-and-steel hilt of his sword, the blade that had separated those very ears from their owners mere hours ago. "The tall one had the burn scar across his neck, just as described. The other had the fox tattoo on his wrist."

He paused. "I brought that too, if you need further proof."

"Gods, no," another councilman muttered, looking pale. "The ears are... sufficient."

Giles nodded, pulling a leather pouch from beneath the table. "Twenty silver crowns was the agreed price. Ten for each bandit's head." He pushed the pouch across the table, careful to avoid the bloody ears.

Alaric took the pouch without counting it. The weight felt right in his palm. "They won't be troubling your eastern road anymore."

"What of the others?" asked a thin, hawk-nosed councilman at the end of the table. "Their band numbered at least five."

"Three fled when they saw what happened to their leaders," Alaric replied, tucking the payment into his belt. "One toward Mistwood, two north. They won't return."

"How can you be so certain?" The hawk-nosed man's voice carried a note of skepticism.

Alaric's eyes, cold as winter steel, fixed on the questioner. "Because I promised them they'd die slower than their brothers if they ever set foot in Morvain again."

The silence that followed was broken only by the nervous swallow of the youngest councilman.

"The village of Thornhaven owes you a debt, mercenary," Giles said finally, regaining his composure. "Though your methods are... direct."

"You didn't hire me for gentleness," Alaric replied. He turned to leave, then paused at the door. "You should burn those. Before nightfall."

"Why?" Giles asked, eyeing the severed ears with renewed wariness.

"Old superstition," Alaric said with a shrug that suggested it was anything but. "In Morvain, parts of the dead should be returned to fire before the first stars appear. Especially those who died... violently."

As Alaric stepped out into the waning afternoon light, a slender figure detached from the shadows beside the council hall. A woman with copper-red hair tied back in a practical braid, her traveling clothes dusty but well-made.

"Master Thornwood," she called, her voice carrying the refined accent of the capital. "I've been waiting for you."

Alaric's hand instinctively tightened on his sword hilt. Few people knew his full name in these parts, and fewer still would have reason to wait for him.

"Do I know you?" he asked, his voice deliberately neutral.

The woman smiled, a flash of confidence that didn't quite reach her eyes. "No. But I know of you. And I have a proposition that pays considerably better than bandit ears."

Alaric studied the woman, noting the quality leather of her boots and the subtle gleam of a dagger hilt beneath her cloak. No ordinary traveler, then.

"Most propositions that pay 'considerably better' involve considerably more risk," he replied, keeping his distance. "What's your name?"

"Lyra Voss," she said, offering no hand to shake. "I represent a merchant from Adrielkeep who requires safe passage to Ravenscrest."

"Ravenscrest is two days' hard ride through Mistwood territory," Alaric said, his brow furrowing. "The main caravan route would be safer."

Lyra's lips curved in a humorless smile. "If safety were the only concern, yes. But time is of greater importance, and the forest path cuts the journey by a full day."

Alaric glanced toward the setting sun. "The merchant must be carrying something valuable to risk the forest path."

"Fifty silver crowns for two days' work," Lyra countered, ignoring his observation. "Half now, half upon arrival."

The sum made Alaric's recent bandit bounty seem paltry. His eyes narrowed with suspicion.

"What aren't you telling me?" he asked bluntly. "Mistwood's dangers aren't worth fifty crowns unless there's something worse than forest predators to worry about."

Lyra glanced around the village square where townsfolk were beginning to light the iron lanterns against the coming darkness. She stepped closer, lowering her voice.

"My employer carries sensitive documents for Mayor Gray in Ravenscrest. There are... interested parties who would prefer those documents never arrive."

"Bandits?"

"Of a sort," she answered cryptically. "We leave at first light. The merchant will meet us at the eastern gate with the horses."

Alaric crossed his arms. "I haven't agreed yet."

"Sixty crowns, then," Lyra said without hesitation. "And a letter of recommendation to the Ravenscrest Guild of Protectors."

The Guild was notoriously selective, offering steady, lucrative work to its members. Such an introduction would be worth nearly as much as the coin.

"I'll need to know what we're facing," Alaric insisted. "No more half-truths."

"Fair enough," Lyra conceded. "Join us for supper at the Broken Shield. My employer will explain everything."

"And if I don't like what I hear?"

"Then take ten crowns for your time and walk away," she said, producing a small pouch that clinked with the unmistakable sound of silver. "No obligation."

Alaric considered the woman before him. Her offer was generous—suspiciously so—but the promise of Guild connections was tempting. The wandering mercenary life had begun to wear on him, and winter approached.

"The Broken Shield in one hour," he agreed finally. "I'll hear your employer out."

Lyra nodded once, satisfied. "One more thing, Thornwood. Come armed."

She turned and walked away, leaving Alaric with the distinct impression that he was missing crucial pieces of a larger puzzle.

The Broken Shield tavern hummed with activity when Alaric arrived, pushing through the heavy oak door into the warmth and noise within. Smoke from the central hearth hung in the air, mingling with the scents of roasted meat and spilled ale.

He spotted Lyra immediately, seated in the corner beside a slight man with scholar's hands and merchant's clothes. Too fine for a village tavern, too plain for nobility. The merchant's fingers drummed nervously on the table as Alaric approached.

"Master Thornwood," Lyra greeted him, gesturing to an empty chair. "This is Elias Blackwood, my employer."

Alaric froze mid-step. "Blackwood?"

The merchant's eyes widened at Alaric's sudden tension. "Is there a problem?"

"I dispatched two men named Blackwood this morning," Alaric said coldly, his hand moving to his sword hilt.

"The Blackwood Brothers?" Elias laughed, though it held a nervous edge.

"No relation, I assure you. It's a common name in the northern provinces."

"A unfortunate coincidence," Lyra added smoothly. "Please, sit. We have much to discuss."

Alaric took the seat cautiously, eyes never leaving Elias. The tavern noise provided a blanket of privacy for their conversation, but he kept his sword hand free.

"Let's not waste time," Elias said, leaning forward. He withdrew a small wooden box from his cloak, no larger than a man's palm. It was carved with intricate symbols that seemed to shift when Alaric tried to focus on them. "This needs to reach Mayor Gray in Ravenscrest by sunset two days hence."

"What's in it?" Alaric asked bluntly.

Elias slid the box back into his cloak. "The contents aren't your concern. What matters is that it arrives intact and on time."

"You're asking me to risk my life escorting a mystery through Mistwood," Alaric said, his voice hardening. "That makes it very much my concern."

"What's in the box isn't dangerous to you," Lyra interjected. "But it's valuable beyond measure to those who would intercept it."

Elias nodded. "Three days from now is the autumn equinox. Mayor Gray must have this before then, or..." He trailed off, glancing nervously around the tavern.

"Or what?"

"Or people will die," Elias finished simply. "Many people."

Alaric studied the merchant's face, searching for deception. He found fear instead – genuine and deep.

"You understand I can't accept that explanation," Alaric said.

Elias sighed, pushing a small leather sack across the table. The heavy clink of coins was unmistakable. "Thirty crowns now. Thirty upon delivery. And this." He produced a sealed letter bearing the wax impression of the Guild of Protectors.

"Your introduction, as promised."

Alaric left the money untouched. "Who's hunting you?"

"Men in red cloaks," Lyra answered when Elias hesitated. "They bear no insignia, but they're well-armed and well-trained. Not ordinary bandits."

"How many?"

"At least five that we know of," she said. "They've been tracking us since we left the capital."

Alaric's mind calculated distances, terrain, potential ambush points along the forest route. "And you're certain they know you're heading to Ravenscrest?"

"They know our destination," Elias confirmed, "but not our route.

We've spread rumors about taking the northern pass."

"A diversion that won't fool them for long," Alaric noted.

Elias leaned closer, desperation creeping into his voice. "Master Thornwood, I cannot overstate the importance of this delivery. If we fail, the consequences will reach far beyond Ravenscrest."

The tavern door banged open, admitting a cold gust of wind and a trio of travelers. Alaric noted how Elias flinched at the sound, how his hand instinctively covered the pocket holding the mysterious box.

"You're scared," Alaric observed. "And not just of these red-cloaked men."

"Wouldn't you be?" Elias whispered. "Please. I need your sword arm and your knowledge of the forest paths."

Alaric weighed his options. The money was exceptional, the Guild connection valuable. But there was something Elias wasn't telling him – something that made the merchant's hands tremble slightly as he reached for his wine cup.

"If we do this," Alaric said finally, "we follow my rules. We travel light and fast. No unnecessary baggage, no detours."

Relief washed over Elias's face. "Agreed."

"And if we encounter these red-cloaked pursuers..."

"Do whatever is necessary," Lyra said coldly. "They cannot be allowed to take the package."

Alaric nodded slowly, then reached for the coin purse. "First light at the eastern gate. Bring sturdy horses and minimal supplies."

As he rose to leave, Elias caught his sleeve. "One more thing. If something happens to me, you must continue to Ravenscrest. The package must reach Mayor Gray before sunset on the equinox."

"Nothing will happen to you if you follow my lead," Alaric replied.

But as he left the tavern and stepped into the chill night air, a sense of unease settled over him. The stars glittered coldly overhead, and somewhere in the distance, a wolf howled – a lonely sound that echoed his own misgivings.

Whatever was in that small wooden box, it was worth killing for. And people who valued mysterious objects that highly rarely balked at sacrificing those who carried them.

Dawn broke gray and misty over Thornhaven as Alaric approached the eastern gate. His pack was light – dried meat, hard bread, a water skin, and the tools of his trade. The obsidian-and-steel sword hung at his hip, its familiar weight reassuring.

Lyra was already there, checking the girth on three horses. Sturdy mountain stock, built for endurance rather than speed. Good choices for the forest paths.

"Where's your employer?" Alaric asked, noting Elias's absence.

"Finalizing arrangements at the inn," Lyra replied, not looking up from her work. "He'll be here shortly."

Alaric examined the horses with a critical eye. "These animals seem well-chosen for our journey."

"I've made this trip before," she said, finally meeting his gaze. "Though never with such... urgency."

"Urgency has a way of finding us regardless of preparation," Alaric muttered, checking his sword belt.

A shout cut through the morning mist, drawing their attention toward the village square. Elias burst from between two buildings, his face contorted with panic, cloak billowing behind him as he sprinted toward them.

"Ride! We must ride now!" he screamed.

Two figures in crimson cloaks emerged in pursuit, their polished breastplates catching the early light. The royal insignia gleamed on their shoulders — the King's own guardsmen.

"Damn it all," Alaric growled, drawing his obsidian-steel blade in one fluid motion. The dark metal seemed to drink in what little light touched it. "Get on the horses!"

Lyra was already moving, swinging herself into the saddle with practiced ease. "Elias, quickly!"

The merchant scrambled onto his mount, fumbling with the reins as the red-cloaked soldiers closed the distance, their own swords now drawn.

"Thornwood!" one called out. "Stand down! This is royal business!"

Instead of answering, Alaric stepped forward, blade leveled. "Get to Ravenscrest," he commanded without looking back. "I'll find you on the forest path."

"We can't wait—" Lyra began.

"Then don't," Alaric cut her off, advancing toward the soldiers. "Go!"

The thunder of hoofbeats told him they'd obeyed, but there was no time to confirm as the first guardsman lunged, steel flashing in the gray morning light. Alaric parried, the impact jarring his arm. These were no common bandits—these men were trained in the capital's fighting pits.

CHAPTER 2 –

INTO THE FOREST WE GO

"Interfering with the King's justice is treason," the second guard warned, circling to Alaric's left.

"Strange," Alaric replied, keeping both men in his sight. "I wasn't aware justice wore a mask and hunted merchants."

The first guard attacked again, a vicious overhead strike that Alaric sidestepped. His counter-slash caught the man across the forearm, drawing first blood. The guardsman hissed but didn't retreat.

"The package the merchant carries is stolen property," the second guard said, feinting forward. "Royal property."

That gave Alaric pause—just long enough for the wounded guard to lunge again. Their blades met with a screech of metal, faces inches apart over the crossed swords.

"Whatever Elias is paying you," the guard grunted, "the King will double it."

Alaric kicked the man's knee, hearing a satisfying crack as the joint gave way. The guard crumpled with a howl of pain. "I don't break contracts," Alaric replied, turning to face the second man.

But the remaining guardsman was already backing away, eyes darting between Alaric and his fallen comrade. "This isn't over, mercenary. The Red Guard doesn't forget a face."

"Neither do I," Alaric promised darkly.

The guardsman helped his injured companion to his feet, both retreating toward the village square. Alaric knew they'd have horses nearby — this delay wouldn't last long.

He sheathed his sword and broke into a run, heading east along the road Lyra and Elias had taken. The forest path lay two miles ahead, and the Red Guard would be close behind once they regrouped.

As he ran, Alaric's mind churned with questions. Royal property? The Red Guard was the King's elite force, deployed only for matters of crown security. Whatever Elias carried in that small wooden box, it was far more significant than "documents for Mayor Gray."

The morning mist began to burn away under the rising sun, revealing the dark line of Mistwood Forest ahead. Somewhere within those ancient trees, Lyra and Elias were making their way toward Ravenscrest—possibly with more of the Red Guard in pursuit.

Alaric had been hired to protect them. Instead, he'd been left behind to face the King's men alone, with no horse and only half-truths to justify his actions.

"Sixty silver crowns," he muttered to himself as he ran. "This job had better be worth it."

The forest loomed closer, its shadows seeming to reach out like grasping fingers. Mistwood had earned its sinister reputation honestly — travelers who strayed from the path rarely emerged again.

And now Alaric would have to navigate those dangers on foot, hunting for companions who might not even wait for him.

The first trees enveloped him like sentinels, the temperature dropping noticeably beneath their ancient boughs. Alaric slowed his pace, scanning the ground for signs of recent passage. Two sets of hoofprints led deeper into the gloom, following a narrow trail barely visible beneath years of fallen leaves.

He drew his sword again, the obsidian edge gleaming dully in the filtered light. The Red Guard would be following soon, but they weren't the only danger in Mistwood. Not by far.

A branch snapped somewhere to his right, and Alaric froze, listening. The forest had gone silent — no birdsong, no rustling leaves, just the sound of his own breathing.

A whispered argument carried through the trees ahead — familiar voices. Alaric crept forward, keeping low to the ground, his tracking skills making his approach silent. Through a gap in the undergrowth, he spotted them — Lyra and Elias, horses tethered nearby, engaged in heated discussion.

"— can't wait for him," Elias was saying, clutching the wooden box to his chest. "The Red Guard will —"

Alaric burst from the trees in a controlled fury, covering the distance between them in three long strides. Before either could react, his fist connected with Elias's jaw, sending the smaller man sprawling backward into the leaf litter. The wooden box tumbled from his grasp.

In the same motion, Alaric pivoted toward Lyra, his obsidian blade materializing at her throat as she reached for her dagger.

"Don't," he growled.

Blood trickled from Elias's split lip as he stared up in shock. "What in seven hells—"

"The King's Guard," Alaric cut him off, pressing the blade closer to Lyra's throat, "called that box 'royal property.' Said it was stolen." His eyes narrowed. "You're not running from bandits or mercenaries. You're running from the crown itself."

Lyra remained perfectly still, her eyes never leaving Alaric's. "Lower your sword, Thornwood. This isn't what you think."

"Then explain it," he demanded. "Now. Or I'll drag you both back to Thornhaven and collect whatever reward the Red Guard is offering."

Elias pushed himself up on his elbows, wiping blood from his mouth.

"We couldn't tell you the full truth. You wouldn't have helped us."

"I'm not helping you now," Alaric reminded him, sword unwavering. "Start talking."

Lyra took a careful breath. "The box contains a royal seal — the King's personal signet. It was taken from the palace three days ago."

"So you are thieves," Alaric said, his suspicions confirmed.

"No," Elias interrupted, reaching slowly for the fallen box. "We're loyal servants of the crown. The true crown."

Alaric's brow furrowed. "What game are you playing?"

"The King is dead," Lyra said quietly. "Poisoned four days ago. The Red Guard has concealed his death while Lord Varen — the King's brother — secures his claim to the throne."

"That's impossible," Alaric scoffed. "Such news would have spread throughout the kingdom."

Elias held up the box. "Why do you think this is so valuable? Without the royal seal, Lord Varen cannot legitimize his rule. And he cannot forge a new one without revealing the King's death."

"The seal must reach Ravenscrest before the equinox," Lyra continued, her eyes never leaving Alaric's. "Princess Helena is there, unaware of her father's death. If the seal reaches her, she can claim her rightful place before Varen consolidates power."

Alaric's sword remained steady, but doubt crept into his mind. "Why should I believe you?"

"Because the Red Guard tried to bribe you rather than arrest you," Lyra pointed out. "They can't afford witnesses or questions. Not yet."

Elias struggled to his feet. "Kill us if you must, Thornwood. But deliver the seal to Princess Helena. The fate of Morvain depends on it."

The forest seemed to hold its breath as Alaric weighed their words. Slowly, he lowered his sword, though he didn't sheath it.

"If you're lying," he said finally, "I'll kill you myself."

Relief washed over Elias's face. "Thank you."

"Don't thank me yet," Alaric warned, wiping Elias's blood from his knuckles. "We're still being hunted by the Red Guard, and Mistwood doesn't suffer fools or liars. We need to move."

"There's a woodsman's cabin half a day's ride deeper in," Lyra offered. "We can rest the horses there."

Alaric nodded grimly. "I'll take the seal."

Elias hesitated, clutching the box tighter. "I was entrusted with—"

"You've proven yourself a target," Alaric cut him off. "And I'm tired of being kept in the dark. The seal stays with me, or our arrangement ends here."

After a tense moment, Elias surrendered the box. Alaric tucked it into his belt pouch, feeling the weight of responsibility settle over him like a shroud.

"If we survive this," he said, mounting the spare horse they'd brought, "you both have much to answer for."

"If we survive this," Lyra replied with a grim smile, "the answers won't matter. We'll either be heroes or traitors, depending on who sits the throne."

As they urged their horses deeper into Mistwood's embrace, Alaric couldn't shake the feeling that he'd been drawn into something far larger than a simple escort mission. The forest closed in around them, swallowing their small party in shadow and silence, while somewhere behind, the Red Guard followed — hunters with the resources of a kingdom at their disposal.

And all for a small wooden box that might determine the future of Morvain itself.

The silence of the forest path stretched between the three riders, broken only by the steady rhythm of hooves on packed earth and the occasional snap of branches overhead. The dense canopy filtered the midday sun into dappled patterns that shifted across their faces as they rode single file through the narrowing trail.

"You handle that blade like you were born with it in your hand," Lyra observed, breaking the uneasy quiet. Her voice carried forward to where Alaric led their small procession, his broad shoulders tense with vigilance.

Alaric didn't turn. "Most children where I'm from were given wooden swords before they could walk. I simply never put mine down."

"And where exactly is 'where you're from'?" Elias asked, his scholarly curiosity momentarily overcoming his nervousness. "Your accent doesn't place you from any particular province of Morvain."

Alaric ducked beneath a low-hanging branch. "That's because I'm not from any particular province. My mother was a camp follower with the King's Army. I grew up wherever the troops were stationed."

"A soldier's son," Lyra mused. "That explains the discipline."

"It explains nothing," Alaric corrected her flatly. "My father was a deserter who fled before I was born. The discipline came later, and at considerable cost."

The bitterness in his voice silenced them for several minutes. The horses picked their way around a fallen log, forcing them to navigate single file through a particularly dense stretch of underbrush.

When they emerged into a slightly wider section of trail, Elias urged his mount forward until he was riding abreast with Alaric.

"How does one become a mercenary with such... particular skills?" he asked, his eyes darting nervously between Alaric's impassive face and the obsidian-steel sword at his hip. "The Red Guard recognized you by name."

A muscle twitched in Alaric's jaw. "I served in the King's infantry for eight years. Rose to captain of a special scouting unit."

"And then?" Lyra prompted from behind them.

"And then I learned that following orders without question has consequences I wasn't willing to live with." His hand tightened on the reins. "A village in the borderlands, suspected of harboring rebels. We were ordered to make an example of it."

The implication hung in the air between them.

"You refused?" Elias guessed.

"Worse." Alaric's voice had gone flat. "I obeyed. Every last detail." He paused, his eyes scanning the trail ahead. "Two days later, I deserted. Been taking private contracts ever since."

"That explains why the Red Guard knew you," Lyra said quietly. "A deserter with your skills would be in their records."

Alaric gave a humorless laugh. "They've tried to recruit me more than once. The Red Guard prefers to employ men who've proven they can do terrible things without hesitation."

"Yet you turned them down," Elias observed.

"I choose my own sins now." Alaric pointed to a barely visible fork in the path ahead. "We go left here. The right trail leads to a bog that's swallowed more than its share of travelers."

As they guided their horses onto the left-hand path, Lyra urged her mount forward until she rode at Alaric's other side. "If you despise the crown's methods, why help us restore the rightful heir? Princess Helena was raised by the same king who ordered that village destroyed."

Alaric's expression darkened. "I don't know the Princess. But I know Lord Varen. Three years ago, I took a contract protecting a nobleman's daughter who caught his eye. The things he did to the servants who tried to shield her..." He trailed off. "Let's just say I'd rather take my chances with unknown royalty than a known monster."

The forest seemed to close in around them as they rode deeper, the trees growing older and more gnarled. Shadows lengthened despite the midday hour, and the air grew noticeably colder.

"We're entering the old heart of Mistwood now," Alaric warned, his hand resting on his sword hilt. "Keep your voices low and your eyes open. This part of the forest has ears—and teeth."

"You seem to know these woods well," Elias observed, his voice dropping to a whisper.

"I've escorted hunters and trappers through here," Alaric replied. "Not all threats in Mistwood wear red cloaks or carry swords."

"What else should we watch for?" Lyra asked, her own hand moving to the dagger at her belt.

Before Alaric could answer, a piercing howl echoed through the trees—too deep and resonant to be a mere wolf. The horses shifted nervously, ears flicking back and forth.

"That," Alaric said grimly, "would be our first concern."

"Wolves?" Elias whispered, his face pale.

"If we're lucky." Alaric urged his horse to a faster pace. "We need to reach the cabin before dusk. After nightfall, we'd be fortunate to face only wolves."

"What exactly lives in these woods?" Lyra demanded, scanning the deepening shadows.

"Nothing natural," Alaric replied. "Not anymore. The old stories say Mistwood was once a battlefield where blood-magic was unleashed. The trees drank it up, and the creatures that survived were... changed."

Another howl sounded, closer this time, followed by a second from a different direction.

"They're coordinating," Alaric muttered. "Hunting us."

"How far to the cabin?" Elias asked, clutching the reins so tightly his knuckles had gone white.

"Too far to outrun what's following us," Alaric said grimly. He drew his obsidian-steel sword, the blade seeming to absorb the forest shadows.

"We make our stand at the clearing ahead. Back-to-back, horses in the center."

As they emerged into a small break in the trees, Alaric dismounted in one fluid motion. "Quickly now. Elias in the middle."

Lyra slid from her saddle with the grace of someone trained in combat, drawing both her dagger and a short sword that had been concealed beneath her cloak. "You've fought these things before?" she asked.

"Once," Alaric confirmed, positioning himself to face the direction of the howls. "Only the obsidian-steel will cut them cleanly. Aim for the throat or eyes."

"And if we miss?" Elias asked, fumbling with a small crossbow from his saddlebag.

Alaric's grim smile held no humor. "Then pray to whatever gods you follow that death comes quickly."

The forest had gone completely silent, not even the rustle of leaves disturbing the unnatural stillness. Then came the sound of branches breaking as something large moved through the underbrush toward them.

"Remember," Alaric said quietly, "no matter what you see, no matter what they say—they are not human. Not anymore."

From the shadows of the ancient trees, a figure emerged—walking upright like a man but moving with the fluid grace of a predator. Its skin was gray-blue and stretched too tight across an elongated face. When it smiled, too many teeth gleamed in the fading light.

"Well met, travelers," it called in a voice like stones grinding together. "What brings you to our woods so close to nightfall?"

"Just passing through," Alaric replied evenly, his blade steady before him. "We seek no quarrel with the forest or its inhabitants."

The creature circled them, its movements unnaturally fluid as it prowled the perimeter of their small defensive triangle. Its eyes—yellow with vertical pupils—never left them as it tested their formation, looking for weakness.

"A polite sword-bearer," it hissed, the words slithering between those too-sharp teeth. "How... refreshing." The creature's gaze lingered on Lyra, nostrils flaring as it inhaled deeply. "The female smells sweet. Like summer berries before the frost." Its tongue—forked and glistening—darted across its lips. "She would make a fine meal."

Alaric shifted his stance slightly, tracking the creature's movements. "Don't do anything rash," he warned his companions in a low voice. "These things feed on fear as much as flesh."

"Clever man," the creature chuckled, the sound like dry bones rattling. "You've met our kind before."

From the dense forest surrounding the clearing, more figures emerged — three, then five, then eight in total. Each resembled the first, though their forms varied slightly — some more bestial, others nearly human but for their gray-blue skin and predatory eyes.

"We rarely have visitors who know what we are," said the first creature, completing its circuit around them. It paused, tilting its head curiously. "Most simply scream."

The creatures began to close the circle, moving with coordinated purpose. The horses whinnied in terror, straining against their reins.

"We have no quarrel with you or yours," Alaric repeated, his voice steady despite the dread pooling in his stomach. "Allow us passage, and we'll be gone from your territory by nightfall."

The lead creature's laugh turned several nearby birds to panicked flight. "And why would we permit such a thing when hunger gnaws at us?" It gestured toward Lyra with elongated fingers ending in yellowed claws. "Especially when you bring such tender meat into our domain?"

Elias trembled visibly, his crossbow wavering in his grip. "Alaric..." he whispered.

"Steady," Alaric commanded. He lowered his sword slightly — not enough to appear defenseless, but enough to signal a willingness to negotiate. "We carry iron and silver. Both would serve you better than our flesh."

The creature paused, interest flickering in those inhuman eyes. "Iron has its uses against the night-walkers. Silver against the moon-touched." It circled closer, sniffing. "How much do you offer for safe passage?"

"Ten silver crowns," Alaric said, watching the creature carefully. "And three iron daggers, forged in Adrielkeep's royal smithy."

The leader's eyes narrowed as it considered. The other creatures had stopped their advance, waiting for its decision.

"Not enough," it finally declared, teeth gleaming. "Not nearly enough for three lives."

"The woman then," Elias blurted suddenly, his voice cracking with panic. "Take her! The seal must reach Ravenscrest—nothing else matters!"

Lyra's head whipped around, shock and betrayal flashing across her face before hardening into cold fury. "You miserable coward—"

"Silence!" Alaric commanded, his voice cutting through their exchange. The creatures had begun to move again, excited by the discord. He raised his obsidian-steel blade, its edge catching what little light penetrated the canopy. "No one is being sacrificed today."

He reached slowly into his belt pouch with his free hand, withdrawing a handful of silver coins that glinted in the dimming light. "Twenty silver crowns," he countered. "All we have. And information worth far more than coin."

The lead creature's eyes fixed on the silver, but its expression remained skeptical. "What information could forest-dwellers possibly need?"

"The Red Guard follows us," Alaric said. "King's men, well-armed and determined. They'll be entering your territory before nightfall."

The creatures hissed in unison, a sound like steam escaping hot metal. The leader's face contorted with anger.

"Red cloaks," it spat. "They burned our southern grove last season. Hunted our younglings for sport."

"They hunt us now," Alaric pressed his advantage. "Help us reach the woodsman's cabin, and you'll have both our silver and the opportunity to settle your score with the Guard."

The creature's clawed fingers flexed as it considered the offer, glancing back at its pack. A silent communication seemed to pass between them before it turned back to Alaric.

"The silver now," it demanded. "And your smallest blade."

Alaric slowly set the coins on the ground, then unsheathed a narrow iron dagger from his boot. He placed it beside the silver, then stepped back.

"Wise choice," the creature purred, scooping up both offerings with startling speed. It examined the dagger closely, testing the edge against its thumb and nodding with satisfaction. "The cabin lies two miles hence, where the stream bends around the lightning-struck oak. We will ensure no pursuit reaches you before dawn."

"You have my thanks," Alaric said formally, not lowering his guard.

The creature's expression shifted into something approximating amusement. "Save your gratitude, sword-bearer. We do this for vengeance, not courtesy." It turned to its companions, barking commands in a language of snarls and clicks. The pack melted back into the forest, disappearing as suddenly as they had appeared.

The leader lingered, those yellow eyes fixing one last time on Lyra. "Perhaps we shall meet again, berry-sweet one. When your protectors are not so... vigilant."

Then it too was gone, leaving only disturbed leaves to mark its passage.

For several heartbeats, none of them moved. Then Elias collapsed to his knees, shaking violently.

"You would have sacrificed me," Lyra hissed, advancing on him with murder in her eyes. "You spineless, worthless—"

Alaric's arm shot out, blocking her path. "Not now. We need to reach the cabin before dark."

"Did you hear what he said?" she demanded.

"I heard a terrified man say something stupid," Alaric replied, hauling Elias roughly to his feet. "We'll deal with his cowardice later. For now, we ride."

Elias wouldn't meet their eyes as he mounted his horse. "The seal must reach Ravenscrest," he mumbled. "Nothing else matters."

"Remember those words when you sleep tonight," Alaric said coldly. "Because we'll be taking watches, and I'm not entirely convinced you deserve protection anymore."

As they urged their mounts forward, following the barely discernible path, Lyra brought her horse alongside Alaric's.

"Would you really have given them all our coin?" she asked quietly.

"I gave them half," Alaric admitted. "And my least favorite dagger."

A ghost of a smile touched her lips. "A mercenary with a favorite dagger. How sentimental."

"A woman who carries hidden blades," he countered. "How unexpected."

CHAPTER 3 – ESCAPE TO RAVENCREST

Their eyes met briefly, a moment of understanding passing between them. Whatever Elias's failings, they were bound together now — by circumstance, by danger, and by the small wooden box that might determine the future of the kingdom.

The forest grew darker around them as they rode, and somewhere behind them, howls echoed through the ancient trees — but whether from their recent acquaintances or their pursuing enemies, Alaric couldn't tell. He only knew that the true dangers of their journey were just beginning.

The twilight deepened around them as they approached the lightning-struck oak, its skeletal branches reaching toward the darkening sky like gnarled fingers. The promised cabin lay just beyond, a squat silhouette against the gloom.

"We'll rest the horses briefly," Alaric said, his voice low. "Then continue at first light."

A distant howl cut through the forest—different from the creatures they'd encountered earlier. This sound was higher, more frantic, almost human in its desperation.

Alaric stiffened in his saddle, hand flying to his sword hilt. Another howl answered the first, closer this time, followed by a bloodcurdling scream that made the horses dance nervously beneath them.

"What in seven hells—" Lyra began, her face paling.

"Ride!" Alaric shouted, spurring his mount forward. "Now! Don't stop, don't look back!"

Elias's eyes widened in terror. "But the cabin—"

"Forget the cabin!" Alaric roared, his voice cracking like a whip. "Keep moving! Get out of the woods now!"

The screaming intensified, joined by wet, guttural howls that seemed to come from all directions at once. Something crashed through the underbrush behind them—something large and fast.

"The Red Guard?" Lyra called, urging her horse to a gallop beside Alaric.

"Worse," Alaric growled, his face grim in the fading light. "The forest has betrayed us."

Through the trees ahead, Alaric could make out flashes of movement—gray-blue skin gleaming with fresh blood, yellow eyes reflecting what little light remained. Their earlier "allies" were slaughtering something—or someone—with savage efficiency.

"They found the Guard patrol," he realized aloud. "And now they're coming for us."

"You said they promised safe passage!" Elias cried, struggling to keep pace.

"They promised no pursuit would reach us," Alaric corrected, ducking beneath a low branch. "They never said they wouldn't hunt us themselves."

The path narrowed dangerously, forcing them to slow as they navigated between ancient trees whose roots seemed to reach for their horses' hooves. Behind them, the sounds of pursuit grew louder — the snap of branches, the padding of feet too swift to be human.

"There's a stream ahead," Alaric called back. "We can use it to mask our scent."

The forest floor began to slope downward, and the gurgle of running water reached their ears. But as they rounded a massive oak, Alaric yanked his reins hard, bringing his mount to a skidding halt.

The stream cut across their path, its waters running red with blood. Three bodies in crimson cloaks lay sprawled along the bank, their throats torn out, entrails glistening wetly in the dying light.

And standing among them, feasting on the remains, were the creatures they'd bargained with—now transformed into something even more horrific.

Their limbs had elongated, joints bending at impossible angles. Their jaws had distended to accommodate rows of needle-like teeth, and their eyes glowed with a hunger that went beyond mere predation.

The lead creature looked up from its grisly meal, blood dripping from its chin. It smiled, that same terrible smile from before.

"Berry-sweet ones," it crooned. "You've returned for supper."

"Back!" Alaric shouted, wheeling his horse around. "Eastern path! Now!"

Lyra and Elias didn't hesitate, turning their mounts and spurring them into a gallop. Alaric followed, drawing his obsidian-steel sword as he rode.

A weight slammed into his back, nearly unseating him—claws raking across his leather armor, seeking purchase. Alaric twisted in the saddle, bringing his blade around in a vicious arc that connected with flesh. The creature shrieked, its grip loosening enough for Alaric to shake it off.

"They're herding us!" Lyra called from ahead, her own sword drawn. "There are more to the east!"

Alaric scanned their surroundings, making split-second calculations. "The ridge!" he decided, pointing to a rocky outcropping visible through the trees. "High ground! They can't surround us there!"

Their horses labored up the incline, foam flecking their mouths as they pushed beyond endurance. Behind them, the pack howled in anticipation, the sound echoing through the darkening forest like a promise of death.

Elias reached the ridge first, his horse stumbling on the loose stones. He dismounted clumsily, nearly falling as he scrambled toward a narrow crevice in the rock face.

"Here!" he called. "We can defend this position!"

Lyra arrived next, sliding from her saddle with practiced grace, her blade at the ready. She positioned herself at the entrance to the crevice, eyes scanning the tree line below.

Alaric was the last to reach the ridge, his horse bleeding from claw marks across its flank. He dismounted and slapped the animal hard, sending it running along the ridge and away from the approaching danger.

"Get inside," he ordered, taking position beside Lyra. "I'll hold them here."

"We fight together," she countered, her voice leaving no room for argument. "Or we die together."

The first of the creatures emerged from the trees, loping on all fours with unnatural speed. It paused at the base of the ridge, those yellow eyes calculating as more of its kind joined it.

"The seal," Alaric said without taking his eyes off the threat below. "Elias, take it. If we fall, try to reach Ravenscrest."

He reached for his belt pouch, but his fingers found only torn leather. The pouch was gone — torn away during the frantic ride or the creature's attack.

"The seal," he repeated, a cold dread settling in his stomach. "Where is it?"

Elias's face went ashen. "You had it..."

"It's gone," Alaric realized, the implications hitting him like a physical blow. "Lost in the forest."

The lead creature below tilted its head, as if sensing their distress. It made a sound that might have been laughter, then began to climb the ridge, its pack following in a wave of gray-blue flesh and gleaming teeth.

"Without that seal, the kingdom falls to Varen," Lyra whispered, raising her blade as the creatures approached. "All for nothing."

"Not nothing," Alaric replied, stepping forward to meet the first attacker. "Not while we still breathe."

The creature lunged, jaws gaping, and Alaric's obsidian-steel blade flashed in the last light of day. The dance of death had begun, and with it, the desperate fight to survive long enough to reclaim what they had lost—if it still existed to be found.

Behind them, hidden in the crevice, Elias clutched something close to his chest—a small wooden box, its carvings seeming to shift in the gathering darkness. His eyes gleamed with a calculation that had nothing to do with fear, and everything to do with opportunity.

Elias's laughter rose above the sounds of battle, a high-pitched, maniacal sound that cut through the chaos. Alaric turned, blade still dripping with the creature's blood, to see the merchant holding the wooden box aloft.

"Looking for this?" Elias's face contorted into a triumphant sneer. "The seal you lost was a worthless replica. I've had the real one all along."

Lyra's sword arm faltered. "What?"

"Insurance," Elias explained, his eyes wild with a newfound boldness. "I needed to ensure my own survival when things inevitably went wrong."

Alaric took a menacing step toward him. "You risked our lives for—"

"For nothing," Elias finished, backing deeper into the crevice. "And now I have a proposition." He gestured toward the advancing creatures. "They want flesh. Give them the woman. One life for two, and the kingdom's future secured."

"You miserable bastard," Lyra hissed.

"It's simple mathematics," Elias continued, his voice eerily calm. "Sacrifice one for the good of —"

Alaric moved with the speed of a striking viper. His fist connected with Elias's jaw, driving the smaller man back against the rock wall with bone-crushing force. Blood sprayed from Elias's mouth as Alaric landed another blow, and another, his face a mask of cold fury.

"You would sacrifice her?" Each word punctuated by another strike. "After she protected you?"

Elias crumpled, the box tumbling from his grasp. Alaric snatched it mid-air, turning to thrust it into Lyra's hands.

"Guard this," he commanded, before returning his attention to the bloodied merchant.

Elias tried to crawl away, but Alaric seized him by the throat, fingers digging into the soft flesh beneath his jaw. With terrifying strength, he dragged the struggling man toward the crevice entrance where the creatures were now clawing their way up.

"Please," Elias gurgled, blood bubbling between his lips. "I can still help—"

"You're worth more to us as bait than as an ally," Alaric growled, his voice dropping to a deadly whisper. "A man who betrays once will betray again."

The lead creature had reached the ridge top, its elongated limbs scrabbling against the stone, yellow eyes fixed on the humans just beyond its reach.

"No!" Elias screamed, clawing at Alaric's grip. "For the love of gods, no!"

"The gods aren't listening," Alaric replied. With a powerful kick, he sent Elias tumbling through the crevice opening.

The merchant landed in a heap before the creatures, scrambling backward on hands and knees. "Wait! I can give you the woman! I can—"

His words dissolved into an unholy shriek as the first creature pounced. Claws raked across Elias's chest, shredding cloth and flesh with equal ease. Blood fountained from the wounds as a second creature joined the feast, its jaws clamping down on Elias's shoulder with an audible crunch of bone.

Lyra turned away, but Alaric watched with cold detachment as the creatures stripped the flesh from the screaming merchant.

Elias's hands flailed uselessly against his attackers, his eyes finding Alaric's in a final, desperate plea for mercy that would never come.

The screams lasted longer than seemed possible, becoming wet, gurgling sounds as the creatures tore into his throat and chest cavity. Only when Elias's body had been reduced to scattered pieces of meat and bone did Alaric step back from the entrance.

"Seal the crevice," he ordered, sheathing his blood-slick sword. "They'll be occupied with him for a while, but not long enough."

Lyra nodded grimly, helping Alaric drag a boulder across the narrow opening. The sounds of feeding continued on the other side, punctuated by growls of satisfaction.

"He deserved it," Lyra said quietly, though her pale face suggested the brutality had affected her more than she cared to admit.

"Deserving has nothing to do with survival," Alaric replied, checking the integrity of their makeshift barrier. "He was a liability we couldn't afford."

The crevice extended deeper into the ridge, narrowing to a tight passage that wound into darkness. Alaric produced a small lantern from his pack, striking flint to steel to light it.

"What now?" Lyra asked, clutching the wooden box to her chest. "We're trapped in here."

Alaric raised the lantern, illuminating the passage ahead. "Not trapped. These old ridges are riddled with caves. If we're lucky, this one connects to the other side."

"And if we're not lucky?"

"Then we die a slower death than Elias," he answered honestly. "Come. We need to put distance between us and them before they finish their meal."

They moved deeper into the passage, the lantern casting grotesque shadows against the stone walls. Behind them, the sounds of feeding gradually faded, replaced by an oppressive silence broken only by their footsteps and breathing.

"You killed him without hesitation," Lyra observed after they had walked for several minutes. It wasn't an accusation, merely a statement of fact.

"He would have killed you with the same lack of hesitation," Alaric replied. "The moment a companion becomes a threat is the moment they forfeit protection."

"Is that your mercenary's code?"

Alaric's expression hardened. "That's survival." He paused, turning to face her. "Would you have preferred I let him sacrifice you to those things?"

"Of course not," she said quickly. "I just... I've never seen someone make that choice so... efficiently."

"It wasn't a choice," Alaric corrected her. "It was a necessity."

The passage widened slightly, allowing them to walk side by side. Lyra studied the box in her hands, running her fingers over the intricate carvings.

"Do you think it's really the royal seal?" she asked, changing the subject.

"Open it," Alaric suggested. "We should know what we're dying for."

Lyra hesitated, then carefully lifted the lid. Inside, nestled on a bed of crimson velvet, lay a heavy gold ring bearing the royal crest of Morvain—a raven with outstretched wings, clutching a crown in its talons. The metal gleamed in the lantern light, seeming to pulse with an importance beyond its physical form.

"It's real," she whispered, a mixture of relief and awe in her voice. "Princess Helena's birthright."

Alaric nodded grimly. "And worth a kingdom, apparently. Close it and keep it safe. We still have a long way to Ravenscrest."

The passage began to slope upward, the air growing fresher. Hope kindled within them as they pushed forward, leaving the horror of Elias's death behind—though the memory of his screams would haunt them long after the echo had faded from the stone walls.

Outside, night had fallen completely over Mistwood Forest. The creatures, having finished their grisly feast, began to search for the scent of their escaped prey, their hunger for flesh only temporarily sated. But the stone passage had done its work, carrying Alaric and Lyra's scent away from their hunters.

Alaric searched their small hideout, finding a small lantern resting against the wall.

The royal seal was secure, its bearers alive—for now. But Ravenscrest remained distant, and the forces of Lord Varen would not rest until they reclaimed the symbol of legitimate rule. The true challenge of their journey was only beginning.

The passage narrowed again as they ventured deeper, the ceiling dropping so low that Alaric had to hunch his broad shoulders to avoid scraping against the jagged stone.

"It's getting tighter," he warned, holding the lantern ahead to reveal a particularly constricted section where the passage squeezed between two massive boulders. "We'll have to crawl through."

Lyra peered past him, her face grim in the flickering light. "Are you certain this leads somewhere? We could be trapping ourselves."

"Feel the air," Alaric replied, lifting his free hand. "There's a current. It means there's an opening somewhere ahead."

He extinguished the lantern, plunging them into darkness to conserve what little oil remained. "I'll go first. Count to thirty, then follow my voice."

Without waiting for her response, he dropped to his hands and knees and began to squeeze through the narrow gap. The rough stone scraped against his shoulders and back, tearing at his leather armor. Halfway through, the passage constricted further, forcing him to turn sideways and inch forward by pressing his palms against the opposing walls.

"Alaric?" Lyra's voice called from behind, an edge of panic creeping in.

"Still here," he grunted, pushing through the final section. "It opens up on this side. Come through carefully."

He heard her begin to navigate the tight space, her breathing quick and controlled. Then a sharp intake of breath followed by a muffled curse.

"I'm stuck," she admitted, frustration evident in her voice.

"Where?"

"My shirt—it's caught on something. And I can't reach back to free it."

Alaric sighed, dropping to his stomach to peer back through the gap. In the darkness, he could just make out her silhouette, trapped halfway through the passage.

"Give me your hand," he instructed, extending his arm into the narrow space.

Their fingers met, and he gripped her wrist firmly, using his other hand to brace against the rock wall. "On three, I'm going to pull. The fabric will either tear or come free."

"Just do it," she said through gritted teeth.

He pulled steadily, feeling resistance as the cloth caught on the jagged stone.

Then came the sound of ripping fabric, and suddenly Lyra lurched forward into his arms, the momentum carrying them both backward onto the cave floor.

For a moment they lay there, Lyra sprawled atop him, her face inches from his. Even in the darkness, he could feel the heat of her breath against his skin.

"Are you hurt?" he asked, his voice rougher than intended.

"Only my pride," she replied, quickly rolling off him. "And my clothing, apparently."

Alaric sat up, reaching for the lantern. When he relit it, the flame illuminated Lyra's torn shirt, a jagged rip exposing her shoulder and part of her back. She tugged at the fabric, trying to cover herself, but the tear was too extensive.

Without comment, Alaric set down the lantern and began to remove his own shirt, the blood-spattered garment stiff with sweat and grime.

"What are you doing?" Lyra asked, watching him with a mixture of wariness and curiosity.

"You need something to wear," he said simply, pulling the shirt over his head. The lantern light played across the defined muscles of his torso, illuminating a network of scars that told their own stories of past violence. He tore the shirt along its seam, creating a long strip of cloth. "This will have to do until we reach Ravenscrest."

Lyra took the offered fabric, wrapping it around her shoulders like a shawl. Her eyes lingered on his bare chest for a moment before she looked away. "Thank you."

Alaric merely nodded, already examining their surroundings. The passage had opened into a larger chamber where water dripped from stalactites overhead, forming shallow pools on the stone floor. The lantern's oil was nearly spent, its flame guttering weakly.

"We need better light," he muttered, searching the ground until he found a sturdy piece of driftwood, carried in by some ancient flooding. He tore another strip from what remained of his shirt, wrapping it around one end of the stick.

"What are you doing now?" Lyra asked, watching as he carefully tipped the lantern to catch the last of its oil on the cloth-wrapped stick.

"Making a torch," he replied, setting the lantern aside. He produced a flint from his belt pouch and struck it against his dagger, sending sparks onto the oil-soaked cloth. It caught immediately, blooming into a bright flame that pushed back the darkness far more effectively than the dying lantern.

"You've done this before," Lyra observed.

"Many times," Alaric confirmed, rising to his feet. He held the torch aloft, revealing a passage on the far side of the chamber. "This way."

As they walked, Lyra studied him in the torchlight, her eyes tracing the contours of his bare torso. "Those scars—they tell quite a story."

Alaric didn't look back at her. "Not one worth telling."

"I disagree," she said quietly. "Each one is a battle survived. A lesson learned."

"The only lesson is that I wasn't fast enough to avoid the blade," he replied, his tone making it clear he didn't wish to discuss the matter further.

They continued in silence for several minutes, the passage gradually sloping upward again. The air grew fresher, carrying a hint of pine and night-blooming flowers.

"We're close to the surface," Alaric said, quickening his pace.

Lyra hurried to keep up, wincing as her torn clothing caught on an outcropping. "Do you think those creatures followed us?"

"They're hunters, not spelunkers," he replied. "They'll search for easier prey."

The passage curved sharply, then opened abruptly into a small cavern where moonlight spilled through a crack in the ceiling. Stars were visible through the opening, a glittering promise of the world beyond their stone prison.

"We made it," Lyra breathed, relief evident in her voice.

Alaric extinguished the torch against the stone floor. "No need to announce our presence with firelight. The moon is bright enough to see by."

He moved to the cavern wall, examining the rough surface. "We can climb out here. The handholds are good."

Lyra approached, the makeshift wrap slipping from her shoulder as she looked up at the opening. In the silvery moonlight, her skin seemed to glow, the curve of her neck and shoulder drawing Alaric's gaze despite his efforts to remain focused on their escape.

CHAPTER 4 –
SLEEP, RUN, PASS OUT

"I'll go first," she said, reaching for the first handhold. "In case you need to catch me."

"A practical decision," Alaric agreed, stepping back to give her room.

As she began to climb, the torn fabric of her shirt slipped further, revealing more of her back. Alaric averted his eyes, though not before noticing a curious scar between her shoulder blades—a deliberate marking that resembled a small crown.

She reached the opening without difficulty, pulling herself through with surprising strength. Her head appeared in the gap a moment later.

"It's clear," she called down softly. "No sign of pursuit."

Alaric climbed swiftly, his powerful arms making short work of the ascent. When he emerged beside her, they found themselves on a rocky outcropping overlooking the forest below.

Mistwood stretched in all directions, a sea of darkness beneath the star-strewn sky.

"Can you tell where we are?" Lyra asked, clutching the torn wrap around her shoulders against the night chill.

Alaric oriented himself by the stars, then pointed northeast. "Ravenscrest lies that way, perhaps a day's journey on foot." He turned slowly, scanning their surroundings. "We've lost the horses, but we've also lost our pursuers, at least for now."

"Small mercies," Lyra murmured, her hand going to the wooden box tucked securely in her belt. "We still have what matters most."

Alaric nodded, his expression grave. "The Red Guard will regroup once they realize what happened to their advance patrol. And they won't be the only ones hunting us."

"Lord Varen's other agents," Lyra agreed, her voice hardening. "They'll be watching all approaches to Ravenscrest."

"Then we avoid the roads entirely," Alaric decided. "Follow the ridgeline as far as possible, then cut through the northern edge of Mistwood where it thins before Ravenscrest."

Lyra shivered, though whether from the cold or the thought of reentering the forest, Alaric couldn't tell. Without thinking, he moved closer, offering the warmth of his body.

"We should rest while we can," he said, gesturing to a sheltered spot beneath an overhanging rock. "A few hours of sleep, then we move at first light."

She looked up at him, moonlight catching in her copper hair. "You saved my life back there. With Elias."

"You would have done the same," Alaric replied, uncomfortable with her gratitude.

"Perhaps," she said, studying his face. "But not with such certainty. You didn't hesitate."

"I've learned the cost of hesitation," he said quietly.

Lyra reached up, her fingers brushing against a jagged scar that ran from his collarbone to his shoulder. "This one?"

Alaric caught her hand, intending to push it away, but found himself holding it instead. Her skin was warm despite the night chill, her pulse quickening beneath his thumb.

"That one came from trusting the wrong person," he admitted, his voice low.

"And this?" Her free hand traced another scar across his ribs.

"A lesson in watching my flank in battle."

She stepped closer, the torn fabric of her shirt brushing against his bare chest. "And this one?" Her finger traced a thin line along his jaw.

"A reminder that beauty can be deadly," he whispered, his eyes never leaving hers.

For a heartbeat, they stood frozen in the moonlight, the air between them charged with something neither had expected to find on this desperate journey. Then Alaric gently released her hand, stepping back.

"We should rest," he repeated, more firmly this time. "Dawn comes early, and we have far to travel."

Lyra nodded, though a hint of disappointment flickered across her face.

"Of course. Practicality above all."

They settled beneath the overhanging rock, the stone wall at their backs providing some protection from the wind that whispered through the ridgeline.

Alaric sat against the wall, legs stretched before him, his eyes scanning the darkness for any sign of pursuit.

Lyra hesitated only a moment before laying down beside him, the makeshift wrap still clutched around her shoulders.

Despite their precarious situation, exhaustion soon overtook her, and she shifted closer to his warmth, her body pressing against his side.

"Cold?" Alaric asked, his voice a low rumble in the darkness.

"Among other things," she murmured, her head finding its way to his lap as naturally as water flowing downhill. "I can't stop thinking about how close we came to death back there."

His hand moved tentatively to her copper hair, fingers gently stroking the tangled strands. The intimacy of the gesture surprised them both, yet neither pulled away.

"Thank you," she whispered, her hand finding his leg, resting there with a deliberate weight that transcended mere gratitude. "For saving my life. For getting us this far."

"We're not safe yet," he reminded her, though his fingers continued their gentle ministrations, tracing patterns against her scalp that made her eyes flutter closed.

"No one is ever truly safe in Morvain," she replied, her hand beginning to move along his thigh in slow, measured strokes. "We take comfort where we can find it."

Alaric's breath caught as her touch grew bolder, more purposeful. "Lyra..."

"Don't tell me this isn't wise," she said, turning to look up at him, her eyes reflecting the starlight. "We both know that. But wisdom has little place in a world where death waits around every corner."

Her hand moved higher, and Alaric's body responded despite his better judgment. Through the fabric of his breeches, her fingers traced the hardening outline of his desire, drawing a sharp intake of breath from his lips.

"This changes nothing," he warned, even as his hand moved from her hair to cup her face, thumb tracing the curve of her cheekbone.

"It changes everything," she countered, rising to her knees before him. The makeshift wrap fell away, her torn shirt hanging open to reveal the pale curve of her breast in the moonlight. "And nothing at all."

Their lips met with the desperate hunger of those who had stared into the abyss and emerged alive. Her hands worked at the fastenings of his breeches while his explored the warm skin beneath her tattered clothing. When she straddled him, taking him inside her with a soft gasp that echoed his own, it felt less like surrender and more like defiance—a claiming of life in the shadow of death.

They moved together in the silver darkness, their bodies finding a rhythm as ancient as the stone that sheltered them. Alaric's hands gripped her hips, guiding her movements as she arched against him, her head thrown back, copper hair cascading down her back like liquid fire.

"Look at me," he commanded softly, and when her eyes met his, something passed between them that transcended mere physical pleasure—a recognition, a promise, a shared secret.

When release claimed them both, they muffled their cries against each other's skin, mindful even in passion of the dangers that lurked beyond their temporary sanctuary.

Afterward, they lay entwined beneath the stars, their breathing gradually slowing, bodies cooling in the night air. Alaric pulled her closer, wrapping his arm around her protectively as she nestled against his chest.

"Sleep," he murmured against her hair. "I'll keep watch."

But sleep eluded him long after Lyra's breathing had deepened and steadied. His eyes remained fixed on the dark canopy of Mistwood below, his mind turning over the complications of what had just transpired between them. He had not allowed himself such vulnerability in years, had not shared his body or his breath with another soul since...

Dawn was still hours away when Alaric stiffened, his senses alert to a change in the night. The forest had gone silent—no night birds called, no insects chirped. Only the wind remained, carrying with it a scent that made his blood run cold.

"Lyra," he whispered, gently shaking her awake. "We need to move. Now."

She came to consciousness instantly, years of training evident in the way she reached for her weapon even before her eyes fully opened. "What is it?"

"Red cloaks," he replied, already gathering their meager possessions. "The wind has shifted. They're following our trail up the ridge."

They dressed quickly, the intimacy of their earlier coupling set aside in the face of immediate danger. Lyra secured the wooden box containing the royal seal, while Alaric scouted the path ahead.

"This way," he indicated, pointing along the ridgeline. "If we hurry, we can reach the northern edge of Mistwood by midday."

As they set off, moving as swiftly and silently as the rocky terrain allowed, Lyra caught his arm. "About what happened —"

"It happened," Alaric cut her off, his voice gentle despite the abruptness of his words. "That's enough for now."

She studied his face for a moment, then nodded. "For now."

They continued along the ridge, leaving behind the shelter that had briefly housed their passion. Neither spoke of what had passed between them, yet both felt its echo with every step they took toward Ravenscrest—and whatever fate awaited them there.

Behind them, the first rays of dawn illuminated a group of riders in crimson cloaks, their faces grim as they followed the trail up the rocky slope. The hunt continued, relentless as the coming day, forcing them to take off into a sprint as the sounds of something trailing them got louder and louder.

The forest thinned as they pushed through the final stretch of dense undergrowth, branches whipping against their faces and arms. Alaric's muscles burned with exhaustion, but determination drove him forward. Behind them, the shouts of the Red Guard echoed through the trees, growing closer with each passing minute.

"There!" Lyra gasped, pointing ahead where the tree line broke. "Open ground!"

They burst from Mistwood's edge into blinding sunlight, momentarily disoriented by the sudden brightness. Before them stretched the vast open fields of Ravenscrest, golden wheat swaying in the breeze. In the distance, the gray stone walls of the city rose against the horizon—so close, yet impossibly far for their weary legs.

"We can make it," Alaric panted, gripping the royal seal tightly in his hand. "If we reach those farmhouses, we can find horses."

The thunder of hoofbeats behind them shattered any hope of reprieve. Alaric glanced back to see crimson cloaks emerging from the tree line, at least six riders spurring their mounts across the open field.

"Run!" he shouted, seizing Lyra's hand. They sprinted through the wheat, the tall stalks whipping against their bodies as they carved a visible path through the golden sea.

Lyra's breath came in ragged gasps beside him. "They're... gaining..."

"Don't stop," Alaric commanded, pulling her forward. "The farmhouses — just ahead."

The first cluster of stone buildings appeared through the wheat — a small hamlet on the outskirts of Ravenscrest's farmland. They altered course, aiming for the narrow lane between two weathered structures.

The pounding of hooves grew louder, accompanied by the metallic ring of swords being drawn. The Red Guard had closed half the distance already, their horses easily outpacing the exhausted fugitives.

"This way!" Alaric veered toward a gap between a stone house and a wooden barn. If they could reach the maze of buildings, they might lose their mounted pursuers in the narrow passages.

As they rounded the first house, Alaric caught a flash of movement in his peripheral vision—a glint of metal from the side of the adjacent building. His combat instincts screamed a warning.

"Lyra, stop!" he bellowed, reaching for her arm. "STOP!"

But his warning was lost in the chaos. Lyra, focused only on escape, sprinted past the corner of the stone house. A crimson-cloaked figure stepped out from the shadows, weapon already in motion. The axe blade caught the sunlight for one terrible moment before it arced through the air with devastating precision.

Alaric watched in horror as the blade connected with Lyra's neck. There was a sickening sound—not the clean slice of flesh he'd expected, but a wet, crushing impact that sent a spray of crimson across the weathered stone wall.

Time seemed to slow. Lyra's body continued forward for two more steps, propelled by momentum, while her head tilted grotesquely, partially severed but still attached by strands of sinew and spine. Her eyes, wide with shock and incomprehension, met Alaric's for one eternal moment before the light within them dimmed forever.

She collapsed in a heap, blood pooling rapidly beneath her ruined neck. The Red Guard soldier yanked his axe free, raising it for another strike.

Something broke inside Alaric—a dam holding back years of carefully controlled rage. With an inhuman roar, he launched himself at the axe-wielder, obsidian-steel blade leading the way. The man barely had time to register the attack before Alaric's sword punched through his breastplate, driving deep into his chest cavity.

Alaric twisted the blade savagely, feeling ribs snap and organs rupture. He withdrew the sword only to strike again, and again, long after the man had stopped moving. Blood soaked his arms to the elbows, splattered across his face like war paint.

More Red Guards rounded the corner, drawn by the commotion. Alaric turned to face them, a feral snarl twisting his features. In his left hand, he clutched the wooden box containing the royal seal; in his right, the blood-slick sword that had already claimed one of their comrades.

"Come then," he growled, his voice barely recognizable. "Come and join your friend."

The first guard hesitated, taking in the scene—his fallen comrade mutilated beyond recognition, the wild-eyed mercenary standing over the headless corpse of the woman. That moment of hesitation cost him his life as Alaric closed the distance with unnatural speed, his blade opening the man's throat in a single, fluid motion.

The remaining guards attacked as one, their training evident in their coordinated movements. But they faced something beyond training now—a man transformed by grief into a weapon of pure destruction. Alaric moved among them like a demon from the old tales, his blade finding gaps in armor, severing tendons, puncturing vital organs.

A sword sliced across his back, cutting deep. He didn't flinch, turning instead to drive his blade through his attacker's eye socket. Another guard's blade pierced his side, and Alaric responded by seizing the man's wrist and snapping it backward, then driving his own dagger up through the soft flesh beneath the jaw.

Blood—his and theirs—soaked the ground, turning the dirt to mud beneath their feet. The combat seemed to last both an eternity and mere seconds. When it ended, Alaric stood alone among the fallen, his chest heaving with exertion, wounds bleeding freely.

He stumbled back to where Lyra lay. Her eyes stared sightlessly at the sky, copper hair matted with blood. With trembling hands, he closed those eyes, his fingers leaving crimson streaks across her pale skin.

"I'm sorry," he whispered, his voice breaking. "I failed you."

The sound of more hoofbeats approached from the direction of the forest. Reinforcements were coming. Alaric knew he should run, should complete the mission and deliver the seal to Princess Helena. It was what Lyra would have wanted — the purpose for which she had given her life.

Instead, he gathered her broken body in his arms, cradling her against his chest as blood continued to seep from her ruined neck, soaking into his already gore-stained clothing. The wooden box containing the royal seal he tucked securely into his belt.

"I will finish this," he promised her unhearing ears. "And then I will come back for you."

With one last look at her face, he gently laid her body down. Standing, he turned toward Ravenscrest, its walls now visible across the wheat fields.

Somewhere within those walls, Princess Helena awaited the seal that would secure her claim to the throne — and somewhere, Lord Varen plotted to seize power that wasn't rightfully his.

Alaric began to walk, each step leaving a bloody footprint in the dust.

The pain of his wounds registered only distantly, overshadowed by the hollow ache in his chest. He had survived countless battles, had dealt death to scores of enemies, had walked away from horrors that would break lesser men.

But this loss—this failure—cut deeper than any blade.

Behind him, the Red Guard reinforcements discovered the carnage he had left in his wake. Their shouts of alarm carried across the fields, but Alaric didn't look back. His path was set now, his purpose crystallized by grief and rage into something harder than the obsidian-steel of his sword.

He would deliver the royal seal to Princess Helena.

And then he would find Lord Varen, the architect of this bloodshed, and introduce him to a suffering beyond imagination.

As he walked, Alaric's fingers absently traced the contours of the wooden box at his belt. Inside lay a simple gold ring that had somehow become worth more than the woman whose life had been sacrificed for it. The absurdity of it all—that kingdoms could rise or fall based on a piece of metal, that lives could be spent like copper coins in the pursuit of power — fueled the cold fury building within him.

The wheat parted before him as he trudged toward Ravenscrest, a blood-soaked harbinger of vengeance with a dead king's seal and a promise to keep.

The city gates of Ravenscrest loomed before him, massive oak reinforced with iron bands that had withstood sieges and centuries alike. Blood trailed behind Alaric in a macabre path, his wounds still weeping freely with each step. The royal seal pressed against his side, its weight insignificant compared to the burden of failure he carried.

"Halt!" A guard called from the watchtower. "State your business!"

Alaric raised his head, revealing a face painted with dried blood and fury. "Open the gate," he commanded, his voice a ragged growl. "I bear a message for Princess Helena."

The guards exchanged wary glances, taking in his blood-soaked appearance and wild eyes. One drew his bow, arrow nocked and pointed at Alaric's chest.

"You'll go no further until you surrender your weapons, stranger," the guard captain called down. "The city is closed to armed travelers without proper documentation."

"I don't have time for this," Alaric snarled, drawing his obsidian-steel blade. The dark metal seemed to drink in the afternoon light, still crusted with the blood of the Red Guard. "Open the gate or I'll open it myself."

More guards appeared along the wall, crossbows trained on him. The captain's face hardened. "Put down your sword or die where you stand."

For a moment, Alaric considered the simplicity of that option — to die here, to join Lyra in whatever darkness awaited. But the seal at his belt demanded otherwise.

"Listen carefully," he said, forcing his voice to steady. "I carry the royal seal of King Adriel. Princess Helena's life depends on me reaching her before sunset. The Red Guard follows close behind me—men loyal not to the crown, but to Lord Varen."

The captain's eyes widened slightly at the mention of the seal. He hesitated, then signaled to his men. "Lower the crossbows." To Alaric, he called, "Show me this seal."

Alaric reached slowly for the wooden box, withdrawing it from his belt. He opened it, letting the afternoon sun catch the gold ring within.

The captain inhaled sharply. "Open the gate!" he commanded, his previous suspicion replaced with urgency. "And send word to the castle—the Princess must be informed immediately!"

With a groaning protest, the massive gates began to swing inward. Alaric sheathed his sword and tucked the seal back into his belt, stumbling forward as his strength began to wane. Blood loss and exhaustion were taking their toll, but he forced himself onward. He could not fail. Not again.

As he passed through the gates, the captain approached, concern evident in his weathered face. "You need a physician—"

"Later," Alaric cut him off. "The Princess first."

"At least take a horse," the captain insisted, gesturing to a bay stallion nearby. "You'll never reach the castle on foot in your condition."

Alaric nodded grimly, allowing two guards to help him into the saddle. The world swam before his eyes, but he gripped the reins with bloody hands and urged the horse forward.

The streets of Ravenscrest blurred around him as he rode, citizens scattering before the blood-soaked rider who drove his mount with single-minded determination toward the castle at the city's heart. Behind him, the alarm bells began to ring — warning of the approaching Red Guard, he presumed.

Market stalls and stone houses gave way to wider avenues lined with the mansions of merchants and lesser nobility. The castle rose before him, its white stone towers gleaming in the late afternoon sun like accusing fingers pointing to the heavens.

"Make way!" he shouted, scattering a group of finely-dressed courtiers who had been crossing the main avenue. "For the Princess!"

The castle gates stood open, but a line of guards formed a barrier across the entrance, spears lowered as he approached.

"Stand aside," Alaric commanded, drawing his sword once more. "I bear the King's seal for Princess Helena."

"The Princess sees no one without appointment," the lead guard replied, though uncertainty flickered in his eyes at the sight of the bloodied warrior before him.

"She'll see me," Alaric growled, sliding from the saddle. His legs nearly buckled beneath him, but rage and determination kept him upright. "Your King is dead. Lord Varen moves to seize the throne. Only this seal—" he patted the box at his belt "—stands between Princess Helena and usurpation."

The guards exchanged glances, clearly torn between their duty to protect and the weight of Alaric's words.

"Let him pass." A new voice rang out from the castle steps.

Alaric turned to see an elderly man in the robes of a royal advisor, his lined face grave beneath a shock of white hair. "I am Lord Harwick, the Princess's seneschal. I will take responsibility for this... visitor."

The guards parted reluctantly, their hands still on their weapons as Alaric stumbled past them. Lord Harwick's eyes widened as he took in the full extent of Alaric's injuries.

"By the gods, man, you're half dead."

"More than half," Alaric muttered, wavering on his feet. "But not yet whole. Take me to the Princess. Now."

Harwick nodded, gesturing to two nearby guards. "Help him. If he falls, carry him."

They moved through the castle corridors, Alaric leaving smears of blood on the polished marble floors. Courtiers and servants pressed themselves against the walls as they passed, whispers following in their wake.

"The Princess is in the east solar," Harwick explained as they climbed a spiral staircase. "She's been... troubled of late. No word from her father in over a week."

"She won't hear from him again," Alaric said bluntly. "He's dead. Poisoned by his brother, if I had to guess."

Harwick's face paled. "These are dangerous accusations."

"Truth often is," Alaric replied, grimacing as pain lanced through his side. One of the wounds had reopened, fresh blood soaking through his tattered clothing.

They reached an ornate door guarded by two women in the distinctive armor of the Princess's personal guard. Harwick addressed them with quiet authority.

"The Princess must see this man immediately. Matters of the highest urgency."

The women exchanged glances, then knocked on the door. After a moment, a soft voice from within bade them enter.

The east solar was a bright, airy chamber with tall windows overlooking the city. Standing before one such window was a slender young woman with auburn hair cascading down her back in loose waves. She turned as they entered, and Alaric found himself looking into eyes that matched the precise shade of the summer sky.

Princess Helena's gaze moved from Harwick to Alaric, widening in shock at his blood-soaked appearance. To her credit, she did not scream or recoil.

"What is the meaning of this, Lord Harwick?" she asked, her voice remarkably steady.

Before the seneschal could answer, Alaric staggered forward, dropping to one knee before her. The movement sent fresh waves of agony through his body, but he ignored them, reaching for the wooden box at his belt.

"Princess Helena," he said, his voice rough with exhaustion and grief.

"I bring grave news... and your birthright."

He opened the box, revealing the royal seal nestled within. With trembling hands, he offered it to her.

"Your father, King Adriel, is dead," he continued, watching her face pale at his words. "Murdered, I believe, by Lord Varen. He seeks to claim the throne before your father's death becomes known throughout the kingdom. This seal — your father's seal — is the key to your legitimacy."

Helena stared at the ring, her composure cracking slightly as she reached for it with slender fingers. "How... how did you come by this?"

"A woman named Lyra brought it from the capital," Alaric answered, his voice catching on her name. "She died ensuring it reached you. As did others."

The Princess closed her fingers around the seal, drawing it to her chest. "Lyra was my father's most trusted agent," she whispered. "If she believed he was dead..."

"Princess," Harwick interjected urgently, "if what this man says is true, we must act quickly. The autumn equinox is tomorrow. According to ancient law—"

"The crown passes to the nearest male heir if no formal succession has been declared by the equinox," Helena finished, her expression hardening. "My uncle knows this well."

She turned to Alaric, studying him with new intensity. "Who are you, that you would risk your life to bring me this seal?"

"My name is Alaric Thornwood," he replied, swaying slightly as his strength continued to ebb. "A mercenary hired to ensure the seal reached you. Nothing more."

"You lie," she said softly, stepping closer. "No mere mercenary would bleed so freely for 'nothing more.' What drives you, Alaric Thornwood?"

The room began to spin around him, Helena's face blurring before his eyes. "That, is a very long story." Alaric spoke.

The last thing Alaric saw before consciousness fled was Princess Helena's face, transformed from shock to steely determination as she clutched her father's seal.

Then Alaric knew no more, his body finally surrendering to its wounds as he collapsed at the feet of the woman for whom Lyra had given her life.

CHAPTER 5 –

WAKING UP IN A NEW CASTLE

Pain was the first sensation that returned to Alaric — a throbbing agony that pulsed through his body with each heartbeat. The second was softness beneath him, a stark contrast to the hard ground he'd grown accustomed to. His eyelids felt weighted with lead as he struggled to open them, light filtering through his lashes in blinding fragments.

White linen canopy. Carved wooden posts. Silk sheets against his skin.

He was in a bed. Not just any bed — the kind reserved for nobility.

Alaric's warrior instincts surged through the fog of pain, sending his hand reaching for a weapon that wasn't there. His fingers clutched at empty air as his vision cleared enough to make out the rest of the chamber — ornate tapestries, a crackling hearth, and a slender figure seated in a high-backed chair across the room.

Princess Helena sat perfectly still, her auburn hair pulled back in a simple braid, her blue eyes fixed on an open book in her lap. She wore a gown of deep emerald that made her pale skin seem to glow in the firelight. As if sensing his gaze, she looked up, their eyes meeting across the space between them.

"You're awake," she said, closing her book and rising in one fluid motion. Her voice carried the same quiet authority he remembered from their brief encounter before he'd collapsed.

Alaric tried to speak, but his throat felt like he'd swallowed sand. He managed only a raspy cough that sent fresh pain lancing through his bandaged torso.

Helena crossed to his bedside, pouring water from a silver pitcher into a goblet. With surprising gentleness, she slipped her hand beneath his head, lifting it slightly as she brought the goblet to his lips.

"Slowly," she cautioned as he drank greedily. "You've been unconscious for three days."

The water soothed his parched throat, allowing him to finally form words. "Three days?"

Helena set the goblet aside, studying his face with those piercing blue eyes. "The physician wasn't certain you would survive. You lost a tremendous amount of blood." She hesitated, then asked, "How do you feel?"

A ghost of a smile touched Alaric's cracked lips. "You look great," he rasped, "and I feel like shit."

Something flickered across her face—surprise, perhaps even amusement—before her expression grew solemn once more. "You brought me my father's seal at great cost. I owe you my gratitude... and my crown."

Alaric closed his eyes briefly, unwilling to face her gratitude when all he could see was Lyra's blood pooling in the dirt. "Don't thank me yet, Princess. I failed more than I succeeded."

"Lyra," Helena said softly, perching on the edge of his bed. "Tell me what happened to her."

The memory crashed over him like a physical blow—the axe catching the sunlight, the spray of crimson against stone, those eyes meeting his one final time. Alaric's hands fisted in the sheets, his knuckles white with tension.

"She was beheaded," he said flatly, the blunt words hanging in the air between them. "Red Guard. They ambushed us outside Ravenscrest."

Helena's face paled, but she didn't flinch from the brutal truth. "And before that? How did you come to be her companion on this journey?"

"I was hired in Thornhaven," Alaric replied, his voice growing stronger as he spoke. "By Lyra and a man named Elias. They offered coin to escort them to Ravenscrest, claimed they carried important documents." His jaw tightened. "They lied."

"About the documents?"

"About everything." Bitterness crept into his tone. "We were pursued through Mistwood by the Red Guard. When we were cornered, Elias revealed his true nature. He tried to sacrifice Lyra to save himself." Alaric's eyes met Helena's, cold and hard as winter steel. "I fed him to the forest creatures instead."

If Helena was shocked by this admission, she didn't show it. "Elias was not known for his courage," she said carefully. "But he was one of my father's most trusted advisors. His expertise in royal law was unmatched."

"His expertise in treachery was considerable as well," Alaric growled. "He carried a false seal to trick any pursuers. Kept the real one hidden until we were cornered."

Helena's brow furrowed. "A precaution, perhaps. The seal's safe delivery was paramount."

"At any cost?" Alaric challenged, anger flaring despite his weakened state. "Lyra died for that trinket. She believed in you—in your right to rule. Her blood paid for your crown, Princess. Remember that when you wear it."

Instead of taking offense, Helena reached out, her cool fingers wrapping around his wrist where it lay atop the covers. "I will remember," she promised, her voice soft but firm. "Every day that I reign, I will remember those who died to put me on the throne."

The sincerity in her eyes caught Alaric off guard, dousing his anger like water on embers. He looked away, uncomfortable with the intensity of her gaze.

"The Red Guard," he said, changing the subject. "They serve your uncle now?"

Helena's expression darkened. "Some, yes. Others remain loyal to the crown—to me. The castle guard prevented Lord Varen's men from entering Ravenscrest after your arrival. There have been... skirmishes at the city gates."

"War is coming," Alaric stated, not a question but a certainty.

"It's already here," Helena replied grimly. "My uncle has declared himself regent, claiming I'm too inexperienced to rule. He controls the capital and three southern provinces. I control Ravenscrest and have the support of the northern lords—for now."

Alaric attempted to sit up, grimacing as pain tore through his bandaged wounds. Helena placed a restraining hand on his shoulder.

"You shouldn't—"

"I need to know where we stand," he insisted, pushing through the pain to prop himself against the headboard.

"Your uncle won't stop until he has the seal. Or until you're dead."

Helena's eyes widened slightly at his bluntness, but she didn't contradict him. "The coronation ceremony is tomorrow at dawn. Once I'm officially crowned, Varen's claim as regent becomes invalid. Many who now sit on the fence will be forced to choose sides."

"And you think a ceremony will stop him?" Alaric asked incredulously. "Men who hunger for power don't surrender it for the sake of tradition."

"No," Helena agreed, rising from the bed to pace before the hearth. "But legitimacy matters in Morvain. The nobles follow strength, yes, but also ancient law. With the royal seal and my father's sword, my claim cannot be disputed."

Alaric watched her move, noting the quiet confidence in her bearing. This was not some frightened girl playing at politics, but a woman who understood the dangerous game unfolding around her.

"Your father's sword?" he questioned.

Helena stopped her pacing, turning to face him. "The Blade of Adriel—named for the first king of our line. It's been passed from monarch to monarch for seven generations. My father always wore it." Her expression clouded. "If he truly was murdered, the sword would have been with him."

"Meaning Varen likely has it now," Alaric concluded grimly.

"Yes. Another reason he must be stopped." Helena returned to his bedside, her face set with determination. "I need your help, Alaric Thornwood."

He gave a short, humorless laugh that pulled painfully at his wounds. "I'm not much use to anyone right now, Princess."

"When you've healed," she clarified. "I need men I can trust. Men who aren't bound by old loyalties or political ambitions." Her blue eyes held his. "Men who understand that sometimes, difficult choices must be made for the greater good."

Alaric studied her face, searching for signs of manipulation or deceit. He found none—only the steady gaze of a woman who had been thrust into power and was determined not to buckle beneath its weight.

"I'm a mercenary," he reminded her. "I fight for coin, not causes."

"And yet you nearly died delivering my father's seal," she countered. "That wasn't about coin."

"It was about a promise," Alaric said quietly, Lyra's face flashing in his memory. "A debt that can never be repaid."

Helena nodded slowly, as if his answer confirmed something she'd already suspected. "Then make me a promise, Alaric. Help me secure my throne and bring my uncle to justice for what he's done. In return, I'll give you whatever is within my power to grant."

The offer hung between them, weighted with implications neither fully understood. Alaric knew he should refuse—should collect whatever payment was owed for the seal's delivery and vanish from Ravenscrest before he became further entangled in royal politics. Yet something in Helena's unwavering gaze held him, reminding him of another pair of eyes that had looked to him with similar trust.

"I'll consider it," he said finally. "After your coronation. Assuming we all live that long."

A small smile curved Helena's lips. "Fair enough." She rose, smoothing her skirts. "Rest now. The physician will return shortly to change your bandages."

As she moved toward the door, Alaric called after her. "Princess." She paused, looking back at him. "Lyra believed in you. Don't make her sacrifice meaningless."

Helena's expression softened. "I won't," she promised. "And Alaric? When we're alone, you may call me Helena."

"Do you want to know what truly drives me?" Alaric asked suddenly, his voice cutting through the silence as Helena reached for the door handle.

She paused, her back still to him, fingers hovering over the ornate brass. For a moment, she seemed to weigh her response, shoulders tensing slightly beneath the emerald fabric of her gown. Then she turned, her face composed but eyes alight with curiosity.

"Yes," she said simply, returning to sit in the high-backed chair beside his bed. "I wish to know everything."

Alaric's laugh was bitter, a sound like steel scraping stone. "No, you don't. But I'll tell you enough." He shifted against the pillows, wincing as the movement pulled at his stitches. "I fight for coin, Princess. Not for honor, not for glory, and certainly not for any cause."

"Yet here you are," Helena observed quietly, "half-dead in my castle, having delivered a seal that secured my claim."

"That was different." His eyes darkened with memory. "Lyra's death demanded completion of her mission. But make no mistake—I am no champion of justice."

Helena leaned forward slightly. "Then what do you want, mercenary? If not coin, if not cause?"

"I want to kill your uncle." The words fell between them like stones, hard and irrevocable. "With my own hands. Slowly, if possible."

Helena's expression didn't change, but something in her eyes sharpened. "Why? What has Lord Varen done to earn such specific hatred?"

Alaric's gaze drifted to the window, where twilight painted the sky in bruised purples and fading golds. "Three years ago, I was part of a mercenary company hired to defend the southern border town of Falwood. Good coin, simple work—or so we thought."

His fingers traced absently over a scar on his forearm, a raised ridge of tissue that disappeared beneath his bandages. "What we didn't know was that Varen had already made a deal with the southern kingdom. He needed a pretext for military intervention, a reason to bring his forces across the border."

"The Southland Campaign," Helena murmured, recognition dawning in her eyes. "My father said it was a necessary response to border raids."

"There were no raids," Alaric said flatly. "Only Varen's ambition. He sacrificed Falwood—gave the southern forces our positions, our numbers, our weaknesses. My company was slaughtered. I survived only because I was scouting when the attack came."

His jaw tightened, a muscle working beneath the stubble. "I returned to find everyone dead—my brothers-in-arms, the townspeople, everyone. But that wasn't the worst of it."

Helena sat perfectly still, waiting.

"I hid in the ruins for three days, watching as Varen's forces finally arrived. He rode in like a conquering hero, as if he hadn't orchestrated the whole bloody massacre." Alaric's voice dropped to a dangerous whisper. "Then I watched him give the order."

"What order?" Helena asked, though something in her expression suggested she already feared the answer.

"'Make an example,' he said. The survivors—women, children, the elderly who'd hidden in root cellars and attics—they were dragged into the town square." Alaric's eyes met hers, cold and flat as winter ice. "The women were raped before their children's eyes. Then the children were butchered while their mothers watched. Finally, the women were killed. Slowly."

Helena's face had gone pale, but she didn't look away. "You witnessed this?"

"Every moment," Alaric confirmed. "I wanted to stop it. Should have tried, even if it meant my death. Instead, I watched. Memorized every face, every name, every scream." His hand fisted in the sheets. "Varen stood on the balcony of the mayor's house, drinking wine while it happened. Smiling."

"Why would he—" Helena began, then stopped herself. "The southern provinces. He needed to ensure their loyalty through fear."

Alaric nodded grimly. "Your uncle returned to the capital a hero, having 'avenged' the massacre at Falwood and secured the southern territories. No one questioned the convenient timing. No one except those of us who knew the truth."

"And you've carried this knowledge alone all this time?"

"Not entirely alone. There were other witnesses—soldiers in Varen's own ranks who were sickened by what they saw. Some tried to speak out. They disappeared. Others kept silent out of fear."

Helena rose from her chair, moving to the window. The last light of day silhouetted her slender form as she gazed out over Ravenscrest. "My father would never have condoned such actions," she said softly. "He must not have known."

"Or perhaps he chose not to know," Alaric suggested, his voice hard. "Kings often find it convenient to look away from the atrocities that secure their power."

She turned to face him, chin lifted in quiet defiance. "I am not my father."

"No," Alaric agreed, studying her with new interest. "You're not. Which is why I'm telling you this now."

"You want my permission to kill him," Helena said, cutting to the heart of the matter with surprising directness. "My uncle. My father's brother."

"I don't need your permission, Princess. Only your lack of interference when the time comes." Alaric's expression was implacable. "Varen is a monster who has done too much evil to still live. The world will be better without him in it."

Helena returned to his bedside, her movements deliberate, controlled. She sat on the edge of the bed rather than the chair, close enough that Alaric could see the fine threads of gold in her auburn hair, could smell the subtle scent of lavender that clung to her skin.

"And if I ordered you to spare him?" she asked, her voice barely above a whisper. "If I commanded that he stand trial for his crimes instead?"

Alaric met her gaze unflinchingly. "Then I would have to disappoint you, Princess. Some debts can only be paid in blood."

For a long moment, they regarded each other in silence, the weight of unspoken possibilities hanging between them. Then Helena nodded, a slight inclination of her head that carried the gravity of royal decree.

"I understand," she said simply.

"Do you?" Alaric challenged, searching her face for signs of deception or manipulation.

Helena's hand moved to rest atop his, her touch cool against his fever-warm skin. "Better than you might think. My uncle's ambition has cast a long shadow over my life. I've spent years watching him whisper in my father's ear, positioning his allies in court, eliminating those who opposed him." Her fingers tightened slightly on his. "I am not naive about what must be done to secure peace."

"And what must be done, Princess?" Alaric asked, suddenly aware of how close she sat, how the firelight caught in her eyes like flames reflected in still water.

"Justice," she replied, the word weighted with meaning beyond its simple syllables. "Swift and final."

Alaric studied her, seeing past the regal bearing to the steel beneath. This was no sheltered royal hiding behind castle walls, but a woman who had learned to navigate treacherous waters while smiling at those who would drown her.

"You surprise me," he admitted.

"Good." A hint of a smile touched her lips. "Underestimation is a weapon I've wielded all my life." She withdrew her hand from his, rising once more. "Rest now. Tomorrow I become Queen, and the real battle begins."

As she moved toward the door, Alaric called after her. "Helena."

She paused, the use of her name without title clearly unexpected.

"Your uncle won't stop until one of you is dead," he said, the words both warning and promise. "Are you prepared for what that means?"

Helena's answer came without hesitation, her voice steady and clear in the gathering darkness.

"I was born ready, Alaric Thornwood." She looked back at him, profile etched in shadow and firelight. "The question is: are you ready to serve a queen who won't flinch from necessary evils?"

Before he could answer, she was gone, the heavy door closing behind her with a sound like distant thunder. Alaric stared at the space she had occupied, his mind turning over this new understanding of the woman whose crown he had helped secure.

Perhaps, he thought, Lyra's faith had not been misplaced after all.

The silence of the room pressed in around Alaric after Helena departed, broken only by the occasional pop and hiss from the hearth. Sleep eluded him despite his exhaustion, his mind churning with thoughts of vengeance, duty, and the unexpected steel he'd discovered in the Princess — no, the Queen-to-be.

He stared at the ornate ceiling, counting the minutes by the burning of his wounds until he could bear the inaction no longer. With a grimace, he pushed back the silk sheets and swung his legs over the edge of the bed. Pain lanced through his torso as he forced himself to stand, the room tilting dangerously before his vision steadied.

"Damn it all," he muttered, gripping the bedpost for support. His bandaged body protested every movement, but three days of unconsciousness had left his muscles stiff and his spirit restless.

Alaric took a tentative step, then another, growing more confident as his body remembered its strength. Across the chamber, a large wooden chest sat beneath the window, moonlight spilling across its polished surface. Something pulled him toward it — instinct perhaps, or simply the warrior's eternal need to know where his weapons lay.

The lid creaked as he raised it, revealing the contents within. His obsidian-steel sword rested atop a folded pile of clothing, the blade cleaned of blood but still bearing the faint, smoky aura that had always marked it as something more than ordinary metal. Beside it lay his daggers, his leather armor — repaired where the creatures' claws had torn it — and a small pouch that clinked with the unmistakable sound of coin.

Alaric lifted the sword, feeling its familiar weight settle in his palm like greeting an old friend. The hilt still bore the imprints of his fingers from countless battles, the leather wrapping worn smooth in places where his skin had rubbed against it.

"Time to move," he told himself, setting the sword aside to examine the clothing. Someone had provided fresh garments—a simple linen shirt, dark breeches, and a leather jerkin dyed the deep blue of Ravenscrest's colors. He dressed slowly, each movement pulling at his stitches, but the pain cleared his mind and focused his thoughts.

Once clothed, he strapped on his sword belt, the weight of the blade against his hip completing him in some essential way. He might be in a royal castle, surrounded by guards and servants, but Alaric Thornwood would not walk unarmed again until Lord Varen lay dead at his feet.

The corridor outside his chamber was dimly lit by wall sconces, their flames casting long shadows across the stone floor. No guard stood at his door—either a sign of trust or evidence that Helena had more pressing concerns than monitoring a wounded mercenary. Alaric suspected the latter.

He moved through the castle like a ghost, his footsteps nearly silent despite his injuries. Servants hurried past without noticing him, their arms laden with linens, silver, and flowers for the coming coronation. The normally sedate pace of castle life had given way to frantic preparation, the corridors humming with purposeful activity even at this late hour.

A grand staircase led down to the main hall, where Alaric paused in the shadows to observe the scene below. Nobles in travel-stained finery were arriving even now, their retinues creating small eddies of chaos as servants scrambled to accommodate them. Heralds announced each new arrival, their voices competing with the general din of conversation and movement.

"Lord Blackthorn of the Northern Marches!"

"Lady Serena Ironwood and her sons!"

"The Delegation from Mistwood Province!"

Each announcement drew reactions from those already gathered—nods of approval, whispers behind hands, calculating glances that measured potential allies and enemies. This was another kind of battlefield, Alaric realized, one where the weapons were words and alliances rather than steel and blood. But the stakes were just as high.

A familiar figure caught his eye—Lord Harwick, the elderly seneschal, directing servants with quiet authority while simultaneously greeting new arrivals. The old man's face showed the strain of the past days, deep lines etched around his eyes and mouth, but his back remained straight, his manner unruffled.

CHAPTER 6 –
KNOW YOUR PLACE

Alaric descended the stairs, drawing curious glances from those who noticed the armed stranger in their midst. He ignored them, moving purposefully toward a side passage where armored knights stood in close conversation, their expressions grave.

"—can't hold the western gate indefinitely," one was saying, his scarred face tight with concern. "Varen's forces grow by the hour."

"The coronation changes everything," replied another, a tall woman whose armor bore the captain's insignia of the royal guard. "Once Her Highness wears the crown, half those troops will switch sides."

"And if they don't?" challenged a third, younger than the others but bearing the confident stance of a battle-tested warrior.

"Then we fight," the captain said simply. "As we've always done."

They fell silent as Alaric approached, hands moving subtly

toward sword hilts. The captain stepped forward, her keen eyes assessing him with professional detachment.

"The Princess's mercenary," she observed, neither approval nor condemnation in her tone. "You should be resting."

"I've rested enough," Alaric replied. "What's the situation at the gates?"

The knights exchanged glances, clearly debating how much to share with an outsider. Finally, the captain nodded, apparently coming to a decision.

"Lord Varen's advance force arrived yesterday — two hundred men flying his personal standard alongside the royal banner. They demand entry to 'witness the Princess's coronation and ensure its legitimacy.'"

"A pretext," Alaric said.

"Obviously," the scarred knight agreed. "They mean to disrupt the ceremony, perhaps even seize the Princess."

"They won't succeed," the captain stated flatly. "We've sealed all gates except the main entrance, which remains heavily guarded. No armed men are permitted entry without direct approval from Her Highness or myself."

Alaric nodded, impressed despite himself. "The city itself?"

"Tense," the younger knight admitted. "Some merchants fear war is coming and have begun to leave. Others are price-gouging, selling provisions at three times their worth to nervous citizens."

"War is already here," Alaric said, echoing Helena's words from earlier. "It just hasn't been declared yet."

The captain studied him with renewed interest. "You speak as one who knows battle."

"I know Varen," Alaric corrected her. "He won't accept defeat through ceremony. The coronation is only the beginning."

Before the conversation could continue, a commotion erupted in the main hall. Alaric turned to see a new group of arrivals being announced — not nobles this time, but envoys in the formal attire of kingdom officials. Their golden tabards bore the royal crest, but with a subtle difference that only those familiar with court protocol would notice: the small mark that identified them as representatives of the King's brother rather than the King himself.

"Lord Varen's envoys," the captain murmured, her hand moving to her sword hilt. "Right on schedule."

"To observe the coronation?" Alaric asked, though he already knew the answer.

"To find a way to stop it," she replied grimly.

Across the hall, Lord Harwick moved to intercept the newcomers, his elderly frame somehow imposing as he drew himself up to his full height. The lead envoy, a thin man with a pinched face and calculating eyes, bowed with exaggerated deference.

"Lord Harwick," the envoy's voice carried clearly across the suddenly hushed hall. "We come bearing a message from Lord Regent Varen for the Princess Helena."

The title 'Lord Regent' sent a ripple of murmurs through the gathered nobles. Harwick's expression remained impassive, but Alaric noted how the old man's hands clasped tightly behind his back—a gesture of restraint rather than deference.

"Her Highness will receive official communications in the morning, after proper verification of their authenticity," Harwick replied, his voice carrying the weight of decades of authority.

The envoy's smile didn't reach his eyes. "I'm afraid this matter cannot wait until morning. It concerns the legitimacy of tomorrow's... ceremony."

The implied challenge hung in the air like the moment before a lightning strike. Nobles shifted uneasily, some moving closer to hear better, others distancing themselves from potential conflict.

Alaric felt the familiar tension before battle settling into his muscles. Whatever game Varen was playing, these envoys were its opening gambit. He stepped forward, intending to intervene, when a clear voice rang out from the top of the grand staircase.

"I will hear Lord Varen's message now."

All eyes turned to see Princess Helena standing above them, resplendent in a gown of midnight blue embroidered with silver stars. Her copper hair was arranged in an elegant coronet of braids, and around her neck hung a simple silver chain bearing a small replica of the royal seal. She descended the stairs with measured grace, her expression serene despite the tension crackling through the hall.

The captain moved immediately to Helena's side as she reached the bottom step, positioning herself between the Princess and the envoys. Alaric found himself doing the same, approaching from the opposite direction until he stood slightly behind Helena's right shoulder, close enough to intervene if needed.

"Your Highness," the lead envoy bowed again, deeper this time. "Lord Varen sends his most sincere condolences on the tragic passing of your father, our beloved King."

A shocked silence fell over the hall. While rumors had circulated, this was the first public acknowledgment of King Adriel's death. Helena's face remained composed, though Alaric, standing close behind her, saw the slight tension in her shoulders.

"How thoughtful of my uncle to confirm what I already knew," Helena replied, her voice carrying clearly to every corner of the hall. "Though I find it curious that he chose to announce my father's death through envoys rather than coming himself to mourn with his family."

The envoy's smile tightened. "Lord Varen is consumed with grief, Your Highness. It is this very grief that compels him to ensure the kingdom's stability during this difficult transition." He produced a sealed document from within his robes. "As the King's only brother and closest male relative, Lord Varen has assumed the role of Lord Regent until such time as the succession can be properly established according to ancient law."

Murmurs rippled through the crowd again, louder this time. Helena extended her hand, and the envoy placed the document in her palm with a flourish that bordered on insolence.

She broke the seal without hesitation, her eyes scanning the contents quickly. When she looked up, her expression had hardened to something that reminded Alaric of a blade fresh from the forge — gleaming and deadly.

"How convenient," she said, her voice now edged with steel, "that my uncle declares himself regent on the very eve of my coronation." She held up the document for all to see. "This paper claims the royal seal is missing, and without it, no coronation can be considered legitimate under Morvain law."

The envoy inclined his head. "The seal disappeared with the King's death, Your Highness. Lord Varen has ordered a kingdom-wide search for this sacred artifact, without which no ruler can be crowned."

Helena's lips curved into a cold smile as she reached for the chain around her neck. "How unfortunate for my uncle that his information is incorrect." She pulled forth not the replica seal that had hung there moments before, but the true royal signet ring, gleaming gold catching the torchlight as she held it aloft for all to witness. "The royal seal is here, in my possession, delivered at great cost by loyal servants of the crown."

Gasps rippled through the hall as nobles pressed forward, straining to see the legendary symbol of Morvain's sovereignty.

"Impossible," the lead envoy hissed, his face draining of color. "That must be a forgery."

"Every noble in this hall knows the true seal on sight," Helena replied, her voice ringing with authority. "At dawn tomorrow, I will be crowned the rightful Queen of Morvain. My uncle's regency is hereby rejected as the desperate grasp for power that it is."

The second envoy stepped forward, his hand moving to his belt.

"Watch your words carefully, Princess," he snarled, abandoning all pretense of diplomacy. "Those who oppose Lord Varen's rightful regency may not live to see tomorrow's dawn."

The captain tensed beside Helena, her hand falling to her sword hilt as the crowd drew back, creating a circle of space around the confrontation. Alaric felt the familiar stillness settle over him—the calm before violence that had served him through countless battles.

Helena drew herself up to her full height, the seal clutched firmly in her hand. "I am the daughter of King Adriel, blood of his blood, heir to the throne of Morvain. I do not require my uncle's permission to claim what is rightfully mine." Her voice carried to every corner of the hall, unwavering and clear. "I am your ruler, and I will assume my rightful place at dawn."

The third envoy's face contorted with rage. "Treasonous bitch!" he spat, his hand darting beneath his golden tabard to produce a slender dagger with a jeweled hilt.

Time seemed to slow as the blade emerged. Alaric moved without conscious thought, his body flowing around Helena's like water around stone. His hand closed over the envoy's wrist, twisting with savage precision until the bones snapped with an audible crack. In the same fluid motion, he wrenched the dagger free and drove it up under the man's jaw, through the soft palate and into the brain.

Blood fountained as Alaric withdrew the blade, spinning toward the second envoy who was reaching for his own weapon. The borrowed dagger flashed again, opening the man's throat in a crimson spray that spattered across the polished marble floor. The envoy clutched futilely at his ruined neck, eyes wide with shock as he collapsed.

The lead envoy backed away, fumbling for a concealed weapon, but

Alaric was on him before his fingers found purchase. A vicious kick shattered the man's knee, dropping him to the floor with a shriek of pain. Alaric's fist connected with his face once, twice, three times — each blow landing with the methodical precision of a butcher at his work. Teeth scattered across the marble, followed by gouts of blood as the envoy's nose collapsed under Alaric's knuckles.

Alaric seized the man by his throat, lifting him half off the ground as he drew back his fist for another strike. The envoy's face was barely recognizable now, a ruined mask of blood and shattered bone.

"Enough!" Helena's voice cut through the shocked silence that had fallen over the hall. "Let him live, Alaric."

Alaric's fist remained poised, every muscle in his body screaming for completion of the violence he'd begun. Blood — not his own — dripped from his knuckles onto the whimpering envoy's chest.

"He's worth more alive than dead," Helena continued, her voice steady despite the carnage before her. "Let him carry word back to my uncle."

Slowly, deliberately, Alaric lowered his fist. He released the envoy, who collapsed in a broken heap on the blood-slick floor, choking on his own teeth.

Helena stepped forward, the royal seal still clutched in her hand, blood spatter marring the pristine blue of her gown. She surveyed the horrified nobles, the dead bodies, and the surviving envoy with the same cool detachment.

"Behold the diplomacy of Lord Varen," she announced, her voice carrying to every corner of the silent hall. "He sends assassins to a coronation. He would kill any who oppose his ambition." Her eyes swept the gathered crowd, challenging and fierce. "But I am not afraid of my uncle's cowardly tactics. I am the rightful heir to the throne of Morvain, and tomorrow I will wear the crown."

She turned to the captain, who stood rigid with shock at the swift violence that had unfolded before her. "Captain Eldric, have this man secured in the eastern tower. Ensure he receives medical attention—enough to keep him alive until I decide his fate."

Captain Eldric bowed stiffly. "At once, Your Highness."

Helena's gaze found Alaric next, taking in his blood-soaked appearance with a look that mingled approval and something darker, more complex. "Master Thornwood, attend me in the council chamber." She turned to Lord Harwick, who had remained remarkably composed throughout the chaos. "Lord Harwick, see to our guests. I believe we all need a moment to collect ourselves before dinner is served."

Without waiting for acknowledgment, Helena swept from the hall, her midnight blue gown trailing through the blood of her would-be assassins. Alaric followed, aware of the eyes that tracked his movement — some fearful, others calculating, all reassessing the mercenary who had just killed two men in the span of heartbeats.

In the relative privacy of the corridor beyond, Helena paused, allowing Alaric to catch up to her. Blood had splashed across her face in a fine mist, giving her the appearance of a warrior queen from ancient legends.

"You didn't hesitate," she observed quietly, studying him with those piercing blue eyes.

"Neither did you," Alaric replied, equally soft. "Most royals would have fled at the first sign of violence."

A ghost of a smile touched her lips. "I am not most royals." She glanced down at her bloodied gown. "I should change before addressing the council. This sends rather the wrong message."

"Or exactly the right one," Alaric countered. "Let them see what challenging your rule will cost them."

Helena considered this, then nodded slowly. "Perhaps you're right. Fear has its uses." She resumed walking, her pace unhurried despite the gravity of what had just occurred. "Walk with me, Alaric. We have much to discuss before dawn."

They walked in silence through the torch-lit corridors, their footsteps echoing against stone walls that had witnessed centuries of royal intrigue. The distant sounds of the castle preparing for tomorrow's coronation faded as they moved deeper into the older sections of Ravenscrest.

"Your uncle's army grows stronger at our gates," Alaric said finally, his voice low. "I counted at least three hundred men from the eastern tower window. They've positioned archers in the tree line."

Helena's face remained impassive, though her fingers tightened around the royal seal she still clutched. "And what would you suggest we do about them, Master Thornwood? You've seen more battles than most of my captains."

"You ask my counsel?" Alaric raised an eyebrow.

"I ask what you would do," she clarified, pausing beside a narrow window that overlooked the shadowy forest beyond Ravenscrest's walls. "If this were your battle to plan."

Alaric studied her profile, illuminated by moonlight that spilled through the leaded glass. "A preemptive strike. Tonight. While they believe us occupied with coronation preparations. A small force could set fire to their siege equipment before they've fully assembled it."

Helena turned to face him fully, something like approval flickering in her eyes. "Interesting. Captain Eldric suggested something similar."

"And yet you hesitate."

"I'm waiting for word from my scouts," she admitted. "There are rumors that not all those soldiers are loyal to Varen. Some wear his colors under duress." Her gaze was steady, calculating. "I would not slaughter men who might yet become my allies."

Alaric inclined his head. "Wise. Though mercy on a battlefield often becomes regret in the aftermath."

"Then I shall rely on your ruthlessness to balance my compassion," Helena replied with the ghost of a smile. She resumed walking, her gown whispering against the stone floor. "Do what you think best, Alaric. I trust your judgment in matters of war."

The casual statement of trust caught him off guard. "You barely know me."

"I know enough," she countered. "You've killed for me twice now. First to deliver the seal, then to protect me from assassins." Her voice softened slightly. "Few men would have survived either task, let alone both."

They reached a heavy wooden door bound with iron. Helena pushed it open, revealing a small private chamber — not the council room he had expected, but something more intimate. A fire burned in the hearth, casting dancing shadows across comfortable furnishings that spoke of regular use.

"My father's thinking room," Helena explained, noticing Alaric's questioning glance. "Where he came to escape the burdens of the crown, if only for an hour." She moved to a side table where a decanter of amber liquid caught the firelight. "Wine?"

"Please."

She poured two goblets, handing one to him before settling onto a cushioned bench near the fire. The blood on her gown had dried to a rusty brown, giving her the appearance of a warrior returned from battle rather than a princess on the eve of her coronation.

"I'm surprised, you know," she said after a moment, swirling the wine in her goblet.

"By what?"

"That you haven't asked for my hand." Her eyes met his over the rim of her cup, a challenge dancing in their blue depths. "It's customary, after all. The hero who saves the princess traditionally claims her as his reward."

Alaric nearly choked on his wine. "I didn't save you for reward."

"No?" She raised an eyebrow, amusement playing at the corners of her mouth. "Then why did you step between me and those blades? Why risk your life for a royal you barely know?"

"It wasn't the time to discuss marriage proposals," he replied dryly. "Not with assassins in our midst."

Helena laughed, the sound surprisingly genuine. "Always so practical." She set her goblet aside and stood, moving toward him with deliberate grace. The fire behind her silhouetted her form through the thin fabric of her gown, revealing curves that the formal cut had previously concealed.

"A pity," she murmured, close enough now that he could smell the subtle scent of lavender beneath the metallic tang of dried blood. "You really are very handsome, Alaric Thornwood. Especially when covered in the blood of my enemies."

CHAPTER 7 –
A DANGEROUS GAME

Her directness disarmed him more effectively than any blade. Alaric set his own goblet down carefully, conscious of the dangerous territory they were entering.

"You play a dangerous game, Princess," he warned, his voice rougher than intended.

"Queen," she corrected him. "By this time tomorrow. And queens take what they want." Her fingers traced the line of his jaw, coming to rest at the pulse point in his throat. "Don't they?"

The heat of her touch burned through him, awakening desires he'd thought long buried beneath duty and vengeance. For a breathless moment, he allowed himself to imagine what it would be like to claim those lips, to lose himself in her warmth and forget the blood-soaked path that had led him to her chamber.

Instead, he gently captured her wrist, lowering her hand. "Not this queen. Not tonight."

Hurt flashed briefly in her eyes before being replaced by the cool mask of royalty. "You refuse me?"

"I respect you," he corrected. "Too much to take advantage of the eve of your coronation, when emotions run high and danger surrounds us." His thumb traced small circles against her pulse, belying the restraint in his words. "If I were to take you to bed, Helena, it would not be as a reward or a conquest, but as a choice made in the clear light of day."

Understanding dawned in her expression, followed by something warmer, more genuine than the calculated seduction of moments before. "You continue to surprise me, mercenary."

"Good," he echoed her earlier sentiment. "Underestimation is a weapon, after all."

A sharp knock at the door interrupted whatever she might have said next. Helena stepped back, composing herself with practiced ease as Captain Eldric entered, her face grave beneath her helmet.

"Your Highness," she bowed stiffly. "We've received word from the scouts. Lord Varen's forces have been joined by the armies of House Blackthorn and House Ironwood. They now number close to a thousand."

Helena's expression hardened, all traces of the woman who had just attempted seduction vanishing beneath the mantle of rulership. "So the northern lords have chosen their side."

"Not all, Your Highness," Eldric continued. "Lord Harwick has received pledges of support from three eastern houses. Their forces march as we speak, but won't arrive before midday tomorrow."

"After the coronation," Alaric noted. "Convenient timing."

"They wait to see which way the wind blows," Helena agreed bitterly. "What of our defenses, Captain?"

"We can hold the walls for three days, perhaps four," Eldric replied, her professional assessment unflinching. "Less if they bring the siege engines I've spotted being assembled in the tree line."

Helena nodded, absorbing this information with remarkable composure. "Double the guard on the walls tonight. And have archers positioned on the eastern tower before dawn. I won't have my coronation disrupted by Varen's forces."

"Yes, Your Highness." Eldric hesitated, then added, "There's one more thing. A messenger arrived an hour ago, claiming to bear information about the King's death. He'll speak only to you directly."

Helena and Alaric exchanged glances. "Another of my uncle's tricks?"

"Possibly," Eldric admitted. "But he knew details about the palace that few outside the royal household would know. And he bears this." She produced a small object from her belt pouch — a broken arrow shaft with distinctive black and red fletching.

Helena's face paled slightly as she took the arrow fragment. "The King's personal guard," she whispered. "This is from Captain Thorne's quiver. He never left my father's side."

"Where is this messenger now?" Alaric demanded.

"Secured in the west tower," Eldric replied. "Under guard, as you ordered, Your Highness."

Helena's fingers closed around the arrow shaft, her decision made. "Bring him to the council chamber in one hour. Master Thornwood and I will hear what he has to say." She turned to Alaric as Eldric bowed and departed. "It seems our evening has been decided for us after all."

"So it would seem," he agreed, retrieving his wine goblet and draining it in one swallow. "Though I doubt this messenger brings good tidings."

"No," Helena sighed, suddenly looking much younger than her years. "Good tidings are in short supply these days." She moved toward the door, pausing to glance back at him. "Coming, Master Thornwood? If we are to face more bad news, I'd prefer to do so with you at my side."

Helena's hand found the door handle when a commotion erupted in the corridor. A young servant boy skidded around the corner, nearly colliding with them, his face flushed with exertion.

"Your Highness!" he gasped, dropping into a hasty bow. "Knights—a dozen at least—emerging from the western edge of the forest! They bear no banners, but their armor gleams silver in the moonlight!"

Alaric's hand flew to his sword hilt, his body tensing like a drawn bowstring. "No banners means they don't want to be identified. Varen's assassins, not his army."

Helena's expression hardened as she processed this new threat. "How far?"

"Minutes from the outer wall, Your Highness," the boy replied, trembling slightly under her intense gaze.

Alaric stepped forward, his decision already made. "Order all guards to battle stations," he told Helena, his voice dropping to the cold, efficient tone of a commander. "Have Captain Eldric double the watch on the prisoner—if these knights are here for him, that confirms his value. Allow no one through the gates, no matter what colors they wear or what words they speak."

"And you?" Helena asked, though the look in her eyes suggested she already knew his answer.

"I'll handle the knights myself." The predatory smile that curved Alaric's lips held no mirth, only the promise of violence. "Twelve men in the dark is hardly a challenge."

"You're still wounded," she reminded him, concern briefly overriding her royal composure.

"Pain clarifies the mind," he replied, already moving toward the servants' stairwell that would take him to the lower levels fastest. "Besides, I've been wanting to test how your uncle trains his killers."

Helena caught his arm, her fingers digging into his flesh with surprising strength. "Don't die for me, Thornwood. I've only just found use for you."

The corner of his mouth twitched upward. "I don't die easily, Princess. Ask your uncle's envoys." He gently disengaged from her grip. "Now go. Alert your guards and secure the castle. I'll return before the council meets."

Without waiting for her response, Alaric disappeared down the narrow stairwell, the darkness swallowing him as he descended into the bowels of Ravenscrest. Helena watched the space where he had been for a heartbeat longer, then turned to the wide-eyed servant.

"Fetch Captain Eldric immediately," she commanded, her voice steady despite the fear clawing at her chest. "Tell her to meet me at the prisoner's cell with her four best guards. Then sound the alarm—quietly. I want every man at his post, but without alerting our 'guests' that we know they're coming."

The boy bowed again and ran, leaving Helena alone in the corridor. She drew a deep breath, steadying herself against the coming storm. "Gods protect you, Alaric Thornwood," she whispered to the empty air. "I still have need of your blade."

*****

Alaric moved through the castle's lower levels like a shadow, his footsteps silent despite his haste. The servant passages were largely deserted at this hour, most staff occupied with preparations for tomorrow's coronation. He encountered only a single kitchen maid, who flattened herself against the wall at the sight of his blood-spattered appearance and drawn blade.

The western postern gate — a small, rarely-used exit designed for messengers and servants — would serve his purpose perfectly. Alaric slipped through it unnoticed, the night air cool against his face as he emerged into the castle gardens.

From here, he could see the western wall and, beyond it, the dark line of the forest. His keen eyes picked out movement at the tree line — armored figures moving with the practiced stealth of trained killers. They were closer than the servant boy had estimated, perhaps five minutes from the wall at most.

Alaric assessed his options quickly. The knights would expect resistance at the gate, but they wouldn't anticipate someone circling behind them. He moved along the garden wall, finding the spot where an ancient oak's branches extended over the stonework. Despite his injuries, he scaled the tree with practiced efficiency, using its limbs to cross over the outer wall and drop silently to the ground on the other side.

The tall grass beyond the wall concealed his approach as he circled wide, aiming to come at the knights from the direction of the forest. His obsidian-steel blade made no sound as he drew it, the dark metal seeming to drink in what little moonlight filtered through the clouds.

The knights had reached the edge of the open field now, their armor indeed gleaming silver in the moonlight. They moved in tight formation, weapons drawn, with the silent coordination that spoke of long training together. Not common mercenaries, then, but Varen's elite — perhaps even former Red Guard who had switched allegiance when the King died.

Alaric counted twelve, as the boy had said. Four with crossbows, eight with swords and shields bearing no insignia. They paused at the field's edge, the leader gesturing toward the postern gate that Alaric had used minutes earlier.

He closed the distance silently, utilizing every shadow, every tuft of tall grass. The night was his ally, as was the knights' focus on the castle wall ahead. They never thought to look behind them, to the forest they had just left.

Their first warning was the wet gurgle as Alaric's blade found the gap between helmet and breastplate of the rearmost knight. The man collapsed without a cry, blood fountaining from his severed artery. Before his body hit the ground, Alaric had already moved to his next target, driving his dagger up through the eye slit of the second knight's helmet.

"Behind us!" The leader's shout came too late as Alaric dropped a third man with a savage slash to the hamstrings, leaving him writhing in the grass.

The remaining knights whirled to face this unexpected threat, crossbows swinging around with deadly intent. Alaric was already moving, using the body of a fallen knight as a shield as two bolts thudded into dead flesh. He rolled, came up inside the guard of a fourth knight, and drove his blade through the man's throat with such force that the point emerged from the back of his neck.

"Demon!" one of the crossbowmen shouted, frantically trying to reload his weapon. Alaric's thrown dagger caught him in the eye before he could finish, sending him toppling backward with a strangled scream.

The remaining seven knights formed a hasty circle, shields raised, trying to contain the whirlwind of death that had erupted in their midst. Their leader, a tall man with a plume of black feathers on his helmet, barked orders in a clipped, authoritative voice.

"Hold formation! He's just one man!"

"One is enough," Alaric growled, launching himself at the weakest point in their circle—a younger knight whose shield arm trembled visibly. His obsidian-steel blade sheared through the shield's edge, taking the knight's fingers with it before reversing to slash across the exposed throat beneath the helmet.

The formation broke as Alaric pressed his advantage, ducking beneath a wild sword swing to hamstring another knight. Blood slicked the grass beneath their feet, making footing treacherous as the desperate melee continued.

A sword caught Alaric across the shoulder, reopening one of his healing wounds. He hissed in pain but used the knight's momentary overextension to drive his blade up through the man's groin, twisting savagely before wrenching it free in a spray of arterial blood.

Five down. Seven remaining.

The leader recognized the losing battle and changed tactics. "Fall back to the trees!" he commanded. "Crossbows cover our retreat!"

Alaric charged forward, determined to prevent their escape. A crossbow bolt grazed his thigh, but he barely felt the sting as battle-fury consumed him. He caught the nearest retreating knight by his cloak, yanking him backward off balance before driving his blade through the man's back with enough force to pierce the breastplate.

The remaining knights broke into a run, all pretense of formation abandoned. Alaric pursued, his longer stride closing the distance despite his injuries. He tackled one from behind, both of them crashing to the ground in a tangle of limbs and armor. The knight fought desperately, landing a gauntleted blow to Alaric's wounded side that sent white-hot agony lancing through him.

Alaric responded by seizing the man's helmet and twisting with brutal strength until the neck snapped with an audible crack. He rolled off the corpse, breathing heavily, blood — both his and theirs — soaking his clothing.

The leader and his last three men had reached the tree line, disappearing into the shadows of the forest. Alaric considered pursuit, then decided against it. His wounds were bleeding freely now, and the advantage of surprise was lost. Better to return to the castle and prepare for their next move, which would surely come before dawn.

He surveyed the carnage he'd left behind — nine bodies scattered across the blood-soaked grass, their silver armor now dulled with gore and dirt.

None bore any identifying marks, but their equipment and fighting style told him what he needed to know. These were Varen's personal guard, men who answered directly to him rather than to the crown.

The fact that they had come in secret, without banners, told him their mission was assassination rather than warfare. Varen was growing desperate — good. Desperate men made mistakes.

Alaric cleaned his blade on the cloak of a fallen knight, then began the laborious process of searching the bodies. He found what he expected — purses of gold, far more than common soldiers would carry, and sealed orders on the leader who had escaped. The wax seal bore no official mark, but the parchment inside confirmed his suspicions.

"Secure the messenger. Kill any who interfere. Return with his head as proof."

So they had come for the mysterious informant. Alaric tucked the orders into his belt pouch—evidence Helena would find useful—and began the painful journey back to the castle, leaving the bodies where they lay as a message to any who might follow.

The postern gate stood ajar as he approached, a lone figure silhouetted against the torchlight from within. As he drew closer, the figure resolved into Helena herself, her copper hair gleaming like fire in the darkness.

"I ordered the guards to their posts," she said by way of explanation, her eyes widening as she took in his blood-soaked appearance. "Are you hurt?"

"Not fatally," he replied, limping past her into the relative safety of the castle walls. "But your uncle's men will not trouble us again tonight."

"All of them?" she asked, securing the gate behind them.

"I left three alive to carry tales of failure back to Varen," Alaric said grimly. "Fear spreads faster than truth."

Helena nodded, her expression hardening as she took in the implications. "Then the messenger truly does hold information my uncle fears." She turned toward the inner keep, her decision made. "Come. We'll hear what he has to say now, before my uncle makes another attempt."

"Let me clean my wounds first," Alaric said, gesturing to his blood-soaked clothing. "I have something to attend to before I join you."

Helena's eyes narrowed slightly. "What are you planning?"

"A message," he replied, his voice flat. "For anyone else who might consider approaching these walls tonight."

She studied him for a long moment, weighing his words against the cold determination in his eyes. Finally, she nodded. "Do what you must. But don't linger in the open too long. My uncle may have more than just knights at his disposal."

"I won't be long," he promised. "Go to the messenger. Learn what he knows."

Helena hesitated, then reached out to touch his blood-spattered cheek, her fingers coming away crimson. "Be careful, Alaric. I need you alive for what's to come."

"As you command, my Queen," he replied, the formality strangely intimate between them.

She withdrew her hand reluctantly and turned toward the inner keep, her midnight blue gown disappearing into the shadows of the corridor.

Once alone, Alaric moved with grim purpose toward the armory adjacent to the gate. Inside, he found what he sought—a rack of iron spikes used to reinforce the defenses during siege. Each was as long as he was tall, wickedly sharp at one end and flat at the other for hammering into place.

He gathered a dozen, the metal cold and heavy in his arms, and returned to the postern gate. The bodies of the knights still lay where they had fallen, silver armor gleaming dully under the rising moon. Perfect.

Alaric slipped through the gate and approached the first corpse—a young knight whose face was frozen in an expression of permanent surprise. With methodical precision, he drove the first spike deep into the soft earth, then hoisted the body onto it, impaling it through the chest until the spike emerged from between the shoulder blades.

The dead weight settled, the body hanging suspended above the ground like a grotesque puppet. Blood, still liquid enough to flow, dripped from the corpse's boots, pattering softly on the grass below.

One by one, Alaric repeated the process with each fallen knight, arranging them in a semi-circle facing the forest. Some he impaled through the chest, others through the throat or belly, positioning their lifeless arms to point accusingly toward the trees where their companions had fled.

The work reopened his wounds, blood seeping through his bandages to mingle with that of the dead. Alaric ignored the pain, focused entirely on crafting his macabre warning. When he drove the final spike through the last knight—the one who had wounded him with the crossbow bolt—he stepped back to survey his handiwork.

Nine bodies suspended in the moonlight, their armor reflecting the cold stars above, blood pooling beneath them in dark puddles that would be visible to any who approached from the forest. A message written in flesh and steel: this is what awaits you.

But Alaric wasn't finished. With careful precision, he removed the helmets from each impaled knight, arranging them in a line at the base of the grisly display. Then, using his dagger and the still-warm blood of the dead, he traced a single word across the breastplate of the centermost corpse:

VAREN.

His grim task complete, Alaric gathered the fallen weapons—swords, daggers, and crossbows that might prove useful in the coming siege—and moved toward the tree line. The forest loomed dark and silent before him, but his trained senses detected subtle movements among the shadows: the watchers Varen had left behind to observe the results of the attack.

Alaric melted into the darkness beneath the first line of trees, moving with the silent grace that had served him through countless battles. He circled wide, using the sound of wind through leaves to mask his approach as he closed in on the first scout.

The man sat motionless on a low branch, a spyglass trained on Ravenscrest's walls. He never heard Alaric's approach, never felt anything beyond a momentary pressure at the base of his skull before the knife severed his spinal cord. Alaric caught the body as it slumped, lowering it silently to the forest floor.

Twenty paces further, he found the second scout—this one on foot, crouched behind a fallen log. The man had just spotted the impaled bodies, his breath catching audibly as he registered the gruesome display. His shock was so complete that he failed to notice Alaric's approach until a hand clamped over his mouth from behind.

"How many more of you are there?" Alaric whispered, his blade pricking the skin beneath the scout's ear.

The man trembled, shaking his head frantically. Alaric eased the pressure of his hand slightly, allowing him to speak.

"Three—three more," the scout gasped, his voice barely audible. "Stationed along the tree line. Please, I'm just a lookout. I'm not even a soldier."

"Where is Varen?" Alaric demanded, twisting the knife enough to draw blood.

"Coming," the scout whimpered. "With the main force. They'll reach the eastern road by midday tomorrow."

Too late for the coronation, but soon enough to pose a serious threat to the newly-crowned queen. Alaric considered his options. He could kill this scout and hunt down the others, but that would take time he didn't have. Better to use the man to send a clearer message.

"What's your name?" Alaric asked, his voice deceptively gentle.

"M-Morris," the scout stammered.

"Well, Morris," Alaric continued, his blade never wavering from the man's throat, "I'm going to give you a choice. You can die here, quietly, and join your friends on those spikes out there. Or you can deliver a message to Lord Varen for me."

"A message," Morris repeated, hope creeping into his voice. "I can do that. I swear it."

Alaric turned the man roughly to face him, keeping the knife pressed against his jugular. "Tell Varen that Alaric Thornwood sends his regards. Tell him I'm coming for him, just as I came for the men at Falwood." He leaned closer, his eyes reflecting the cold light of the stars above. "Tell him I remember the faces of everyone who died there. Tell him I've been practicing what I'll do to him when we meet."

Morris's face had gone white with terror, his eyes wide as he stared into Alaric's implacable gaze. "F-Falwood? But that was —"

"Tell him," Alaric continued, pressing the blade deeper until a thin trickle of blood ran down the scout's neck, "that the Princess has the royal seal, and by dawn she will be Queen. And tell him that every man he sends against these walls will end up like those knights out there."

He released Morris with a shove that sent the smaller man stumbling backward. "Now run. If you're still within sight of these walls when I count to ten, I'll hunt you down and skin you alive."

Morris needed no further encouragement. He turned and fled into the forest, crashing through underbrush in his haste to escape. Alaric watched him go, counting silently.

At "ten," he turned back toward Ravenscrest, his grim task complete. The remaining scouts could wait—they would either flee after seeing Morris's panic, or they would stay and report what they had witnessed. Either way, the message would reach Varen: death awaited at Ravenscrest's walls.

As Alaric approached the postern gate, the full moon emerged from behind a cloud, illuminating the field of impaled knights in stark relief. Their shadows stretched long and dark across the grass, reaching toward the castle like accusing fingers. In the morning, all who approached the western wall would see Alaric's warning—a promise written in blood and steel of what awaited those who threatened the soon-to-be Queen.

The gate opened at his approach, a guard ushering him quickly inside. "The Princess awaits you in the west tower, sir," the man said, eyeing Alaric's blood-soaked appearance with poorly concealed apprehension. "The prisoner has begun to talk."

Alaric nodded, casting one final glance at his handiwork before the gate closed behind him. The night was still young, and much remained to be done before dawn brought Helena's coronation—and with it, the war that would determine the fate of Morvain itself.

He climbed the winding stairs to the west tower, each step sending fresh pain through his reopened wounds. The guard outside the tower door straightened as he approached, knocking twice before opening it to announce his arrival.

"Master Thornwood, Your Highness."

Alaric stepped into the chamber to find Helena standing over a seated figure—a man in the tattered remains of what had once been the uniform of the King's personal guard. The prisoner's face was bruised, one eye swollen shut, but his remaining eye widened with recognition as Alaric entered.

"You," the prisoner whispered, his voice hoarse with disuse. "The mercenary from Thornhaven."

Alaric froze, recognition dawning as he studied the battered face before him. "Captain Thorne. I thought you were dead."

Helena's gaze darted between them. "You know each other?"

"We've met," Alaric replied grimly, his hand instinctively moving to his sword hilt. "The last time I saw him, he was giving orders to the Red Guard who were hunting us through Mistwood."

Captain Thorne's remaining eye darted nervously between Alaric and Helena. "Not by choice," he rasped, his split lip cracking as he spoke. "Varen had my family. Said he'd kill them if I didn't lead the hunt for you."

"A convenient excuse," Alaric replied coldly.

"It's the truth!" Thorne's voice cracked with desperation. "I led them into Mistwood deliberately, hoping to lose them in the depths. I never expected..." His voice trailed off, a visible shudder running through his battered frame.

"Expected what?" Helena pressed, leaning closer.

CHAPTER 8 –

MORE QUESTIONS UNANSWERED

Thorne's face contorted with remembered horror. "The creatures. They came from nowhere — gray-blue skin, yellow eyes, teeth like needles. My men..." He swallowed hard, Adam's apple bobbing beneath the bruises on his throat. "The creatures took them. Skinned them alive while they screamed. Ate them piece by piece, starting with the softest parts."

Alaric let out a dark chuckle that raised gooseflesh on the arms of the guards present.

"You should never have followed me into Mistwood," he said, his voice deadly quiet. "The forest and I have an understanding."

Thorne stared at him with dawning comprehension. "You knew. You led us there deliberately."

"Perhaps," Alaric shrugged, neither confirming nor denying. "How did you escape?"

"I didn't," Thorne whispered. "They let me go. Said to tell the others what awaited them." His gaze shifted to Helena. "Your Highness, you must understand — Varen is coming. Not just with the knights you've seen, but with an army a thousand strong. Mercenaries, conscripts, soldiers loyal to his gold rather than any crown."

"A thousand men won't matter," Alaric stated flatly.

Helena turned to him, brow furrowed. "How can you be so certain? Our walls are strong, but a force that size could overwhelm us before reinforcements arrive."

"They'll never reach the gate," Alaric replied, a predatory smile spreading across his face. "Trust me on this."

"Why are you so sure?" Helena demanded, her regal composure slipping slightly to reveal genuine concern.

Alaric's eyes met hers, something ancient and cold flickering in their depths. "There is much you don't know about me, Princess. Much your uncle doesn't know either." He placed a hand on her shoulder, his touch surprisingly gentle despite the blood still caking his knuckles. "But you needn't worry. By this time tomorrow, you'll be queen, and Varen will understand exactly what kind of enemy he's made."

Captain Thorne looked between them, his remaining eye wide. "You don't understand. Varen doesn't just want the throne—he wants you dead, Princess. He believes the throne is his by right of strength. The royal seal means nothing to him."

"Then he will learn differently," Helena replied, drawing herself up to her full height. "Captain Thorne, you've risked much to bring this warning. Will you stand with us now, against the man who threatened your family?"

Thorne hesitated, conflict evident on his battered face. "My family—"

"Is safe," Alaric interrupted. "I had them moved to a secure location three days ago."

Both Helena and Thorne stared at him in shock.

"How did you —" Thorne began.

"I have resources beyond these walls," Alaric said dismissively. "Your wife and daughters are under protection in a place Varen will never find them."

Helena's eyes narrowed slightly. "You never mentioned this."

"You never asked." Alaric's gaze remained fixed on Thorne. "So, Captain. Where do your loyalties lie now?"

Thorne straightened in his chair, a new resolve hardening his features. "With the true heir. With Princess Helena."

"Good." Alaric turned to Helena. "We should move him somewhere more secure. The western tower is too exposed if Varen's men breach the walls."

Helena nodded, her mind already racing ahead. "Captain Eldric, have quarters prepared in the inner keep. Captain Thorne's knowledge of my uncle's plans may prove invaluable." She paused, studying Alaric with newfound curiosity. "And you, Master Thornwood, will join me in my father's study. It seems we have much to discuss before dawn."

As they descended the tower stairs, Helena kept her voice low. "You speak as if you command forces beyond these walls. What aren't you telling me?"

Alaric's smile was grim in the torchlight. "Let's just say I've been planning for this confrontation longer than you realize. Varen's ambitions didn't begin with your father's death."

"And these... creatures from Mistwood? You imply they answer to you somehow."

"Not to me," Alaric corrected. "But we share a common enemy. Varen's men burned their southern grove, remember? The forest has a long memory and little mercy."

They reached the bottom of the stairs, where the corridor branched toward the private royal apartments. Helena dismissed her guards with a gesture, waiting until they were alone before continuing.

"If what Thorne says is true, we face overwhelming odds."

"Numbers mean nothing if they never reach their target," Alaric replied. "Besides, you have something Varen doesn't."

"The royal seal?"

"Me," he said simply, without arrogance—a statement of fact.

Helena studied him in the flickering torchlight, seeing beyond the blood-soaked mercenary to something else entirely—something older and more dangerous than she had first realized.

"Who are you really, Alaric Thornwood?" she whispered.

He took her hand, his blood-stained fingers entwining with hers in a gesture too intimate for subject and sovereign. "Someone who has waited a very long time for tomorrow's dawn." He lifted her hand to his lips, pressing a kiss against her knuckles that left a smear of blood like a crimson promise. "Someone who will see you crowned, no matter the cost."

The torches flickered as if disturbed by an unfelt breeze, casting strange shadows across Alaric's face—shadows that seemed to shift and change in ways that defied explanation. Helena felt a shiver run down her spine, not entirely from fear.

"Then let us prepare," she said, tightening her grip on his hand. "Dawn comes quickly, and with it, my reign begins."

As they walked toward the king's study, servants scurried past with final preparations for the coronation. None noticed the blood-soaked mercenary and the soon-to-be queen, hands still clasped in silent understanding, nor the shadows that seemed to follow in their wake—shadows that moved with purpose of their own.

In the forest beyond Ravenscrest's walls, yellow eyes gleamed in the darkness, watching, waiting. The wind carried whispers between the ancient trees, a promise of blood and vengeance when the sun rose on a new day and a new queen. Lord Varen's army approached, a thousand strong, unaware that they marched not toward victory, but toward a reckoning long overdue.

The king's study was silent save for the crackling fire and the soft clink of crystal as Helena poured wine into two goblets. Moonlight spilled through the tall windows, casting long shadows across the ancient tomes and maps that had guided her father's rule for decades.

"You truly saved Thorne's family?" Helena asked, handing Alaric a goblet. "His wife and daughters are safe?"

Alaric accepted the wine but didn't drink, his eyes reflecting the firelight like a predator's. "Yes. I've been taking bounty jobs in Thornhaven for months. Watching, waiting."

"For what?" She settled into her father's chair, the weight of imminent coronation visible in the set of her shoulders.

"For Elias and Lyra to appear." A ghost of a smile touched his lips. "I knew they would eventually. The royal seal had to move, and Varen's ambitions were growing too bold to ignore."

Helena's brow furrowed. "You were waiting for them specifically? How could you possibly know—"

"I've been orchestrating this confrontation for years, Helena." Alaric set his untouched wine aside. "It was mere chance they tried to hire me, though. A fortunate coincidence that allowed me to guide them more directly."

Helena studied him, the blood-spattered mercenary who had killed with such frightening efficiency, who spoke of years-long plans with the casual certainty of a master tactician.

"What are you really, Alaric Thornwood?" she asked quietly. "How can you be so certain Varen will lose? Why do you hate him with such... consuming passion?"

Alaric held her gaze for a long moment, then set his goblet on the table with deliberate care. "I think it's time you knew the truth."

He stepped back from the table, rolling his shoulders as if to ease some long-held tension. The air around him seemed to thicken, to darken, and then—

Helena gasped as massive wings unfurled from his back, tearing through his shirt to spread across the study like great sails of midnight darkness. Each feather gleamed with an iridescent black sheen, reflecting blue and purple in the firelight. His face transformed subtly, cheekbones sharpening, eyes taking on a crimson glow as elongated fangs descended from his upper jaw.

"I am not a mercenary," he said, his voice deeper, resonating with power that made the windows vibrate slightly. "At least, not merely a mercenary."

Helena's hand flew to the dagger at her belt, her face pale with shock. "Vampire," she whispered, the ancient word falling from her lips like a prayer or a curse.

"Yes." Alaric made no move toward her, allowing her to process the revelation. "I have walked this earth for centuries, Helena. I have seen empires rise and fall, kings crowned and deposed." His wings shifted, adjusting to the confines of the room. "And I have waited decades for the chance to end Varen's bloodline."

"Why?" she managed, her hand still on her dagger though she hadn't drawn it. "What did he do to earn the enmity of... of your kind?"

"Not my kind. Me, specifically." Alaric's eyes blazed brighter. "Falwood was not the first village Varen sacrificed for his ambition. Three hundred years ago, he was a different man with a different name, but the same black soul. He led a purge against my people—burned our sanctuary, slaughtered the children first to draw out the adults." His voice dropped to a deadly whisper. "My wife and daughter were among them."

Helena's hand slowly released the dagger, horror and fascination warring in her expression. "He's lived that long? How is that possible?"

"Dark magic. Blood rituals. He steals the life force of others to extend his own." Alaric's wings trembled with barely contained rage. "He is an abomination even by my standards."

Silence fell between them, broken only by the soft rustling of Alaric's wings as they shifted in the firelight. Helena rose from her chair, approaching him with cautious steps.

"May I..." she hesitated, hand outstretched toward his wing.

Alaric nodded once, extending the massive appendage slightly toward her.

Her fingers brushed the edge of his wing, tracing the contour of a feather. "They're warm," she said with surprise. "I expected them to be cold."

"A common misconception about my kind," Alaric replied, watching her face closely. "We are not dead, merely... transformed."

Helena moved closer, her initial fear giving way to curiosity as she examined the intricate structure of his wing. "How do you hide them?"

"Practice. Centuries of it." His expression softened slightly as she continued her exploration. "Most humans react with considerably more terror than you're displaying, Your Highness."

"I've studied the old texts," she murmured, her fingers tracing where wing joined shoulder. "The ones my father kept locked away. They spoke of your kind as guardians once, before the hunts began." She looked up at him, her blue eyes meeting his crimson gaze without flinching. "Is that true?"

"For some of us, yes." Alaric's wings folded slightly, curving around her like a protective canopy. "We lived alongside humans, shared our knowledge, used our gifts to protect those who could not protect themselves."

"Until Varen's ancestor turned the humans against you," Helena finished, understanding dawning in her eyes. "That's why you hate him so deeply. His bloodline destroyed that peace."

"His bloodline is his bloodline," Alaric corrected her. "Varen is not a descendant. He is the same man, preserved through dark rituals and stolen life." His fangs gleamed in the firelight. "A parasite who has fed on the suffering of others for centuries."

Helena's hand moved from his wing to his face, her touch feather-light against his cheek. "And tomorrow, you will end him."

"Yes." The word was a promise and a threat wrapped in one. "After you are crowned, I will find him and tear out his heart — the proper way to end his kind of immortality."

"And after that?" she asked, her hand still against his face. "What happens to the vampire who helps a queen claim her throne?"

Alaric's wings shifted, enfolding them both in a cocoon of darkness that seemed to shut out the world beyond. "That depends on the queen," he said softly. "Some might see a monster to be hunted. Others..."

"Others might see an ally," Helena finished, her fingers tracing the sharp line of his jaw. "A protector with gifts beyond mortal men."

"And which do you see, Helena of Morvain?" he asked, her name on his lips like a sacred invocation.

Her answer came not in words but in action as she rose on her toes and pressed her lips to his, heedless of the fangs that could tear her flesh with a single misstep. The kiss was brief but deliberate, a queen making her choice with full knowledge of its meaning.

When she pulled back, her eyes shone with determination. "I see the future of my kingdom," she said simply. "And it includes you, Alaric Thornwood, in whatever form you choose to serve."

His wings unfurled slowly, revealing them once more to the moonlight that spilled through the windows. Outside, the first hints of pre-dawn gray touched the eastern horizon—the coronation would begin in mere hours, and with it, the confrontation they had both been orchestrating for so long.

"Then let us prepare," Alaric said, his wings folding back into nothingness as his features returned to their human guise. Only his eyes retained a hint of their true nature, crimson embers banked but not extinguished. "Your reign begins today, Helena. And with it, Varen's long-overdue reckoning."

Alaric reached out, grasping Helena's wrist as she turned toward the door. "Wait," he said, his voice dropping to a whisper. "What I've shown you tonight—my true nature—it must remain between us alone."

Helena's eyes widened. "You don't trust my council?"

"This isn't about trust," Alaric replied, drawing her closer. "It's about survival. If word spreads that a vampire aids the new queen, many who would support you might turn against you instead. The old fears run deep."

She studied his face, the crimson glow still faintly visible in his eyes. "Your secret is safe with me," she promised, then hesitated, her fingers tracing the line of his jaw. "But if tomorrow brings what we both fear—if Varen's forces overwhelm us—I don't want to die with regrets."

"What regrets would those be?" Alaric asked, his voice rough with sudden tension.

Helena's answer came as she pressed her body against his, her lips finding his with fierce determination. "This," she whispered against his mouth. "I want this, tonight, while we still have time."

The kiss deepened, her tongue darting between his lips, heedless of the fangs that could tear her flesh. Alaric growled low in his throat, his hands sliding down to her waist, lifting her effortlessly onto the edge of her father's desk.

"You don't know what you're asking for," he warned, even as his hands bunched in the fabric of her gown, drawing it up her thighs.

"I know exactly what I'm asking for," Helena replied, her fingers working at the fastenings of his blood-stained shirt. "I want you, Alaric Thornwood, vampire or man or both—I want all of you."

The last threads of his restraint snapped. With a snarl, Alaric tore her gown down the middle, the expensive fabric giving way beneath his inhuman strength. Helena gasped, not in fear but in wanton approval, her hands raking down his chest, leaving red welts that healed almost as quickly as they formed.

"Show me," she demanded, her voice husky with desire. "Show me what you really are."

His wings unfurled once more, midnight black and terrible in their beauty, casting them both in shadow as he claimed her mouth again. This kiss was brutal, possessive, his fangs nicking her lower lip and drawing a bead of blood that he licked away with a groan of pleasure.

"Your blood," he murmured against her throat, "it sings to me."

"Then taste it," Helena challenged, tilting her head to expose the pale column of her neck. "Take what you need."

Alaric's eyes blazed crimson as he lowered his mouth to her throat, fangs grazing the delicate skin over her pulse. He didn't bite—not yet—instead trailing kisses down to the swell of her breasts, now exposed by her ruined gown.

Helena arched beneath him, her hands tangling in his hair as he took one nipple into his mouth, the careful scrape of fangs against sensitive flesh drawing a cry from her lips. Maps and documents scattered to the floor as he laid her back across the desk, her copper hair fanning out around her like flames.

"I've wanted this since I first saw you," she confessed, her legs wrapping around his waist, drawing him against the heat between her thighs. "Even covered in blood and half-dead, you were the most magnificent thing I'd ever seen."

Alaric tore away the remnants of her gown, leaving her naked beneath him save for the silver chain bearing the royal seal. The metal gleamed against her flushed skin, a reminder of the crown she would wear come dawn — and all that stood between her and that destiny.

"If we do this," he warned, his voice thick with restrained passion, "there's no going back. You'll be changed."

"I'm already changed," she replied, reaching between them to unfasten his breeches. "Now stop talking and take me like you want to."

His control shattered completely. With a growl that was more beast than man, Alaric seized her hips, his fingers digging into her flesh hard enough to bruise as he positioned himself at her entrance. He thrust into her without gentleness, burying himself to the hilt in one savage motion that tore a scream from her throat—pain and pleasure intermingled in equal measure.

For a moment, he stilled, giving her body time to adjust to his invasion. Helena's eyes were wide, her breath coming in short gasps, but there was no fear in her gaze—only hunger to match his own.

"More," she demanded, her nails raking down his back between the juncture of his wings. "Don't hold back."

Alaric needed no further encouragement. He withdrew almost completely before driving into her again, setting a punishing rhythm that had the heavy desk creaking beneath them. Each thrust pushed her further across the polished surface until her head hung over the edge, copper hair cascading toward the floor.

Helena matched his ferocity, her hips rising to meet each brutal thrust, her cries of pleasure echoing off the stone walls of the study. She was glorious in her abandon, a queen who took her pleasure as she took her crown — by right and with absolute authority.

"Look at me," Alaric commanded, one hand sliding up to grasp her throat, applying just enough pressure to make her gasp. "I want to see your eyes when you come apart."

Her gaze locked with his, blue meeting crimson in a clash of wills and desire. His wings created a canopy of darkness above them, feathers rustling with each powerful thrust as the tension built between them.

"Bite me," Helena gasped, her body tightening around him as she approached her peak. "I want to feel everything—everything you are."

Alaric lowered his head to her throat, his rhythm never faltering as his fangs grazed her skin. "Are you certain?" he asked, his voice barely recognizable through his haze of desire.

"Yes," she hissed, her fingers digging into his shoulders. "Now!"

His fangs sank into her flesh at the exact moment her climax crashed over her. Helena's scream of ecstasy echoed through the chamber as her body convulsed around him, her back arching off the desk with such force that only his arm around her waist kept her from falling.

The taste of her blood—royal blood, power incarnate—pushed Alaric over the edge. He drank deeply as his own release tore through him, his seed spilling into her womb as his wings unfurled to their full span, knocking books and artifacts from nearby shelves.

For several heartbeats, they remained locked together, his mouth at her throat, her body trembling with aftershocks of pleasure. Then, with careful tenderness that belied the violence of their coupling, Alaric withdrew his fangs and licked the wounds closed, leaving only two small puncture marks as evidence.

Helena lay boneless beneath him, her chest heaving, a sheen of sweat making her skin glow in the firelight. Blood—her blood—stained Alaric's lips as he gazed down at her with an expression caught between awe and possessiveness.

"You taste like destiny," he murmured, brushing a strand of copper hair from her flushed face.

A lazy smile curved her lips as she reached up to trace the outline of his wing. "Is that a vampire's way of saying I taste good?"

Alaric chuckled, the sound rusty as if long unused. "Among other things." He withdrew from her body gently, then gathered her into his arms, carrying her to the chaise longue near the hearth. His wings folded around them both as he settled her against his chest, their limbs entangled in sated intimacy.

"Will I become like you now?" Helena asked, her fingers tracing the rapidly healing scratches she'd left on his chest. "A vampire?"

"No," Alaric assured her, pressing a kiss to her temple. "That requires a more... deliberate exchange. Though you may find your senses heightened for a day or two. My saliva has certain properties."

She hummed thoughtfully, nestling closer against him. "Useful, perhaps, for the battle to come."

Even in the aftermath of passion, her mind turned to strategy—a quality that made Alaric's admiration for her deepen further. She was no fragile maiden to be protected, but a warrior queen who had just taken a vampire to her bed with the same decisive confidence with which she would take her throne.

"Dawn approaches," he murmured, noting the gradual lightening of the sky outside the windows. "Your coronation awaits."

Helena sighed, her hand coming to rest over his heart. "A few more minutes," she pleaded, sounding suddenly young despite the regal authority she wielded so naturally. "Let me have this moment before I must become queen."

Alaric tightened his embrace, his wings creating a cocoon of darkness around them both. "As you wish, my queen," he whispered against her hair. "Though crowned or not, you already rule more than you know."

They lay together in comfortable silence as the first birdsong heralded the approaching dawn. Outside the study walls, Ravenscrest stirred to life, servants and soldiers preparing for the coronation that would forever change the kingdom's fate. Beyond the castle's protection, Varen's forces gathered, unaware of the ancient predator who waited within—a vampire who had found something worth fighting for beyond mere vengeance.

And in his arms, Helena of Morvain drifted on the edge of sleep, her body bearing the marks of their passion, her blood mingled with his in a bond more profound than either had anticipated. Whatever came with the new day—coronation or battle, triumph or tragedy—this night had sealed their fates together in ways that would echo through the centuries to come.

"We should dress," Alaric said finally, pressing a kiss to her forehead. "Your handmaidens will be looking for you soon."

CHAPTER 10 –

STRANGE BEDFELLOWS, STRANGER ALLIES

Helena stirred reluctantly, wincing slightly as she sat up. The marks of their encounter were evident across her pale skin—bruises in the shape of his fingers on her hips, the puncture wounds at her throat, the general tenderness between her thighs.

"They'll talk," she mused, surveying the damage with a sort of detached pride rather than dismay.

"Let them," Alaric replied, his wings retracting as he rose to retrieve what remained of their clothing. "Queens have taken lovers throughout history. It changes nothing about your right to rule."

Helena accepted the remnants of her gown with a rueful smile. "This, however, will be harder to explain." The midnight blue fabric hung in tatters, completely unwearable.

Alaric moved to a cabinet in the corner, retrieving a cloak of deep green velvet that had hung there. "Your father's, I believe," he said, draping it around her shoulders. "It will serve until you reach your chambers."

She wrapped herself in the cloak, inhaling deeply. "It still smells like him," she murmured, a flash of grief crossing her features before being replaced by resolve. "By sunset today, I will avenge him. We both will."

Alaric nodded, fastening his breeches and retrieving his sword from where it had fallen during their frenzied coupling. "Varen won't expect what awaits him. The vampire he thought he destroyed centuries ago, and the queen he underestimated."

Helena's expression hardened into something regal and dangerous.

"Wait," Helena said, pausing at the threshold. She turned back to face him, her brow furrowed in thought. "If Varen has lived for centuries as you have, how has no one noticed? Surely my father would have recognized something amiss about his own brother?"

Alaric's expression darkened as he buckled his sword belt. "Your uncle isn't like me. My immortality is my nature—his is stolen through ritual and sacrifice."

"That doesn't answer my question," Helena pressed, pulling the green cloak tighter around her shoulders.

"Because the man you know as Varen isn't the same physical form he's always worn." Alaric moved to the window, gazing out at the lightening sky. "Every few decades, when suspicions grow or his body begins to fail, he performs a ritual. He transfers his consciousness, his very essence, into a new vessel—a body he's prepared through blood magic."

"You mean he..." Helena's face paled with horror.

"Yes. He becomes someone else entirely. New face, new name, new life." Alaric's voice hardened. "Sometimes he inserts himself into noble families as a distant relative. Other times he simply kills and replaces someone whose position serves his purposes."

"And now he wears the face of my uncle," Helena whispered.

"In this lifetime, yes. Varen is merely the latest identity he's stolen." Alaric turned back to her. "That's why he's so dangerous—he's had centuries to perfect his deceptions, to place loyal servants throughout the kingdom who help facilitate his transformations."

Helena shook her head in disbelief. "How can we fight something like that? Even if we kill this body—"

"We won't just kill the body," Alaric interrupted, his eyes flashing crimson. "I know how to end him permanently. I've spent centuries learning his weaknesses, tracking his movements across generations. This time, he won't escape me."

Helena studied him for a long moment, then nodded once. "I'll see you at the coronation," she said, her voice regaining its regal authority. "By sunset, we'll both have our vengeance."

She slipped from the study without another word, leaving Alaric alone with the scattered evidence of their passion. He gathered the torn remnants of her gown, tossing them into the fire where they curled and blackened, erasing the physical proof of their encounter.

Dawn had broken fully now, golden light spilling across Ravenscrest's stone walls. Alaric strode through the corridors, ignoring the curious glances of servants preparing for the day's ceremony. In the great hall, nobles were already gathering, their finery a riot of color against the ancient tapestries.

He moved through them like a shadow, his blood-stained appearance drawing whispers and sidelong glances. None dared approach him directly — the memory of his swift violence against the assassins still fresh in their minds.

The castle courtyard bustled with activity as Alaric emerged into the morning light. Guards patrolled the walls, their armor gleaming in the sun, while servants hung banners bearing Helena's royal crest from every available surface. The atmosphere hummed with nervous anticipation—a kingdom poised on the edge of transformation.

Alaric made his way toward the main gate, nodding to Captain Eldric as he passed. The woman returned his acknowledgment with a respectful inclination of her head, her eyes tracking his movement with professional assessment.

"The western approach is secure," she reported without preamble. "Your... display... seems to have discouraged further incursions from that direction."

"Good." Alaric glanced toward the forest edge, where the impaled bodies of Varen's knights remained visible—a grotesque warning to any who might follow. "And the eastern road?"

"Our scouts report movement," Eldric admitted, her voice dropping. "A large force, perhaps a day's march away. Flying Varen's personal standard alongside the royal banner."

"He claims legitimacy even as he marches to overthrow the rightful heir," Alaric observed coldly. "Typical."

"The coronation begins in one hour," Eldric continued, her hand resting on her sword hilt. "We've doubled the guard, checked every guest personally. No one enters without direct approval."

Alaric nodded, his gaze sweeping the castle walls. From this vantage point, Ravenscrest appeared impregnable—ancient stone rising proudly against the morning sky, banners snapping in the breeze, archers positioned at regular intervals along the battlements.

But he knew better. No fortress was truly impregnable, especially against an enemy who had centuries to plan his assault. Varen would have contingencies, secret approaches, loyal agents already within the walls.

"I need to check something," he told Eldric, moving toward the gate. "Continue your preparations. I'll return before the ceremony begins."

The captain looked as if she might object, then thought better of it. "As you wish," she said, turning back to her duties.

Alaric stepped through the massive gates, nodding to the guards who stood at attention as he passed. Beyond the walls, the road stretched toward the distant forest—the same forest that had claimed so many of Varen's men. Its dark green canopy seemed to shimmer slightly in the morning light, as if stirred by an unfelt breeze.

He smiled grimly. The forest was awake, aware, and hungry for the blood of those who had desecrated its southern grove. Varen's approaching army would find more than mere trees standing between them and Ravenscrest.

Alaric closed his eyes, reaching out with senses beyond human comprehension. The forest responded to his silent call, a whisper of ancient power brushing against his consciousness like the caress of a familiar lover.

Soon, he promised the waiting darkness. *Soon you will feast on the blood of our common enemy.*

The trees rustled in anticipation, though no wind disturbed their branches.

Alaric opened his eyes, satisfaction curling through him like smoke. Helena would be crowned queen today, and Varen—the man who had worn a hundred faces across the centuries—would finally face judgment for his crimes.

The bell tower began to toll, signaling one hour until the coronation ceremony. Alaric turned back toward the castle, his pace unhurried despite the momentous events about to unfold. He had waited centuries for this day—what was one more hour in the grand scheme of such vengeance?

Behind him, yellow eyes blinked open within the shadowed forest, watching, waiting for the feast to come.

A low rumble shook the ground beneath Alaric's feet, the vibration traveling up through his boots as he turned back toward Ravenscrest. At first, he thought it an earthquake—until a massive shadow fell across the road ahead.

He spun just as the boulder sailed over his head, a jagged mass of stone larger than a wagon hurtling through the air with impossible force. It struck the castle wall with a thunderous crash, stone chips exploding outward as guards shouted in alarm.

From the forest edge, five hulking shapes emerged — trolls, their gray-green skin glistening in the morning sun, muscles rippling beneath hides thick as armor. Behind them surged a mass of men, hundreds strong, brandishing weapons and screaming battle cries.

"Sound the alarm!" Alaric roared, drawing his obsidian-steel sword in one fluid motion. "Archers to the wall!"

The warning bells began to toll frantically as archers scrambled to position, their first volley arcing through the clear morning sky to rain down upon the advancing horde. Men fell, but the trolls merely grunted as arrows bounced harmlessly off their thick hides.

One troll wrenched an entire pine tree from the ground, roots and all, hurling it toward the gate with devastating force. The ancient wood splintered against stone, but the wall held. Another boulder followed, then another, the trolls using their unnatural strength to bombard Ravenscrest's defenses.

Alaric didn't wait for the enemy to reach the walls. He charged forward, a lone figure racing toward the advancing army, his blade gleaming with deadly purpose. The first line of attackers met him with shocked expressions that quickly turned to terror as his sword carved through their ranks.

He moved with inhuman speed and precision, each strike finding a vital point—throats, hearts, the vulnerable juncture where helmet met breastplate. Men fell around him like wheat before a scythe, their blood soaking into the earth as he cut deeper into their formation.

Behind him, the castle gates swung open as Ravenscrest's guards poured forth, Captain Eldric at their head, her voice rising above the din as she rallied her soldiers to Alaric's aid. The defenders formed a wedge, driving into the enemy's flank while Alaric continued his bloody work at their center.

"Push them back!" Eldric shouted, her sword flashing in the morning light as she parried a blow and ran her attacker through. "For the Queen!"

The battle devolved into chaos, the air thick with screams and the metallic tang of blood. Alaric fought with cold efficiency, never transforming, never revealing his true nature despite the temptation. This was a human battle, to be won with steel and courage rather than supernatural power.

A troll smashed through the front line of defenders, massive fists swinging in deadly arcs that sent men flying like broken dolls. Alaric ducked beneath its grasp, slicing hamstrings as he rolled past. The creature bellowed in pain, dropping to one knee as guards swarmed it, driving spears into its vulnerable eyes and mouth.

Another troll fell to a coordinated attack from Ravenscrest's archers, dozens of arrows finding the soft tissue of its throat when it roared in challenge. It collapsed in a spray of dark blood, crushing several of its own allies beneath its massive bulk.

The remaining three trolls reached the castle wall, hammering at the ancient stone with fists like battering rams. Cracks spread across the lower sections as dust and debris rained down upon the defenders.

Alaric sprinted toward the armory wagon that had followed the guards from the gate. He seized a heavy spear, testing its weight for a moment before hurling it with preternatural strength. The weapon flew true, piercing the back of the nearest troll's skull and erupting from its eye socket in a spray of gore.

Without pausing, he grabbed another spear, then another, each throw finding a vital target. The second troll collapsed with a shaft protruding from the base of its spine, its legs going instantly limp as it howled in agony.

The last troll turned at its companions' cries, beady eyes focusing on Alaric with primitive hatred. It abandoned the wall, charging across the battlefield with surprising speed for something so massive. Defenders scattered from its path as it barreled toward the man who had felled its kin.

Alaric stood his ground, sword raised, a cold smile playing across his blood-spattered face. The troll was five strides away — then three — then one —

A dozen spears struck it simultaneously from different angles, the castle guards coordinating their attack with practiced precision. The creature staggered, momentum carrying it forward even as its life ebbed away. It crashed to the ground at Alaric's feet, massive hand still reaching for him as death glazed its eyes.

Silence fell across the battlefield, broken only by the moans of the wounded and the hiss of arrows as archers dispatched the few remaining attackers attempting to flee. Alaric surveyed the carnage with clinical detachment—hundreds of bodies strewn across the field, blood soaking into the earth in dark pools.

Captain Eldric approached, her armor dented and splashed with blood, a fresh cut bleeding above her eye. "That was no random attack," she said, wiping her blade clean on a fallen enemy's cloak. "Trolls don't ally with humans willingly."

"No," Alaric agreed, his gaze turning toward the forest where yellow eyes still watched from the shadows. "Someone sent them. Someone desperate enough to sacrifice these men as a distraction."

"Distraction from what?" Eldric asked, following his gaze toward the trees.

Before Alaric could answer, a runner approached from the castle, his face pale with urgency. "Captain! Master Thornwood! The prisoner—Captain Thorne—he's been taken!"

Alaric's blood ran cold. "What?"

"Assassins," the runner gasped, struggling to catch his breath. "They came through the old tunnels beneath the east tower. Killed the guards and took him. The Princess—I mean, Her Majesty—she's calling for you both immediately."

Understanding dawned like ice in Alaric's veins. Varen had never intended this attack to succeed—it was merely a diversion while his real agents infiltrated the castle through forgotten passages. And now he had Thorne—the one man who could testify to Varen's true nature and crimes.

"Secure the walls," Alaric commanded, already striding toward the gate. "This isn't over. Not by far."

Inside the castle, he found Helena in the council chamber, her coronation gown replaced by practical riding leathers, a sword belted at her waist. Her copper hair was pulled back in a severe braid, her face set with cold fury as she bent over maps spread across the table.

"They took him right from under our noses," she said without preamble as Alaric entered. "Four men in servants' garb. They knew exactly where he was being held and exactly how to reach him."

"Varen has spies within your household," Alaric replied, moving to her side. "He always has."

Helena's hand clenched around the hilt of her sword. "The coronation is postponed until we secure the castle. I won't wear the crown while traitors walk my halls."

"No," Alaric contradicted her, his voice firm. "The coronation proceeds as planned. It's what Varen fears most — your legitimate claim recognized before all of Morvain."

"While my castle is compromised? While assassins could strike at any moment?" Helena challenged, eyes flashing.

"Especially then," Alaric insisted. "Show strength, not fear. Besides—" he smiled grimly "—I believe I know where they've taken Thorne. And I promise you, they won't keep him long."

Helena studied his face, recognizing the deadly promise in his eyes. "Where?"

"The old temple in Mistwood," Alaric replied, his fingers tracing the location on the map before them. "Sacred ground, once. Now corrupted by Varen's blood rituals. He'll want to silence Thorne permanently, and that's where he conducts his darkest work."

"Then we'll mount a rescue," Helena decided, already calculating distances and forces in her mind. "After the coronation. A small, elite force—"

"No," Alaric cut her off gently. "You will be crowned queen. You will secure your castle and prepare for Varen's main assault." His eyes flickered briefly crimson. "I will retrieve Thorne alone."

"That's suicide," Captain Eldric protested, having entered in time to hear his declaration. "Even for you."

Alaric's smile held no warmth. "For a man, perhaps. But I am not merely a man, as Her Majesty can attest."

Understanding passed between him and Helena—a silent acknowledgment of secrets shared in the night.

"Very well," Helena conceded after a moment. "The coronation proceeds in one hour. And you—" she placed her hand on Alaric's arm "—will return with Captain Thorne before sunset, or I will lead the army of Morvain into Mistwood myself to find you both."

"As my queen commands," Alaric replied, the formal words carrying a deeper meaning than any present could fully grasp.

The bells began to toll again, calling nobles and commoners alike to witness the crowning of their new ruler. Helena straightened, royal bearing settling over her like a familiar cloak.

"Go," she told Alaric, her voice softening slightly. "But remember your promise. I expect both vengeance and victory before this day ends."

Alaric bowed, a gesture of genuine respect rather than mere formality. "On my immortal soul, I swear it."

As he turned to leave, Helena called after him, her voice pitched for his ears alone. "And Alaric? The forest hungers. Feed it well."

He didn't look back, but a smile curved his lips as he strode from the chamber. Behind him, Helena of Morvain prepared to take her crown, while ahead, the ancient woods waited to unleash centuries of pent-up vengeance against those who had wronged them both.

The day of reckoning had dawned at last, written in blood and crowned in gold, with a vampire's promise binding it all together.

CHAPTER 11 –
PRELUDE

Captain Eldric fell into step beside Alaric as he strode through the castle corridors, his black cloak billowing behind him like wings folded in shadow. The captain's armor gleamed in the morning light streaming through the high windows, a stark contrast to Alaric's blood-darkened attire.

"Your immortal soul," Eldric said abruptly, breaking the tense silence between them. "That was quite the oath you swore to Princess Helena."

Alaric kept his gaze fixed ahead, his pace never faltering. "Was it?"

"Most men swear on their honor, their family name, or simply their lives." Eldric's voice carried an edge of suspicion. "But you chose your immortal soul. Why?"

"Perhaps I value it more than those other things," Alaric replied, his tone revealing nothing.

They descended the grand staircase, servants scurrying out of their path as they recognized the blood-spattered mercenary and the stern-faced captain.

"Or perhaps," Eldric pressed, "you believe your soul truly is immortal. Are you a particularly religious man, Master Thornwood?"

Alaric's mouth quirked in the ghost of a smile. "Not in any way you'd recognize, Captain."

They passed through the great hall, now empty of nobles as all prepared for Helena's coronation in the cathedral adjoining the castle grounds. Sunlight streamed through stained glass, casting colored patterns across the stone floor.

"You're not what you appear to be," Eldric stated flatly, her hand resting casually on her sword hilt. "I've fought alongside men for twenty years. I know killers, mercenaries, soldiers of fortune. You're something else entirely."

"Your point?" Alaric asked, turning down the corridor that led to the eastern gate.

"My point is that Princess Helena—soon to be Queen Helena—trusts you with her life and her kingdom." Eldric moved to block his path, forcing him to stop. "I need to know if that trust is misplaced."

Alaric met her gaze, his eyes cold and ancient in a face that appeared no older than thirty. "What you need, Captain, is to prepare your men for what's coming. Not to question the one ally who might ensure your queen survives the day."

"And what exactly is coming?" Eldric demanded. "What do you know that you're not telling us?"

"Death," Alaric said simply. "On a scale this kingdom hasn't seen in centuries." He stepped around her, continuing toward the gate. "Now, either help me or get out of my way."

Eldric cursed under her breath but followed, her longer strides bringing her alongside him again. "The scouts report movement in the eastern forest, but nothing immediate. We have time to prepare."

"No," Alaric corrected her, "we don't."

They reached the gatehouse, guards snapping to attention as Eldric approached. Alaric paused, scanning the tree line with eyes that saw more than any human could — movement in the shadows, the gleam of armor, the gathering of forces just beyond normal sight.

"Why won't you tell me what you are?" Eldric asked, lowering her voice so the guards couldn't hear. "What hold do you have over our princess that she would trust a blood-soaked stranger over lifelong advisors?"

"Perhaps she recognizes the value of allies who aren't bound by politics or tradition," Alaric replied, his patience wearing thin. "Now open the gate. I have business in the forest."

"Not until you answer me," Eldric insisted. "What did you mean by your immortal soul? Why would you —"

A horn blast cut through the morning air — deep, resonant, and unmistakably hostile. Both Alaric and Eldric whipped toward the sound as a second horn joined the first, then a third, the cacophony rolling across the open field between castle and forest.

"Open the gate!" Alaric commanded, drawing his obsidian-steel sword in one fluid motion.

The guards moved to obey, cranking the mechanism that slowly raised the massive portcullis. As the barrier lifted, revealing the view beyond, Eldric sucked in a sharp breath.

The tree line erupted with movement — a seething mass of soldiers pouring from the forest shadows like ants from a disturbed hill. Sunlight glinted off armor and weapons as they formed into rough battle lines, their standards snapping in the morning breeze. At their center, mounted on massive warhorses, rode commanders in ornate armor bearing Varen's personal crest.

"Gods above," Eldric whispered, her face paling. "There must be a thousand of them."

"One thousand, four hundred and seventy-three," Alaric corrected with cold precision. "Plus the three hundred already positioned in the western approach."

Eldric shot him a disbelieving look. "How could you possibly—"

"Sound the alarm," Alaric cut her off, stepping through the partially raised gate. "Get every able-bodied defender on the walls. And get Helena to the cathedral—now. The coronation must proceed, regardless of what happens here."

"You can't go out there alone!" Eldric protested, seizing his arm. "That's suicide!"

Alaric looked down at her hand, then back to her face. Something in his eyes made her release him instantly, a primal fear flickering across her features.

"I'm not going to fight them, Captain," he said quietly. "Not yet. First, I'm going to offer them a choice."

"What choice?"

"The same one I always offer," Alaric replied, his voice dropping to a register that seemed to vibrate in the stones beneath their feet. "Retreat, or die."

He strode through the gate and out onto the open field, a solitary figure against the backdrop of Ravenscrest's imposing walls. Behind him, Eldric barked orders, sending runners to alert the castle while archers scrambled to position along the battlements.

The advancing army slowed as they spotted the lone man walking calmly toward them, his black cloak billowing around him, sword gleaming at his side. Confusion rippled through their ranks—this was not the desperate defense they had expected.

Alaric stopped halfway across the field, planted his feet, and waited. The morning sun beat down on his shoulders, the weight of his true nature straining against the human guise he maintained. Not yet, he told himself. Not until they've made their choice.

A horseman detached from the main force, spurring his mount forward. As he drew closer, Alaric recognized the ornate armor and distinctive plume—Lord Blackthorn, one of the northern lords who had pledged fealty to Varen.

"In the name of Lord Regent Varen, rightful ruler of Morvain, I demand the surrender of Ravenscrest Castle and all within!" Blackthorn called, his voice carrying across the field. "The false queen must relinquish her claim and submit to the regent's judgment!"

Alaric's laugh cut through the morning air like a blade—cold, sharp, and utterly devoid of humor. "Lord Blackthorn," he called back, "you've chosen poorly. I offer you one chance to correct your mistake. Take your men and leave. Now."

Blackthorn's face flushed with anger. "Who are you to make demands of me, mercenary? One man against an army?"

"I am Alaric Thornwood," he replied, his voice carrying unnaturally far, reaching every ear in the assembled host. "I have come to deliver a message from Queen Helena, rightful ruler of Morvain."

"And what message is that?" Blackthorn sneered.

Alaric smiled, a predator's baring of teeth. "That those who stand against her will not live to see tomorrow's dawn."

Laughter rippled through the front ranks of soldiers, nervous at first, then growing in confidence as they took in the absurdity of the situation — one man threatening an army.

"Seize him," Blackthorn ordered, gesturing to the nearest soldiers. "Bring him to me alive if possible. Dead if necessary."

Ten men broke from the front line, weapons drawn as they advanced on Alaric. He stood motionless, waiting, his sword still sheathed at his side.

The first soldier reached him, swinging a heavy mace in a crushing arc toward Alaric's head. Alaric moved — a blur of motion too fast for human eyes to track. The soldier's head separated from his shoulders, rolling across the grass as his body crumpled.

The remaining nine hesitated, shock evident on their faces. Alaric hadn't even drawn his sword — the man's own weapon had somehow been turned against him with impossible speed and precision.

"I said," Alaric repeated, his voice dropping to a growl that seemed to shake the earth beneath their feet, "retreat or die."

"Kill him!" Blackthorn screamed, his composure shattering. "Kill him now!"

The soldiers rushed forward together, weapons raised. Alaric finally drew his obsidian-steel blade, the dark metal seeming to drink in the sunlight rather than reflect it. What followed wasn't combat so much as slaughter — Alaric moved through their formation like smoke, his blade finding vital points with surgical precision. Throats opened, limbs separated, torsos split from shoulder to hip in sprays of arterial blood.

In less than ten heartbeats, all nine men lay dead or dying at his feet, their blood soaking into the grass. Alaric stood among the carnage, not a single scratch on him, his blade dripping crimson onto the earth.

A stunned silence fell over the battlefield. From the castle walls, Eldric watched with wide eyes, her hand gripping her sword hilt so tightly her knuckles showed white.

"Last chance," Alaric called to Blackthorn, who sat frozen atop his warhorse. "Take your army and go. Tell Varen his time is ending."

Blackthorn's shock gave way to rage. He raised his sword, pointing it at Alaric. "Forward!" he bellowed to his troops. "Kill the demon! For Lord Varen!"

The front line surged forward with a collective roar, hundreds of men charging across the field toward the solitary figure standing amid the bodies of their comrades.

Alaric closed his eyes briefly, a sigh escaping his lips. "So be it."

His form blurred, darkness gathering around him like a storm cloud. When it cleared, massive wings extended from his back, obsidian feathers gleaming in the sunlight. His eyes blazed crimson, fangs extending as his true nature emerged in all its terrible glory.

A collective gasp rose from the charging soldiers, many faltering mid-stride at the sight of the transformed creature before them. On the castle walls, Eldric dropped to one knee, a prayer falling from her lips as she finally understood the truth of Alaric's oath.

"Immortal soul indeed," she whispered.

Alaric rose into the air, wings beating powerfully as he hovered above the battlefield. His voice, when it came, seemed to emanate from everywhere at once—the ground, the sky, the very air they breathed.

"You were warned," he intoned, raising his sword toward the forest behind the army. "Now witness the price of your choice."

The tree line shuddered, ancient trunks swaying though no wind disturbed their branches. Then, with a sound like the earth itself groaning in pain, the forest moved.

"Your blood will feed the earth that you sought to conquer!" Alaric's voice thundered across the battlefield, each word vibrating through bone and soil alike. "None shall be spared! None shall escape! Your lives are forfeit for your allegiance to a monster!"

From the forest edge emerged nightmares given flesh — creatures with elongated limbs and mottled blue-gray skin, their yellow eyes gleaming with ancient hunger. They moved with terrible speed, flowing across the field like living shadows, their needle-teeth gleaming in twisted grins.

The front line of soldiers broke, screaming as the first creatures reached them. Claws ripped through armor as if it were parchment, tearing men apart in fountains of gore. The creatures fought with savage efficiency, targeting throats, bellies, and eyes—any soft tissue they could reach.

Captain Eldric watched in horror from the castle wall, her hand frozen on her sword hilt. Around her, guards fell to their knees, prayers spilling from trembling lips as they witnessed power beyond mortal comprehension.

"Sweet mercy," Eldric whispered, her face ashen. "What have we allied ourselves with?"

Alaric descended into the thick of battle, his wings creating gusts that knocked soldiers from their feet. With a savage gesture, he plunged his obsidian blade into the earth. Crimson light pulsed from the point of impact, spreading outward in glowing veins that raced beneath the soldiers' feet.

The men closest to him screamed as their blood responded to his call—bursting from their eyes, mouths, and every pore. It flowed through the air in ribbons of scarlet that twisted toward Alaric's outstretched hand, coalescing into a sphere of writhing crimson between his palms.

"By ancient right, by blood spilled and promises broken," Alaric chanted, his voice carrying unnaturally across the battlefield, "I claim your life force as payment for your trespass!"

With each word, another dozen soldiers collapsed, their bodies withering as blood and life essence were ripped from them. The crimson sphere grew, pulsing with stolen vitality, its light casting Alaric's face in demonic relief.

Lord Blackthorn tried to flee, wheeling his horse toward the tree line, but the forest creatures cut off his retreat. His mount reared in terror, throwing him to the ground where clawed hands seized his limbs. His screams rose above the din as the creatures methodically dismembered him, passing pieces of his still-living body between them like grim trophies.

"Fall back! For the love of God, fall back!" a commander shouted, trying to rally what remained of the front ranks. His head separated from his shoulders a moment later, removed by a casual sweep of Alaric's hand.

Halfway across the battlefield, the forest itself had begun to advance — trees uprooting themselves to lumber forward on twisted root-legs, their branches seizing fleeing soldiers and impaling them on sharpened limbs. Blood ran down ancient bark, absorbed greedily as the trees seemed to shudder with pleasure.

Eldric tore her gaze away, turning to the white-faced guards beside her. "Seal the gates," she ordered, her voice steadier than she felt. "No one enters or leaves until this... until it's over."

"But Captain," a young guard protested, "shouldn't we help? They're being slaughtered!"

"That's not a battle," Eldric replied grimly. "It's a feeding. And we are not meant to interfere."

On the field below, Alaric rose higher into the air, the sphere of blood and life-force now large enough to cast its own shadow. With a gesture of terrible finality, he hurled it toward the remaining mass of soldiers who had formed a desperate defensive circle.

The sphere exploded on impact, its contents raining down in a caustic deluge that melted flesh from bone wherever it touched. Men writhed in agony as their bodies dissolved, muscle and sinew liquefying while they remained horribly conscious.

"Remember this day!" Alaric's voice boomed across the carnage. "Remember what awaits those who stand against the rightful Queen of Morvain!"

From the castle, the coronation bells began to toll—Helena was being crowned even as her enemies died by the hundreds outside her walls. The sound seemed to drive the forest creatures into greater frenzy, their attacks becoming more frenzied as they tore through the dwindling ranks of soldiers.

Some men threw down their weapons, falling to their knees in surrender or prayer. The creatures showed no mercy, ripping throats and shattering spines with methodical brutality. Others ran, only to be caught by animated roots that erupted from the earth to ensnare their ankles, dragging them screaming into the soil.

Alaric landed amid a knot of elite guards who had formed around one of Varen's commanders. These men fought with the desperation of the damned, their blades slick with the ichor of forest creatures they had managed to wound or kill.

"You fight well," Alaric acknowledged, his wings folding

slightly as he assessed them. "But futilely."

"Demon!" the commander spat, raising his sword. "Return to hell!"

"After you," Alaric replied, his hand shooting forward to seize the man by his throat.

The commander's eyes bulged as Alaric's fangs sank into his neck. Unlike the mass feeding before, this was intimate, almost tender in its execution. Alaric drank deeply, the commander's struggles growing weaker with each swallow until he hung limp in the vampire's grasp.

When Alaric released him, the commander's body crumpled to the ground—not dead, but transformed. His eyes opened, now glowing with the same crimson light as his maker's.

"Rise," Alaric commanded. "Find Varen. Tell him what you've witnessed here today."

The newly-made vampire nodded once, then fled with inhuman

speed toward the forest, passing unharmed through the ranks of creatures still feasting on the dead and dying.

Alaric surveyed the battlefield, satisfaction evident in his blood-smeared face. Where an army had stood, now only corpses remained — hundreds of bodies in various states of dismemberment, the ground so saturated with blood it squelched beneath his boots as he walked.

The forest creatures were retreating, dragging choice pieces of their prey back toward the tree line. The animated trees, too, were returning to their original positions, roots sliding back into the earth as they resumed their ancient vigil.

Alaric's wings spread wide as he took to the air once more, circling the field of carnage before landing at the castle gate. The guards stationed there shrank back, terror evident in their faces as they beheld their blood-soaked ally in his true form.

Captain Eldric alone stood her ground, though her face had gone the color of old parchment. "The coronation is complete," she reported, her voice remarkably steady. "Queen Helena awaits your report in the throne room."

Alaric nodded, his wings folding against his back but not disappearing entirely. "And the prisoners?" he asked.

"Those who surrendered?" Eldric swallowed hard. "There... there are none, my lord. Your creatures were... thorough."

Something like regret flickered across Alaric's inhuman features. "A pity. Information would have been useful." He gestured toward the gate. "Lead on, Captain. Let us inform Her Majesty that her reign begins with victory."

CHAPTER 12 –

WHAT DO YOU SEE AS A MONSTER?

As they passed through the castle corridors, servants and nobles alike pressed themselves against the walls, many making signs of protection or whispering prayers. Alaric ignored them, his focus entirely on the throne room ahead where Helena awaited news of her first battle as queen.

The massive doors swung open to reveal the court assembled in full regalia, with Helena seated upon the ancient throne of Morvain. The royal crown gleamed upon her copper hair, the royal seal now hanging from a golden chain around her neck rather than the silver one she had worn before.

She rose as Alaric entered, her expression betraying nothing of the shock she must have felt at his blood-drenched appearance and still-manifest wings.

"Lord Thornwood," she greeted him formally, using a title he had never claimed. "What news from the field?"

Alaric approached the throne, stopping at the proper distance before dropping to one knee in a gesture of fealty that sent murmurs rippling through the assembled court.

"Victory, Your Majesty," he replied, his voice carrying to every corner of the vast chamber. "Your enemies lie dead beyond your walls. Those who survive will carry tales of the price of opposing Morvain's rightful queen."

Helena descended the dais steps, her coronation gown whispering against the stone floor as she approached him. With regal grace, she extended her hand—not to be kissed, as protocol would dictate, but to touch his blood-spattered cheek in a gesture too intimate for queen and subject.

"Rise, Lord Thornwood," she commanded softly. "And tell me of Captain Thorne."

Alaric stood, towering over her despite her considerable height. "He awaits rescue still, Your Majesty. I was... delayed." His wings shifted slightly, sending droplets of blood pattering to the floor. "With your permission, I will retrieve him now."

"Permission granted," Helena replied, her fingers lingering against his face a moment longer than necessary. "But first, there is the matter of your reward."

Alaric's brow furrowed slightly. "I require no reward beyond serving your cause, Your Majesty."

"Nevertheless," Helena continued, turning to address the court, "a queen must recognize exceptional service. Kneel, Alaric Thornwood."

Surprise flickered across his features, but he obeyed, dropping once more to one knee before her. Helena drew a ceremonial sword from the scabbard of the royal guard captain who stood at her right hand.

"For valor beyond measure, for loyalty beyond question, and for service to the crown of Morvain," she intoned, touching the flat of the blade to each of his shoulders in turn, "I name you Lord Protector of the Realm, with all rights and privileges thereto."

Gasps and murmurs swept through the court as Helena returned the sword to its bearer. "Rise, Lord Protector," she commanded, loud enough for all to hear. "And go with my blessing to complete your mission."

Alaric stood, his wings unfurling to their full impressive span as he bowed deeply. "As my queen commands," he replied, the formal words carrying the weight of an oath more binding than any mortal vow.

As he straightened, their eyes met in silent communication—queen and vampire, bound by blood and purpose and something deeper still. The court might witness their formal exchange, but none could see the true current that flowed between them, forged in the night's passion and sealed in the day's carnage.

"I shall return by sunset," Alaric intoned, his gaze fixed dead ahead — even as his wings unfurled behind him in a slow, deliberate display of menace. The ragged pennants of crimson and black caught the light from the candelabras, casting monstrous shapes on the stone walls and sending a fresh ripple of panic through the courtiers pressed against them.

"With Captain Thorne," he continued, voice ringing with unnatural resonance that made even seasoned knights flinch, "and Lord Varen's head."

A few of the bolder nobles had begun to edge toward the exits, but at Helena's next words, they froze mid-step.

"I shall have a spike prepared for it above the castle gate," declared Queen Helena of Morvain, each syllable clipped and deadly. Her smile was cold—beautiful as hoarfrost—and it held every soul in the room captive.

For a moment only the wind could be heard, snaking through the shattered windows and stirring blood-tinged banners. No one moved. No one spoke. Even the guards stared at their new queen with expressions that mingled awe and terror.

Alaric fixed his eyes on Helena and inclined his head in wordless salute. Then he turned with a liquid predatory grace that defied human anatomy and strode down the length of the throne room. The crowd parted before him like water fleeing a ship's prow, men and women flattening themselves against columns or diving beneath clerestory arches to avoid even the brush of his shadow.

He did not pause at the heavy doors. Instead, Alaric vaulted directly onto one of the marble balustrades, planted both taloned feet on its narrow edge, and leapt—upward, outward—

shattering through a grand arched window set high on the wall. The sound was thunderous: a thousand shards of colored glass exploding into air, raining down upon the court below in glittering slivers that sliced silk sleeves and exposed skin alike.

The last glimpse anyone had of him was his silhouette backlit by sun and sky: black wings fully spread, cloak streaming behind him like a funeral banner, face thrown upward in ecstasy as he soared toward vengeance.

In his wake chaos reigned for an instant—a few courtiers openly wept; others merely trembled where they stood, hands pressed over hearts or mouths as if trying to stanch an invisible wound. A young page fainted outright to the floor; two older councilors exchanged a look of pure panic before dropping to their knees in prayer.

But Helena gave them no time to gather themselves. She advanced from her throne in three measured steps and raised her scepter high so that all might see it trembling faintly in her gloved fist. The light played along its length; somewhere within its crystal tip, something red seemed to flare briefly before subsiding into a dull glow.

CHAPTER 13 –

HELENA – FIRST QUEEN OF MORVAIN

"Attend me," Helena commanded — not shouting but somehow louder than any scream — and all conversation ceased instantly.

She surveyed her court as a general might survey battered but surviving troops after battle. Her gaze lingered on those who had flinched or tried to flee; she marked them quietly with little more than an upturn at one corner of her mouth. The effect was more terrifying than any curse.

"You have all borne witness," she said, voice steady now as she paced slowly down from the dais. "Let none say this day was anything but necessary."

Helena reached Lady Ashcombe first: matronly advisor with trembling hands clasped so tightly her knuckles gleamed white as bone.

"Lady Ashcombe," Helena purred softly enough that only those nearest could hear, "have your scribes record every detail for posterity — and let them not spare any mention of our enemies' fate." The woman nodded frantically and nearly dropped her fan in her haste to obey.

Next came Chancellor Rowan Blackthorn—who bowed deeply but risked glancing up from beneath heavy brows when she drew near.

"Summon all surviving captains," Helena instructed him coldly. "We must take inventory of our strength while our enemies are still reeling."

He did not look at her again as he shuffled away at once. None dared linger under Helena's scrutiny; each noble she addressed turned pale and made haste to carry out her command, even if it meant volunteering for work beneath their rank or dignity.

Within minutes what had been an audience chamber transformed itself into an impromptu war council. Messengers were dispatched. Bloodied pages scurried to sweep up broken glass; servants moved silently about distributing handkerchiefs for dabbing wounds or mopping sweat from feverish brows. No one attempted escape—not while Queen Helena stood watchful over all with eyes bright as molten coin.

Only when satisfied that order had been restored did Helena allow herself to relax—fractionally—and return to her throne.

She eased herself onto its carved seat as if lowering an iron weight onto her own shoulders; then she settled the royal crown more firmly onto her brow. It fit better this time—not just physically but in some intangible sense as well. If anyone doubted whether she belonged there before today's carnage, none would ever voice it again within these walls.

The hush inside grew absolute: not even a cough or shuffling foot disturbed Helena's dominion over all that remained.

As noon sunlight slanted through ruined windows and painted crimson mosaics along polished stone floors, Queen Helena sat enthroned amid devastation—supreme architect of survival and savagery alike—while far above them all Alaric Thornwood's shadow circled closer toward its final act.

If any had expected tears or tremors from their queen they found none; there was only resolve chiselled into features too young for such burdens yet wearing them better than most men twice her age ever could.

Outside Adrielkeep's gates the city lay quiet under siege of rumor already spreading faster than fire: stories about what had transpired inside those ancient walls—about monsters unleashed beyond reckoning—about how Queen Helena had faced them down without blinking once.

Inside, beneath ancient banners dripping with history (and not a little blood), newly minted lords and wary old power brokers waited hunched over maps and ledgers for Her Majesty's next decree… hoping only that they would survive long enough to carry it out.

Helena watched them — all of them — with silent calculation until one by one they wilted under her attention like flowers scorched by frost.

She waited until Captain Eldric limped back into view: armor dented but eyes clear despite all she'd seen this day.

"Report," said Queen Helena.

Eldric's voice wavered only slightly as she recounted lost numbers and tallied weapons left fit for use; then she added (with something dangerously close to pride) that no soldier had deserted their post during or after the slaughter.

"And Lord Thornwood?"

Helena smiled — the first real smile since morning — though it showed teeth.

"He will return before sunset…
with Captain Thorne," said Eldric.

"And Lord Varen's head, there is
not doubt in my mind."

She said it lightly enough for
those nearby to think perhaps she meant
it figuratively—but no one present was
fool enough anymore to doubt what
Queen Helena took literally.

She leaned back in the throne,
elbows resting on its arms as sunlight
gilded both crown and hair until even
those who hated her could admit she
looked every inch born for rule.

She felt power settle around her
shoulders against velvet gown like an
old friend come home again after many
years lost wandering foreign roads.

Below in streets already
thickening with fearsome rumors—from
panicked survivors who'd glimpsed
wings like night or howling things that
tore men limb from limb—the city
braced itself for whatever new law

would issue forth from this blood-slick day.

Within Adrielkeep? Silence reigned—until finally someone remembered protocol well enough to call out:

"Long live Queen Helena!"

The echo came back ragged at first—from throats raw with terror—but then caught fire throughout great hall,

And so Morvain passed into new rule: unbroken line from slaughterhouse birthright straight on toward dusk.

Helena swept from the throne room with the train of her blood-spattered gown hissing across the stone floor. The buzz of whispered conversations erupted the moment the doors closed behind her, courtiers huddling together like frightened birds after a hawk's passing. She paid them no mind, her thoughts already racing ahead to what must be done before Alaric returned with his grim trophies.

Captain Eldric followed close behind, her armor clanking with each hurried step. The captain's face was ashen, jaw clenched tight enough to crack teeth. They walked in tense silence through the winding corridors until they reached the king's study — now Helena's by right of succession.

Once inside, Helena moved to the window, gazing out at the field of carnage beyond the castle walls. Carrion birds had already begun to circle, dark specks against the afternoon sky.

"Speak your mind, Captain," Helena said without turning. "Your silence screams louder than any battle cry."

Eldric shut the door with more force than necessary, the heavy oak slamming against its frame. "What have you done?" she demanded, her voice hoarse. "What unholy alliance have you forged?"

Helena turned slowly, one eyebrow arched. "I've secured my

throne and saved countless lives within these walls. Would you prefer I'd surrendered to Varen's forces?"

"There are lines that shouldn't be crossed," Eldric said, taking a step forward. Her hand rested on her sword hilt, though whether from habit or threat, Helena couldn't tell. "That... creature... is not human. He slaughtered hundreds without mercy, without humanity. I saw men's blood boil in their veins at his command!"

"Yes," Helena replied calmly. "Impressive, wasn't it?"

Eldric recoiled as if struck. "Impressive? It was an abomination! The men on those walls will have nightmares until their dying day. Some are already saying you've made a pact with demons to secure your rule."

"And if I have?" Helena challenged, moving to her father's desk — her desk now — and pouring wine from the crystal decanter. She offered none to Eldric. "Would that be so different from the alliances other monarchs have made throughout history? Marriage to secure borders, treaties signed in blood—"

"This is different and you know it," Eldric cut in. "Thornwood is a monster. Whatever he is—vampire, demon, I don't know—he's not natural. And he's not loyal to you or Morvain. He serves his own purpose."

Helena sipped her wine, studying Eldric over the rim of her goblet. "Of course he does. As do we all."

"Your Majesty," Eldric said, making a visible effort to soften her tone, "Varen is not yet defeated. His main force may be destroyed, but he himself remains at large. We need allies, yes, but not... not this. Not at the cost of our humanity."

"Our humanity," Helena repeated, setting down her goblet with a sharp click against the polished wood. "Was it humanity that killed my father?

Was it humanity that sent assassins into my castle? Was it humanity that would have seen me dead before I could wear my rightful crown?"

She stepped around the desk, closing the distance between them until they stood face to face. "Varen surrendered his claim to humanity centuries ago, Captain. Yes, I know what he is — what he's done to extend his life far beyond natural limits. He has slaughtered innocents, consumed their essence, violated every law of God and nature to feed his ambition."

"Then fight him with steel and courage," Eldric pleaded. "Not with dark powers that will corrupt you as surely as they've corrupted him."

Helena laughed, the sound brittle in the quiet room. "Steel against sorcery? Courage against centuries of cunning? You would have me bring a sword to a battle of shadows."

"Better to die with honor than live with the taint of such alliances," Eldric insisted.

"Is that what you truly believe?" Helena asked, her voice dropping to a dangerous whisper. "That honor matters more than survival? More than victory?"

Eldric met her gaze unflinchingly. "I believe there are some prices too steep to pay, Your Majesty. Even for a crown."

"Then you are a fool," Helena said coldly. "A brave fool, perhaps, but a fool nonetheless." She turned away, moving back to the window. "Do you know what Varen did to the last village that resisted him? Falwood, it was called. A small settlement at the edge of Mistwood."

"I've heard rumors—"

"Not rumors. Truth." Helena's fingers tightened around her goblet. "He ordered every man, woman, and child gathered in the village square. Then he had his soldiers nail them to the walls of their own homes — still alive, screaming for mercy. The children went first, so their parents would be forced to watch."

Eldric paled further, her hand falling away from her sword.

"When the nailing was done," Helena continued relentlessly, "he ordered the houses set ablaze. Hundreds burned alive, their screams lasting until their lungs filled with smoke." She turned back to face Eldric. "That is the enemy we face, Captain. That is the monster who would take my throne."

"And you think allying with another monster is the answer?" Eldric asked, though with less conviction than before.

"I think survival requires difficult choices," Helena replied. "I think a queen must be willing to make those choices, even when they cost her sleep at night." She set down her goblet and straightened, every inch the ruler she had become. "Alaric Thornwood may be a monster, but he is my monster. And he will help me destroy a greater evil before it destroys us all."

Eldric's shoulders slumped slightly, the fight draining from her stance. "And afterward? When Varen is dead and his head adorns our gates? What then? Do you truly believe Thornwood will simply bow and return to whatever darkness spawned him?"

A small, secretive smile played at the corners of Helena's mouth. "That, Captain, is a concern for another day. For now, we have a kingdom to secure and a war to win." She moved to her desk and unrolled a map of the surrounding territories. "Now, tell me of our defenses. I want every approach to the castle patrolled. Varen may have lost his army, but he's far from powerless."

Eldric hesitated, clearly wanting to pursue her line of questioning, but years of military discipline won out. She stepped forward, pointing to the western approach. "We've doubled the guard here, where the forest comes closest to the walls. If there's another attack—"

"There won't be," Helena interrupted. "Not today, at least. Varen will be regrouping, considering his options. And Alaric..." Her voice softened slightly at his name. "Alaric will find him before he can mount another assault."

"You trust him that much?" Eldric asked, incredulous.

Helena's eyes met hers, something ancient and knowing in their blue depths. "I trust his hatred of Varen more than I trust most men's love of country. Some grudges transcend time, Captain. Some vengeance demands satisfaction regardless of cost."

Before Eldric could respond, a sharp knock sounded at the door. A young guard entered, his face pale with urgency.

"Your Majesty," he said, bowing hastily. "Lord Harwick sends word. A rider approaches from the east—a single horseman bearing no standard. He requests entry to the castle."

Helena and Eldric exchanged glances. "A messenger from Varen?" Eldric suggested.

"Or a trap," Helena countered. She turned to the guard. "Have archers ready on the walls. Bring this rider to the courtyard—not inside the castle proper—and search him thoroughly for weapons. I will hear what he has to say."

The guard bowed again and hurried away. Helena moved to a small cabinet against the far wall, withdrawing a slender dagger with an ornate hilt. She slipped it into a hidden sheath within her sleeve.

"Shall I summon more guards?" Eldric asked, watching the queen arm herself.

Helena shook her head. "No. Just you and Lord Harwick. I want to keep this quiet until we know what we're dealing with." She paused at the door, looking back at her captain. "And Eldric? Whatever your personal feelings about Lord Thornwood, keep them to yourself in public. The court must see unity among the crown's closest advisors."

"As you command, Your Majesty," Eldric replied stiffly.

They made their way to the eastern courtyard, where the afternoon sun cast long shadows across the cobblestones. Lord Harwick awaited them, his elderly frame still straight with dignity despite the day's events.

"Your Majesty," he bowed, his voice lowered for privacy. "The rider approaches the gate now. He claims to bear urgent news regarding Lord Varen's whereabouts."

"A defector?" Helena asked, her interest piqued.

"Or bait for a trap," Eldric muttered, echoing Helena's earlier concern.

The great iron gates creaked open just enough to admit a single rider. The horse that entered was lathered with sweat, its sides heaving from hard riding. Its rider wore a plain brown cloak, hood pulled low over his face. Two guards flanked him immediately, spears at the ready.

"Dismount and identify yourself," Lord Harwick commanded as the rider halted before them.

Slowly, the figure slid from the saddle, movements betraying exhaustion or injury. When he pushed back his hood, gasps escaped from all present.

It was Captain Thorne—or what remained of him. His face was a mass of fresh bruises, one eye swollen completely shut. Blood matted his hair and beard, and his left arm hung at an unnatural angle, clearly broken.

CHAPTER 14 –
THE VAMPIRE'S WHORE

"Your Majesty," he croaked, attempting to bow but nearly collapsing instead. Eldric rushed forward to support him. "I... I escaped. Varen's men... they were taking me to the old temple in Mistwood. But something attacked our party on the road. Something terrible. In the confusion, I managed to steal a horse and flee."

Helena stepped closer, her eyes narrowing with suspicion. "What attacked you?"

Thorne shuddered visibly. "Creatures... like those from before. Blue-gray skin, yellow eyes... They came from nowhere, tore men apart like parchment. One moment we were riding, the next..." He swallowed hard. "It was a slaughter."

"Alaric's creatures," Eldric murmured, exchanging a significant look with Helena.

"Where is Varen now?" Helena demanded.

"The old temple, as Lord Thornwood guessed," Thorne replied, wincing as he shifted his weight. "He's preparing some kind of ritual. I heard his men talking—something about transferring his essence when the moon rises. He knows his armies have failed. He's desperate."

Helena's mind raced with implications. If Varen was indeed preparing the ritual Alaric had described—the one that would allow him to inhabit a new body—then they had precious little time.

Helena's eyes narrowed, something about Thorne's story not quite fitting together. "Why ride back to me, Captain? You escaped your captors—why not flee to safety? Why return to a castle you knew would be under siege?"

Thorne's one good eye darted between the faces surrounding him. "I... I had to warn you, Your Majesty. About Varen's plans."

"And risk recapture? Risk torture?" Helena stepped closer, her voice dropping to a dangerous whisper. "A wounded man on a stolen horse, riding straight into danger rather than away from it?"

"My loyalty is to the crown," Thorne insisted, sweat beading on his brow despite the cool afternoon air. "Always has been."

"Your loyalty was to my father," Helena corrected him. "Yet you vanished when he needed you most. Found yourself conveniently captured rather than defending your king."

Thorne's breathing quickened. "That's not—I was ambushed—"

"The captain of the King's Guard, ambushed?" Helena laughed, the sound sharp as breaking glass. "A man who survived a dozen assassination attempts against my father, suddenly helpless when it mattered most?"

"Your Majesty," Eldric cautioned, sensing the dangerous shift in Helena's tone.

Helena ignored her, circling Thorne like a predator. "Tell me, Captain. What did Varen promise you? Gold? Lands? A title when he took the throne?"

"Nothing! I swear it!" Thorne's voice cracked with desperation. "I serve only—"

He stopped mid-sentence, his body going rigid. A strange gurgling sound escaped his throat as his head snapped back at an unnatural angle.

"Step back!" Eldric shouted, drawing her sword as she pulled Helena away from the convulsing man.

Thorne's good eye rolled back in his head until only white showed. When he spoke again, his voice had changed—deeper, resonating with unnatural power.

"The false queen makes pacts with demons," he intoned, blood beginning to trickle from his nostrils. "Helena of Morvain has sold her soul to darkness."

The guards backed away, making signs of protection as Thorne's body contorted, his broken arm twisting further with sickening cracks.

"She has taken the vampire Thornewood to her bed," Thorne continued, his lips barely moving though the words rang clear in the courtyard. "Drunk his blood. Shared her flesh. The crown sits upon a tainted brow."

Lord Harwick gasped, his aged face paling as he looked at Helena with dawning horror.

"Silence him," Helena commanded, her voice steady despite the accusation.

But Thorne wasn't finished. "Helena is not your true queen," he rasped, bloody spittle flying from his lips. "She is a vessel for ancient evil. The vampire's whore. The —"

The wet sound of steel meeting flesh cut off his words. Eldric stood before him, her sword buried to the hilt in his chest. Their eyes met for one frozen moment—Thorne's suddenly clear and filled with something like gratitude—before she wrenched the blade free.

He crumpled to the cobblestones, blood pooling beneath him. Eldric turned to Helena, her sword still dripping red.

"Forgive me, Your Majesty," she said, her voice tight. "He was clearly bewitched. Varen's puppet, sent to spread lies and discord."

Helena stared down at Thorne's body, her expression unreadable. "Have the corpse burned immediately," she ordered. "Salt the ashes and scatter them in running water."

The guards exchanged uneasy glances, but moved to obey. Lord Harwick remained frozen, his rheumy eyes fixed on Helena with naked suspicion.

"Your Majesty," he began carefully, "these accusations—"

"Were the desperate ravings of a dying man," Helena cut him off. "Or worse, dark magic meant to turn us against each other." She turned to face him fully, royal authority radiating from her like heat from flame. "Would you take the word of a traitor over that of your anointed queen?"

Harwick hesitated, years of political instinct warring with the horror of what he'd just witnessed. "Of course not, Your Majesty," he said finally, bowing low. "I merely thought—"

"You thought to question your sovereign based on the utterances of a corpse," Helena finished for him, her voice like ice. "A dangerous path, Lord Harwick. One I suggest you reconsider."

The old man's face drained of what little color remained. "Forgive an old man's foolishness," he murmured, bowing again more deeply.

Helena's gaze swept over the gathered guards, each of whom suddenly found great interest in the cobblestones at their feet. "Return to your posts," she commanded. "Speak of this to no one, on pain of death."

They scattered like leaves before a storm, leaving only Helena, Eldric, and the rapidly cooling body of Captain Thorne in the courtyard.

"Eldric," Helena said quietly once they were alone, "walk with me."

They left Thorne's body for the guards to dispose of, making their way toward the private royal gardens where ivy-covered walls ensured their conversation would remain private.

"Thank you," Helena said finally, breaking the tense silence between them. "For acting so decisively."

Eldric's face remained impassive. "I serve the crown, Your Majesty."

"Do you?" Helena stopped beside a stone bench, turning to face her captain directly. "Or do you serve Morvain? There is a difference, though few recognize it."

"I serve both," Eldric replied carefully. "When the crown acts in Morvain's best interests."

Helena smiled thinly. "A diplomatic answer."

"The only honest one I can give." Eldric's hand still rested on her sword hilt, the blade now cleaned of Thorne's blood but no less deadly. "Was it true? What he said about you and Lord Thornwood?"

Helena considered her options carefully. Denial would be easiest, but Eldric had seen too much today to be easily deceived. Truth might cost her a loyal captain—or gain her a true ally.

"Some of it," she admitted finally. "Alaric Thornwood is indeed a vampire. And I have allied myself with him against Varen."

"And the rest?" Eldric pressed, her gaze unwavering.

Helena met that gaze without flinching. "My personal affairs are my own, Captain. But know this—I have not been corrupted or bewitched. Every choice I've made has been with Morvain's survival as my sole concern."

Eldric absorbed this, her expression troubled. "The court will talk. The guards who heard Thorne's accusations—"

"Will keep silent if they value their lives," Helena finished. "As for the court, let them talk. Rumors of royal liaisons are hardly new."

"This is different," Eldric insisted. "Thornwood isn't just a controversial lover—he's not human. If word spreads that Morvain's queen consorts with the undead—"

"Then I will deal with it," Helena cut her off sharply. "As I have dealt with everything else today."

A distant horn blast interrupted their conversation—three short bursts followed by a longer note. The signal for an approaching ally.

Eldric straightened immediately, professional instincts overriding personal concerns. "That would be Lord Fennwick's forces," she said. "They were due to arrive by sunset."

"Go," Helena ordered. "See them settled and bring Lord Fennwick to me immediately. We'll need to coordinate our defense in case Varen launches another assault."

Eldric bowed and turned to leave, but Helena called after her.

"Captain—one more thing."

Eldric paused, looking back over her shoulder.

"I need to know where you stand," Helena said quietly. "Not just today, but in the days to come. Varen isn't our only enemy. Once word spreads of what happened here—of what Alaric is—there will be those who turn against us. I need to know if you're one of them."

Eldric was silent for a long moment, her face unreadable in the fading afternoon light. Finally, she spoke, each word carefully chosen.

"I serve Morvain first. Always have. If your alliance with... Lord Thornwood... protects our people from Varen's cruelty, then I stand with you." Her eyes hardened. "But if I ever believe you've been corrupted — if I see evidence that you no longer act in Morvain's best interests — my loyalty will end there."

Helena nodded, accepting the conditional support for what it was. "Fair enough. Go see to Lord Fennwick."

Alone in the garden, Helena sank onto the stone bench, suddenly exhausted. The weight of the crown, both literal and figurative, pressed down on her shoulders like a physical burden. She reached up to touch the puncture wounds on her neck, still tender beneath her high collar.

Thorne's accusations echoed in her mind. Vampire's whore. Vessel for ancient evil. False queen. How much had Varen discovered? How much was merely lucky guesswork designed to sow discord?

More importantly, how many others would raise similar questions once Alaric's true nature became common knowledge?

The sun was sinking toward the horizon, casting long shadows across the garden. Soon Alaric would return — hopefully with Varen's head as promised. But what then? Would her people accept a vampire as Lord Protector once the immediate threat was eliminated?

Would they accept her as queen, knowing what she had done — what she had become — to secure her throne?

Helena closed her eyes, feeling the changes within her body that Alaric's blood had wrought. Her senses sharpened beyond human norm, her strength and speed subtly enhanced. Not vampire, not yet, but no longer entirely human either.

A queen caught between worlds, just as her kingdom stood balanced between darkness and light.

In the distance, the sound of approaching horses announced Lord Fennwick's arrival. Helena rose, composing herself with practiced ease. Whatever doubts plagued her private thoughts, her public face must show nothing but absolute confidence.

CHAPTER 15 –
THE 1ST NIGHT OF MANY

Night was falling over Morvain, and with it, the promise of Alaric's return. Whatever happened next — whatever price she must pay for her choices — Helena would face it as she had faced everything else today.

Not as a vessel or a whore or a false queen.

But as Helena of Morvain, rightful ruler of her father's kingdom, with the blood of ancient kings in her veins — and now, something older still.

The clash of steel against steel tore Helena from uneasy slumber. Her eyes snapped open in the darkness, momentarily disoriented until another crash echoed through the corridor outside her chambers. She rolled from bed in one fluid motion, bare feet silent against the cold stone floor.

"Guards!" she called, but no response came.

Helena snatched her father's sword from its stand beside her bed, the blade gleaming dully in the moonlight that streamed through her window. She didn't bother with a robe over her thin nightgown, knowing each second might mean life or death.

The corridor outside her chambers was chaos—two bodies already lay crumpled against the wall, the crimson stains identifying them as her own guards. Ahead, Captain Eldric fought desperately against two soldiers in unmarked armor, their blades catching torchlight as they pressed her back toward Helena's door.

"Behind you!" Helena shouted, charging forward with her sword raised.

One attacker turned, his eyes widening at the sight of her. "The vampire queen!" he spat, face contorted with hatred. "Death to the blood witch!"

He lunged toward her, blade aimed at her heart. Helena parried, the impact jarring her arms but her form remained perfect—the result of years of secret training her father had insisted upon. She countered with a slash that opened the man's forearm, drawing a howl of pain.

Eldric seized the moment of distraction to drive her sword through the back of the second attacker, the blade erupting from his chest in a spray of crimson. "Your Majesty!" she gasped, yanking her weapon free as the man collapsed. "Get back to your chambers!"

"I think not," Helena snarled, advancing on the remaining soldier who now backed away, clutching his wounded arm.

"Demon-lover," he hissed, spittle flying from his lips. "Unholy abomination. The people know what you are!"

Helena's blade flashed once, twice—a perfect cross-cut that left the man's head tumbling from his shoulders before his body had time to fall.

Silence descended on the corridor, broken only by Eldric's ragged breathing and the soft patter of blood dripping onto stone.

"Report," Helena commanded, wiping her father's blade clean on the dead man's cloak.

Eldric straightened, wincing at what appeared to be a shallow cut across her ribs. "A small group infiltrated through the servants' quarters. Eight, maybe ten men. We've neutralized most, but—"

A scream echoed from somewhere deeper in the castle, cutting off her words.

"How many of our people are dead?" Helena demanded, already moving toward the sound.

"At least six guards that I've seen," Eldric replied, falling into step beside her. "They knew exactly where to strike—the night watch points, your personal guards—"

"Traitors within our walls," Helena concluded, her voice deadly calm even as rage built within her. "Again."

They rounded a corner to find three more bodies—two attackers and one of Helena's handmaidens, her throat cut so deeply she was nearly decapitated. Helena knelt briefly beside the girl—Elise, barely sixteen—touching her cooling cheek in a silent farewell.

When she rose, something had changed in her face. The composed queen was gone, replaced by something colder, harder.

"Enough," she whispered, the word carrying more menace than any shout. "I have endured assassination attempts, slander, and betrayal. I have been patient. I have been merciful." Her fingers tightened around her sword hilt until her knuckles shone white in the torchlight. "No more."

Eldric took an involuntary step back, something in Helena's expression triggering a primal warning in her soldier's instincts.

"Your Majesty —"

"Sound the alarm," Helena cut her off, already striding toward the great hall. "Every knight, every guard, every noble with a claim to loyalty — I want them in the main courtyard immediately."

"It's the middle of the night," Eldric protested, hurrying to keep pace. "Many will be —"

"Did I stutter, Captain?" Helena's voice cracked like a whip. "Immediately. Those who delay will be considered complicit in tonight's attack."

Eldric paled but nodded, gesturing to a guard who had appeared at the end of the corridor. "Sound the assembly bell. Full muster in the courtyard. The Queen commands it."

The guard's eyes widened at the sight of his blood-spattered queen in her nightclothes, but he saluted and ran to obey.

Helena continued her relentless pace toward the great hall, servants flattening themselves against walls as she passed. Blood dripped from the hem of her nightgown, leaving a trail of crimson droplets on the stone floor. She looked like something risen from ancient legend—a vengeful spirit with copper hair streaming unbound down her back and a naked sword in her hand.

"What do you intend?" Eldric asked quietly as they reached the massive oak doors of the great hall.

Helena paused, her face illuminated by the wall sconces. In the flickering light, her features seemed sharper, her eyes reflecting the flames with an almost preternatural glow.

"Justice," she replied, the word falling from her lips like a death sentence. "No more half-measures. No more political maneuvering. Tonight, everyone in Ravenscrest will learn exactly what happens to those who move against their queen."

The great bell began to toll, its deep voice echoing across the sleeping castle. Three times it rang—the signal for immediate assembly, not used since the night of the old king's death. Throughout Ravenscrest, lights began to appear in windows as confused residents were jolted from sleep.

Helena pushed open the doors to the great hall and strode to the dais where her throne stood. She did not sit, but instead stood before it, sword still in hand, waiting as the first bewildered nobles and knights began to trickle in.

Lord Harwick appeared, hastily dressed but dignified despite being roused from sleep. His eyes widened at the sight of Helena, still in her bloodied nightgown.

"Your Majesty, what has—"

"Take your place, Lord Harwick," Helena interrupted coldly. "All will be explained when everyone is present."

More arrived with each passing minute—knights in partial armor, ladies in nightgowns and hastily donned robes, servants and guards looking confused and frightened. The murmurs grew as they took in their queen's appearance and the bodies being carried past the open doors.

Captain Eldric positioned guards at each entrance, her face grim as she surveyed the growing crowd. When the great hall was nearly full, she approached the dais.

"All present who could be accounted for, Your Majesty," she reported. "Three nobles are notably absent: Lord Blackwell, Lady Marienne, and Baron Folson."

"Have their chambers searched," Helena commanded, her voice carrying across the now-hushed hall. "Bring them here—willing or not."

A ripple of shock passed through the assembled crowd. Blackwell and Folson were among the most powerful lords in Morvain, their families' histories intertwined with the kingdom's for generations.

Helena stepped forward, the bloodied sword in her hand catching the light from the hastily lit chandeliers. The great hall fell silent, hundreds of eyes fixed on their queen as she surveyed them with cold fury.

"Tonight," she began, her voice clear and terrible in the stillness, "assassins entered my castle. They killed my guards. They murdered an innocent handmaiden who had the misfortune to cross their path." She paused, letting the words sink in. "They called me 'vampire queen' and 'blood witch' as they tried to take my life."

Whispers erupted throughout the hall, quickly silenced by Helena's raised hand.

"These were not common mercenaries. They knew our defenses, our rotations, the secret passages that few outside the royal family should know exist." Her gaze swept across the assembled nobles, lingering on certain faces. "They had help from within these walls."

"Impossible!" Lord Harwick protested, stepping forward. "Your Majesty, no true noble of Morvain would—"

"Silence!" Helena's command cracked like a whip, and Harwick fell back as if physically struck. "I have been patient. I have been understanding. I have allowed whispers and doubts and questions of my rule because I believed time would prove my worth as your queen."

She descended the dais steps, her bloodied nightgown trailing behind her like a macabre wedding train. The crowd parted before her as she walked among them, her sword still naked in her hand.

"That patience ends tonight," she continued, stopping before a cluster of younger nobles who had been among the most vocal critics of her alliance with Alaric. "You have questions about Lord Thornwood? About the nature of our alliance? Ask them now, openly, instead of plotting in shadows and sending killers in the night."

The nobles exchanged nervous glances, none willing to speak first. Finally, young Lord Terrick stepped forward, swallowing hard before addressing his queen.

"Your Majesty, there are... rumors. About Lord Thornwood's nature. About what happened on the battlefield." His voice strengthened slightly as he continued. "The people deserve to know if their queen consorts with—"

"With what, Lord Terrick?" Helena cut in, her voice dangerously soft. "Say the word you whisper behind closed doors. Say it here, before your queen and your peers."

Terrick paled, but lifted his chin defiantly. "With a vampire, Your Majesty. They say Lord Thornwood is a creature of darkness, and that you have... welcomed him into more than just your council chambers."

A collective gasp rose from the assembled court, followed by tense silence as all eyes fixed on Helena, waiting for her reaction to this unprecedented accusation.

To their surprise, she smiled — a cold, terrible smile that transformed her face into something both beautiful and frightening.

"At last," she said softly, "honesty." She turned, addressing the entire hall once more. "Yes, Lord Alaric Thornwood is a vampire. Yes, he commands powers beyond mortal men. And yes, I have allied Morvain with him against those who would see us all dead or enslaved under Varen's rule."

The admission sent shockwaves through the great hall. Some made signs of protection; others reached for weapons that weren't there. Guards exchanged uneasy glances, uncertain where their duty lay in this unprecedented situation.

A second of stunned, electric silence held the great hall suspended; then a hundred voices exploded in whispers and sharp intakes of breath. Lords and ladies leaned toward one another, white-knuckled hands trembling on the hilts of ornamental daggers or prayer beads. Even the guards tensed, uncertain if this was the moment the old order shattered. In that charged hush, Queen Helena strode forward and cut through their fear with words as precise as the blade in her hand.

"Before you judge," she called out, voice ringing off marble and stone like the tolling of a bell, "remember what Varen would have brought upon you. Remember the army that stood at our gates. Remember the centuries of suffering he has inflicted on this kingdom while wearing different faces, consuming innocent lives to extend his own."

She let her gaze linger on each pocket of resistance in the crowd — on House Vexley's drought-eyed matron who had lost three sons to Varen's wars; on Lord Armitage, his face cratered and gray from wounds barely healed after the siege; on Lady Hestera, clutching her husband's arm so fiercely he winced despite himself. They remembered — she could see it in their eyes — and she pressed that wound before it could begin to scab.

"Do you forget so quickly?" Helena went on, her voice softening only to become more dangerous. "What we endured at Starfall? The way Varen fed on your friends and kin and returned them as hollow wraiths? I make no apologies for using every weapon at my disposal to protect this kingdom and its people. If that weapon bears fangs instead of a banner, it is because your loyalty alone was not enough."

Her sword lifted—never pointed at any one man or woman, but hanging in the air as a silent threat over all of them—as she gestured to the eastern windows where dawn's first pallor grazed stained glass with hints of blood and gold. "Out there lies a field of bodies—evidence of what awaits those who stand against Morvain," she said. "We survived because we were willing to do what others would not."

Among those closest to Helena, even her allies hesitated before meeting her gaze now. She read their hunger for conviction—for some justification that would let them hold onto faith in crown and country—and she gave it to them, patient but merciless.

"Do you think I do not see your suspicion?" Helena continued, striding from one end of the dais to the other so every face felt her scrutiny. "You think me tainted by Thornwood's blood; you wonder if I am still fit to rule." She stopped beside Lord Harwick and laid her hand on his shoulder as if granting absolution—or marking him for later judgment. "But I have never betrayed Morvain," she vowed, each word hammered into its own iron law. "I will die before I hand this realm over to monsters—or cowering traitors hiding behind noble crests."

The doors at the far end banged open with a thunderclap that drowned even Helena's rhetoric. Two burly guards half-dragged, half-carried three figures into view: Lord Blackwell limping, cloak torn from an unceremonious struggle; Lady Marienne pale with fury but trying to preserve what dignity she could behind a mask of haughty disdain; Baron Folson disheveled, his face split by panic and sweat. Each bore bruises from having been forcibly extracted from private chambers—or perhaps from having attempted flight through less dignified means.

All eyes snapped to them as they stumbled under escort down the center aisle. It was brutally clear they had not come willingly.

Helena did not hide her satisfaction; it twisted her lips into something just shy of triumphant cruelty as she watched Folson try — and fail — to meet her eye. She waited until all three stood before her throne, surrounded by an expanding ring of armed guards.

"Ah," Helena purred, voice thick with sarcasm sharpened by contempt. "Our missing guests arrive at last."

Blackwell straightened his back with soldierly reflex but bled uncertainty from every other pore; Marienne stood rigid as statuary, looking nowhere except at some fixed point above Helena's head; Folson tried once more for defiance but only managed a strangled whimper when Helena took an ominous step closer.

She circled them slowly, making sure every soul present watched how power shifted — not by birthright or tradition but by will alone.

"Ladies and gentlemen," Helena announced to the assembly in a tone that dared anyone to interrupt, "these three were caught attempting to slip away while loyal men and women bled defending this castle." She reached out suddenly and snatched Blackwell's signet ring from his left hand with a motion almost too quick for human sight — a parlor trick learned from Alaric — or perhaps something deeper now animated her fingers.

"This is how traitors behave," she spat, tossing the ring into the assembled nobles like throwing raw meat into a pen of wolves. "They run when confronted by consequence."

A quiver ran through the massed nobility; several stepped back instinctively while others surged forward as though proximity alone could keep them safe from implication.

"You are accused," Helena continued icily over Blackwell's stammered protestations, "of conspiring with enemies both foreign and domestic against your sovereign." She paused briefly over Marienne, whose lined face twisted in silent rage but could not muster words sufficient to defend herself.

"In light of tonight's events," Helena declared loud enough for even kitchen servants lining the rear walls to hear, "we shall dispense with weeks of tedious inquiry." She turned slowly so every corner could see: "You will answer now—and publicly."

Blackwell's pride flickered weakly before dying out altogether. "Your Majesty," he croaked past split lips," we acted only out of concern for Morvain! You align yourself with...things! You bring unnatural darkness into our halls while outlawing dissent!"

"Our Queen brings life where you bring cowardice," Eldric muttered under her breath—a low oath caught only by those nearest but echoing up toward the vaults regardless.

Helena fixed Blackwell with an arctic stare. "Is that your defense? That you plotted regicide because my methods offend your delicate sensibilities?"

Around them nobles shifted uncomfortably—some involuntarily nodding along with Helena's logic; others shrinking into themselves lest their own clandestine doubts be exposed next.

Lady Marienne found her voice then—knifing through tension with barbed precision: "We do not recognize this...this reign by terror! We followed only those who still remember when Morvain was ruled by daylight—not whatever nameless thing you have become!"

For a heartbeat it seemed even Helena might falter—but then she threw back her head and laughed; not cruelly at first but as if genuinely entertained by how little these supposed leaders understood power.

"I am no more monster than any man or woman who has ever sat upon this throne," she said at last through cold mirth." The only difference is that I refuse hypocrisy—I declare my darkness openly rather than hide it behind pious words while slaughtering rivals in secret passages."

She turned again to address all present: "You will bear witness tonight—not merely to justice but to truth unveiled." Then softer yet somehow more menacing: "Let none say again that your Queen lacks transparency."

CHAPTER 16 –

BLIND LOYALTY BRINGS ONLY FALSE PROPHETS

As dawn brightened beyond stained glass windows now running red beneath rising sunbeams, two robed priests entered bearing lit tapers — a tradition reserved only for occasions demanding absolute solemnity or divine approval. The crowd parted reverently; even those who moments ago doubted bowed heads instinctively against forces they no longer understood.

Helena motioned for silence until nothing breathed except flame and expectation.

"In ancient days," she intoned in ritual cadence none had heard since childhood catechism, "traitors were broken upon wheels or cast into tombs alive — but such measures breed only martyrs." Her eyes swept across Blackwell's crumbling poise before locking onto Folson's last shreds of bravado." Tonight we set precedent anew — a reckoning not just for these three but for all who would conspire in darkness against Morvain's unity."

She stepped directly in front of Lady Marienne then — so close their faces nearly touched — and spoke softly enough for only Marienne (and those who listened hardest) to hear: "If you had succeeded tonight there would be fire in every window from here to Shadowspine." Her next words were venom whispered sweetly: "You failed because you mistook my mercy for weakness."

Marienne blanched but did not reply.

Helena turned to face the assembled court, her bloodied nightgown catching the first rays of dawn filtering through the stained glass windows.

"My lords and ladies of Morvain," she called out, her voice carrying to every corner of the great hall, "these three stand accused of high treason against the crown. The evidence of their guilt lies in the blood of those who died tonight." She gestured to the three trembling nobles. "What say you? What punishment befits those who would murder their queen in her bed?"

Silence fell over the great hall, thick and oppressive. The nobles exchanged uneasy glances, none willing to be the first to speak. The silence stretched, becoming almost unbearable as Helena stood motionless, waiting.

Lord Harwick cleared his throat as if to speak, then thought better of it. Lady Ashcombe clutched her pendant, lips moving in silent prayer. Even Captain Eldric shifted uncomfortably, her hand resting on her sword hilt.

Just as Helena opened her mouth to break the silence herself, a voice called from the back of the hall:

"Hold them until Lord Thornwood returns!"

Heads turned, searching for the speaker. Then another voice joined, louder:

"Yes! Let Lord Thornwood decide their fate!"

Like a wave building strength, the cry was taken up throughout the hall, growing from scattered voices to a thunderous chant:

"Thornwood! Let Thornwood judge them! Hold them for Thornwood!"

Helena's expression remained impassive, though something flickered in her eyes—surprise, perhaps, or satisfaction. She raised a hand, and the chanting gradually subsided.

"You would entrust this judgment to Lord Thornwood?" she asked, her gaze sweeping the assembled court. "The same man some of you whispered was a monster mere days ago?"

"He defended Morvain when these cowards plotted against it," shouted a knight near the front, his face still bandaged from the battle. "Let him decide their punishment!"

Murmurs of agreement rippled through the crowd. Helena nodded slowly, a small smile playing at the corners of her mouth.

"Very well. The traitors will be held in the north tower until Lord Thornwood returns." She gestured to the guards. "Take them away."

As the three nobles were dragged from the hall, their faces ashen with terror, Helena addressed the court once more.

"Are there any who still harbor doubts? Any who question my rule or my methods? Speak now, openly, and receive honest answers. Or forever hold your peace."

For a moment, it seemed no one would dare speak. Then a man stepped forward—Lord Kerner, a devout follower of the old faith, his weathered face grave beneath a shock of white hair.

"Your Majesty," he said, bowing stiffly, "I have served the crown of Morvain for sixty years. I served your father, and his father before him." He straightened, meeting her gaze directly.

"But what I witnessed in the fields yesterday... the slaughter, the unnatural creatures, the blood magic... it was unholy. There are some powers that should not be wielded, even against our enemies."

A collective intake of breath followed his words. Many expected Helena to strike him down where he stood for such boldness. Instead, she descended the dais steps until she stood before him, close enough to see the faint tremor in his aged hands.

"Lord Kerner," she said, her voice carrying clearly despite its softness, "if we had not had Lord Thornwood's aid—if we had not unleashed those powers you find so disturbing—would you prefer to be Varen's enemy instead of mine?"

Kerner paled, memories of Varen's previous atrocities clearly flashing behind his eyes. "No, Your Majesty," he admitted. "I would not."

"The old ways failed us," Helena continued, raising her voice so all could hear. "My father's traditional alliances, his conventional armies — they could not stand against Varen's dark powers. Should I have clung to tradition and watched Morvain fall? Or should I have seized every advantage available to protect my people?"

She turned, addressing the entire hall once more. "I do not ask you to love the darkness, my lords and ladies. I ask only that you recognize its necessity — and be grateful it fights for us rather than against us."

Lord Kerner bowed his head. "Wisdom beyond your years, Your Majesty. Forgive an old man's fears."

Helena touched his shoulder lightly. "Fear is natural, Lord Kerner. But let it be directed toward our true enemies, not toward those who stand between us and annihilation."

The court dismissed, Helena strode from the great hall with Captain

Eldric following close behind. The first rays of morning sun streamed through the high windows, illuminating the blood that had dried in rusty patterns across Helena's nightgown.

"Captain," she called over her shoulder as they reached the royal wing, "attend me."

Helena pushed open the door to her private study and immediately moved toward the adjoining chamber where her ladies kept her wardrobe. She began unlacing her ruined nightgown, seemingly unconcerned with Eldric's presence.

"Your Majesty," Eldric said, averting her eyes and fixing her gaze on a tapestry depicting one of Helena's ancestors in battle. "That was... unexpected. The court rallying behind Lord Thornwood."

Helena stepped behind a carved wooden screen, tossing the bloodied nightgown over the top. "Not entirely unexpected," she replied, her voice muffled as she pulled a clean chemise over her head. "Fear is a powerful motivator, Captain. They've seen what Varen can do. They've seen what Alaric can do. They're simply choosing the monster they believe will keep them alive."

"And will he?" Eldric asked, her voice carefully neutral. "Keep them alive, I mean."

Helena emerged from behind the screen in a simple blue gown, her copper hair still loose around her shoulders. "As long as they remain loyal to me." She moved to her dressing table, selecting a silver brush and beginning to work it through her tangled hair. "What troubles you, Captain? Speak freely."

Eldric shifted uncomfortably, her armor creaking with the movement. "Your alliance with Lord Thornwood... it's one thing in wartime. But after? When Varen is defeated? The nobles may have cheered for him today, but fear and gratitude can quickly turn to resentment and superstition."

"You're concerned about the future," Helena observed, setting down the brush and beginning to braid her hair with practiced fingers.

"I'm concerned about your future," Eldric corrected her. "Your reign has just begun. To tie it so closely to a... to someone like Thornwood..."

"A vampire," Helena supplied calmly. "You can say the word, Captain. I've acknowledged it before the entire court."

Eldric's jaw tightened. "Yes. A vampire. The old texts speak of their kind as manipulative, dangerous. Using mortals for their own purposes."

"And what purpose do you believe Alaric is using me for?" Helena asked, securing her braid with a silver clasp.

"Vengeance against Varen, clearly. But after that? Power? A kingdom under his influence? Access to royal blood?" Eldric's hand unconsciously moved to her sword hilt. "The histories say vampires were driven from Morvain centuries ago for good reason."

Helena rose, moving to the window where she could see the aftermath of yesterday's battle still visible on the field beyond the walls. Workers had begun the grim task of collecting bodies for mass burial, the distant figures moving like ants across the blood-soaked ground.

"The histories," she said softly, "were written by the victors, Captain. By those who feared power they couldn't control." She turned back to face Eldric. "What if I told you Alaric was here in Morvain long before Varen? That he protected these lands when my ancestors were still petty warlords squabbling over hunting rights?"

Eldric's eyes widened. "That would make him..."

"Very old indeed," Helena finished with a slight smile. "And perhaps more invested in Morvain's wellbeing than even its most loyal human subjects."

"You believe his loyalty to the kingdom supersedes his... nature?" Eldric asked skeptically.

Helena moved to her desk, sorting through documents with deliberate care. "I believe Alaric Thornwood is bound to me by ties stronger than mere political alliance, Captain. And I believe that when Varen is defeated, those ties will only strengthen."

"What ties?" Eldric pressed, a note of dread creeping into her voice.

Helena looked up, her blue eyes meeting Eldric's dark ones directly. "Blood, Captain. The most ancient bond of all." She rolled up a map and tucked it into a leather case. "Now, I need you to prepare our forces. When Alaric returns with Varen's head, I want a formal execution announced. The people must see their enemy defeated, must witness the end of his tyranny with their own eyes."

"And if Lord Thornwood fails?" Eldric asked quietly.

Helena's expression hardened. "He won't. But if by some chance Varen should prevail..." She moved to a small cabinet, unlocking it with a key she wore around her neck. From within, she withdrew a slender dagger with strange symbols etched along its blade. "I have contingencies in place. Always."

Eldric stared at the weapon, recognition dawning in her eyes. "That's a blood-steel blade. They're forbidden except for royal executions."

"Yes," Helena confirmed, sliding the dagger into a sheath at her waist. "Capable of killing even those who have prolonged their lives through unnatural means. My father kept it locked away, too afraid to use it even when he suspected Varen's true nature." Her mouth twisted with contempt. "His hesitation cost him his life. I will not make the same mistake."

"Your Majesty," Eldric began, then hesitated, choosing her words carefully. "The court may have accepted Lord Thornwood's... nature... for now. But there will be consequences. Religious leaders, common folk — not everyone will embrace a vampire as the queen's protector."

"I'm counting on it," Helena replied with a cold smile. "Those who cannot accept the new order will reveal themselves soon enough. And when they do..." She left the sentence unfinished, but her meaning was clear.

Eldric's face paled slightly. "You intend to purge the kingdom."

"I intend to secure it," Helena corrected, her voice sharp. "Those who stand with me will prosper. Those who stand against me will not stand for long. It's really quite simple, Captain."

She moved to the door, signaling the end of their conversation. "Have riders ready. The moment Alaric returns, I want messengers dispatched to every corner of Morvain announcing Varen's defeat and my uncontested rule."

"And what of the rumors?" Eldric asked, following her reluctantly. "About you and Lord Thornwood? About what happened between you?"

Helena paused, her hand on the door latch. "Let them talk, Captain. Soon enough, they'll have more to discuss than palace gossip." She opened the door, stepping into the corridor where guards snapped to attention at her approach. "After all, a kingdom ruled by a queen with a vampire at her side? That's just the beginning of the changes Morvain will see under my reign."

CHAPTER 17 –
LORD VAREN.

Miles from Ravenscrest, deep within the shadows of Mistwood Forest, Lord Varen emerged from his tent into the pale dawn light. His weathered face was drawn with fury, dark eyes scanning the makeshift camp where two dozen men huddled around small fires. These weren't ordinary soldiers — they were specially trained, each one versed in dark magic and assassination techniques. The remnants of his once-great army.

"You," Varen barked, pointing at a soldier warming his hands by the nearest fire. "Report. What news of the advance force?"

The soldier scrambled to his feet, his face paling beneath the dirt and grime of travel. He approached Varen with the caution of a man nearing a venomous serpent, stopping just out of arm's reach and dropping to one knee.

"My lord," he began, his voice trembling slightly, "the advance force was intercepted at the castle gates. They... they were all killed."

"By whom?" Varen's voice dropped to a dangerous whisper.

The soldier swallowed hard. "Thornwood, my lord. Witnesses say he... he tore through them like they were nothing. Some speak of wings, of inhuman speed—"

"Speak plainly, fool," Varen snarled, closing the distance between them in two swift strides. "Was it him? The vampire?"

"Yes, my lord. It appears he has... revealed himself."

Varen's face contorted with rage. His hand shot out, seizing the soldier by the throat and lifting him off his feet with unnatural strength. "And the girl? What of Helena?"

"C-crowned," the soldier choked out, clawing desperately at Varen's iron grip. "She's been crowned queen—"

Something snapped in Varen then. With a roar that sent birds scattering from nearby trees, he hurled the soldier to the ground and descended upon him like a beast. His fists rose and fell in a brutal rhythm, each impact accompanied by a wet crunch as bone gave way beneath supernatural strength.

"Useless!" Varen screamed, his knuckles splitting as they connected with the soldier's increasingly unrecognizable face. "Centuries of planning! Centuries of patience! Undone by incompetence!"

The other soldiers backed away, horror etched on their faces as their commander continued his savage assault long after the man had ceased moving. Blood sprayed across Varen's fine clothes, spattering his face and beard until he resembled a butcher more than a nobleman.

When he finally stopped, breathing heavily as he knelt over the pulverized remains, an unnatural silence had fallen over the camp. Varen rose slowly, wiping bloody hands on his cloak as he surveyed the terrified faces of his remaining men.

"Prepare the ritual chamber," he ordered, his voice eerily calm after such violence. "We move to the temple immediately."

A soldier braver—or perhaps more foolish—than the others stepped forward. "My lord, shouldn't we wait for reinforcements from the northern houses? Lady Marienne promised—"

"Lady Marienne is likely dead or captured by now," Varen cut him off. "As are Blackwell and Folson, if the vampire has revealed himself." He turned toward the darkest part of the forest, where ancient trees grew so densely that perpetual twilight reigned beneath their canopy. "We no longer have the luxury of time."

"But my lord," the soldier persisted, "without an army, how can we hope to—"

Varen moved with blinding speed, his hand closing around the man's throat just tightly enough to silence him without crushing his windpipe. "You question me?" he hissed, his face inches from the soldier's. "After three centuries, you think I haven't prepared for every contingency?"

He released the man, who collapsed gasping to his knees. Varen addressed the entire camp, his voice carrying unnaturally in the still morning air.

"Thornwood believes he has won. He thinks this body—" Varen gestured to himself with contempt, "—is all that I am. He forgets what I achieved in the Temple of Whispers while he wasted centuries nursing his grudge."

Varen strode to a covered wagon at the edge of the camp, throwing back the canvas to reveal an ornate chest bound with iron bands inscribed with eldritch symbols. "The ritual requires blood. Fresh, royal blood." A terrible smile spread across his face, revealing teeth too sharp to be entirely human. "Fortunately, we have exactly what we need."

He reached into the wagon, dragging forth a bound and gagged figure—a young man, barely twenty, with dark hair and the unmistakable features of the royal line.

"Prince Corwin," Varen announced, yanking the gag from the prisoner's mouth. "Helena's cousin from the eastern branch. Third in line to the throne... until today."

The young man's eyes were wide with terror, his face bruised from rough handling. "My father will pay whatever ransom—"

"Your father is dead," Varen interrupted coldly. "As is your brother. Your blood is worth far more to me than gold, boy."

Understanding dawned in Corwin's eyes, followed by a desperate surge of struggle against his bonds. Varen struck him casually across the temple, sending him slumping back into unconsciousness.

"Pack everything," he ordered his men. "We reach the temple by midday. When night falls, we begin the ritual." His gaze lifted to the distant shape of Ravenscrest Castle, barely visible through the trees. "Let Thornwood and his queen celebrate their victory. By midnight, I will have a new body, and they will face an enemy they cannot possibly anticipate."

"Bring the boy," Varen commanded, his voice cutting through the forest's unnatural silence. "It's time."

Two soldiers dragged Prince Corwin's limp form toward the clearing where an ancient stone altar stood beneath gnarled branches. The young man had regained consciousness, his eyes wild with terror as he struggled against his captors.

"Please," Corwin begged, his voice cracking. "I have gold — estates — anything you want!"

Varen ignored his pleas, drawing a curved ceremonial dagger from his belt. The blade gleamed with an oily iridescence that seemed to absorb rather than reflect the dappled sunlight filtering through the canopy.

"Hold him down," Varen ordered, approaching the altar with methodical calm.

The soldiers forced Corwin onto the cold stone, pinning his limbs as he thrashed and screamed. Varen stood over him, studying the young man's features with detached curiosity.

"You have your grandmother's eyes," he remarked conversationally, pressing the tip of the blade against Corwin's cheek. "I remember when she begged for mercy too. Before I took her head."

"Monster!" Corwin spat, summoning what courage remained to him. "Helena will destroy you for this!"

Something darkened in Varen's expression. "Helena," he repeated, the name sounding like a curse on his lips. "That girl thinks she understands power. She knows nothing."

With sudden savagery, Varen plunged the dagger into Corwin's shoulder, twisting it with deliberate cruelty. The prince's scream echoed through the forest, sending birds scattering from nearby branches. Blood welled around the blade, dark and rich against the pale stone.

"I require sustenance for what comes next," Varen announced to his watching men. "And royal flesh has... particular properties."

Understanding dawned in the soldiers' eyes as Varen withdrew the blade and began to methodically slice away a strip of flesh from Corwin's arm. The prince's screams intensified, then choked off into broken sobs as shock began to set in.

One by one, the soldiers backed away, revulsion evident on their faces despite their hardened natures. None dared speak against their lord, but their disgust was palpable in the heavy forest air.

Varen seemed oblivious to their reaction, focused entirely on his grisly task. He held up a strip of bloody flesh, examining it with the critical eye of a gourmand before placing it between his teeth. His eyes closed briefly in apparent satisfaction as he chewed.

"The blood remembers," he murmured, almost to himself. "It carries the memory of power through generations."

He cut again, this time taking a larger piece from Corwin's thigh. The prince had gone silent now, his eyes glassy with shock and blood loss, though his chest still rose and fell in shallow, irregular gasps.

Sergeant Frey, a veteran of a dozen campaigns under Varen's command, turned away first. His weathered face had gone ashen beneath his beard, jaw clenched against the bile rising in his throat. Twenty years of warfare had hardened him to all manner of brutality, but this—this abomination—was beyond even his capacity to witness unmoved.

"Back to camp," he muttered to the men nearest him. "He doesn't need an audience."

The soldiers followed gratefully, abandoning their posts without waiting for Varen's permission. None looked back as they retreated through the trees, the sounds of cutting and tearing fading mercifully with distance.

Frey moved with deliberate casualness toward the makeshift barracks they'd established among the trees. His mind raced beneath his carefully composed expression. He'd served Varen loyally for two decades, believing the promises of glory and wealth. He'd ignored rumors, justified atrocities, convinced himself that power required necessary evils.

But this was different. This was madness.

Behind him, Corwin's weakening cries gave way to an awful silence. Frey didn't turn to look, but he heard the drag of something heavy across forest loam — Varen hauling what remained of the prince toward the central fire.

Inside the cramped tent that served as officers' quarters, Frey moved with quiet efficiency. He gathered only essentials — his sword, a water skin, a small pouch of silver coins he'd hoarded over years of service. His fingers trembled slightly as he rolled these items into his bedroll, securing it with leather straps worn smooth from years of use.

"Planning a trip?"

Frey froze, then slowly straightened to face the tent's entrance.

Caldwell, one of Varen's personal guards, stood silhouetted against the daylight, hand resting casually on his sword hilt.

"Scouting mission," Frey replied smoothly, decades of soldiering lending credibility to the lie. "Lord Varen wants the eastern approach checked before nightfall."

Caldwell's eyes narrowed skeptically. "Funny. He didn't mention that to me."

"Perhaps he doesn't tell you everything," Frey countered, slinging his pack over one shoulder while keeping his other hand near his weapon. "You want to question his orders? Go ahead. I'm sure he'd be delighted to explain himself while he's enjoying his... meal."

The reference to what was happening at the fire made Caldwell blanch visibly. He stepped aside, no longer blocking the tent entrance.

"Tell the sentries I sent you," he muttered, unable to meet Frey's eyes. "Otherwise they might put an arrow in your back."

Frey nodded curtly and pushed past him into the afternoon light. The camp had fallen unnaturally quiet, men huddled in small groups, speaking in whispers if at all. Near the central fire, Varen crouched over Corwin's mutilated body, tearing strips of charred flesh from bone with bloody fingers.

Frey kept his gaze averted, moving with practiced nonchalance toward the perimeter. The two sentries at the eastern edge barely glanced at him as he approached.

"Caldwell sent me to check the ravine," he told them, jerking his head toward the forest beyond. "Keep your eyes open. I'll be back by dusk."

The younger guard nodded, clearly relieved to have something to focus on besides the horrors at camp. The older one—Bannon, a grizzled veteran who'd served alongside Frey for years — held his gaze a moment longer.

"Watch yourself out there," Bannon said quietly. "Woods aren't safe anymore."

Something passed between them — understanding, perhaps, or a silent farewell. Frey clapped him once on the shoulder, then slipped between the trees into deeper forest.

He walked steadily for nearly an hour, putting distance between himself and the camp before allowing his pace to quicken. The forest grew denser here, ancient trees crowding out the light, their massive roots creating natural barriers that forced him to zigzag rather than travel in a straight line.

When he judged himself far enough away, Frey paused to get his bearings. Ravenscrest lay to the northwest, perhaps two days' hard travel through difficult terrain. The border of Morvain stretched east, a three-day journey to neutral territory.

South led deeper into Mistwood, where few ventured and fewer returned.

Frey chewed his lip, weighing his options. Ravenscrest meant possible execution if Helena's forces captured him. The border meant exile, a life of wandering without purpose or place. The deep forest meant almost certain death from the creatures that prowled its heart.

No good choices. But then, he'd made his first bad choice years ago when he'd sworn allegiance to Varen.

A twig snapped somewhere behind him. Frey whirled, sword half-drawn before he registered the sound's source—a young deer, frozen in alarm at his sudden movement. They stared at each other for a heartbeat before the animal bounded away, white tail flashing between trees.

Frey exhaled slowly, sheathing his blade. Nerves. He needed to get control of himself if he hoped to survive.

He'd taken three steps toward the east when a low chuckle froze him in place.

"Going somewhere, Sergeant?"

Varen's voice seemed to come from everywhere and nowhere, echoing strangely among the trees. Frey turned slowly, his hand falling to his sword hilt once more.

Lord Varen stood twenty paces away, his fine clothes stained with Corwin's blood, his beard and mouth still glistening with grease from his unholy feast. Despite the distance between them, his eyes seemed to bore into Frey's with unnerving intensity.

"My lord," Frey managed, falling back on military formality while his mind raced for excuses. "I was scouting the eastern—"

"Spare me your lies," Varen cut him off, his voice deceptively gentle. "I've always valued your loyalty, Frey. More than most. I'm disappointed."

"What I saw back there..." Frey abandoned pretense, gesturing vaguely toward the camp. "That wasn't war. That wasn't even human."

"No," Varen agreed, taking a step forward. "It wasn't human at all. It was so much more." He spread his arms, indicating the forest around them. "We stand at the threshold of transformation, Sergeant. By dawn tomorrow, I will transcend this failing flesh and become something greater. History pivots on this moment."

"You're mad," Frey whispered, backing away. "You've always been mad. I just couldn't see it."

Varen's smile chilled him to the marrow. "Mad? Perhaps. But madness and greatness often wear the same face." He took another step forward. "I could use you still, Frey. There's a place for you in what comes after. A place of honor."

For a moment, Frey wavered. Twenty years of obedience didn't dissolve easily, and Varen's charisma remained potent even now, splattered with a prince's blood and reeking of charred human flesh.

Then he remembered Corwin's screams. The way Varen had savored each bite, the almost sensual pleasure he'd taken in the boy's suffering.

"No," Frey said firmly, drawing his sword. "I've followed you into darkness before, but not this time. Not anymore."

Sorrow seemed to pass across Varen's features — genuine regret that made Frey hesitate a crucial moment. Then the mask slipped, revealing the predatory coldness beneath.

"Such a waste," Varen sighed, and raised his hand.

Pain exploded in Frey's chest — not a physical blow, but something worse, as if invisible fingers had plunged between his ribs to squeeze his heart. He dropped to one knee, sword falling from nerveless fingers as he clutched at his chest.

"Did you think you could simply walk away?" Varen asked, approaching with unhurried steps. "After everything you've witnessed? Everything you've done in my name?"

"Kill me then," Frey gasped through clenched teeth. "But I won't go back."

Varen crouched before him, studying his face with the detached curiosity of a naturalist examining an insect. "Oh, I'm not going to kill you, old friend." He reached out, placing his palm against Frey's forehead. "I have a far better use for you."

Darkness swallowed Frey, a blessed reprieve from the agony in his chest. When consciousness returned, it came in waves of searing pain that tore screams from his throat before he could even open his eyes.

Heat. Unbearable heat against his back.

His eyes flew open to find himself suspended above a roaring fire, his arms and legs bound to a thick wooden pole that rotated slowly, mechanically. The skin of his back blistered and cracked as it passed over the flames, the smell of his own cooking flesh filling his nostrils.

"Ah, you're awake." Varen's voice came from somewhere beyond the blinding firelight. "I was beginning to think you'd miss the experience entirely."

Frey tried to speak, but only a ragged howl escaped as the rotation brought his shoulder blades directly over the hottest part of the flames. His skin blackened instantly, fat beginning to render and drip into the fire below with sickening hisses.

"The secret," Varen continued conversationally, stepping into view with a small knife in hand, "is slow cooking. Too fast and the meat toughens. Too slow and the subject dies before the best parts are ready."

The spit continued its relentless turning, bringing Frey's chest away from the flames momentarily. In that brief respite from the worst agony, he managed to gasp: "Why?"

"Waste not, want not," Varen replied, his eyes reflecting the firelight as he approached. "Your betrayal disappointed me, but your body still serves a purpose. Sustenance for the ritual to come."

With clinical precision, Varen sliced a strip of cooked flesh from Frey's outer thigh. Steam rose from the exposed wound as Frey's scream echoed through the clearing. Varen examined the morsel, then placed it delicately in his mouth, chewing thoughtfully.

"A touch overdone," he critiqued, swallowing. "But the fear adds a pleasant complexity."

The spit rotated again, bringing Frey's back once more to the flames.

This time, the fire reached bone where his skin had already been burned away. The pain transcended anything he had imagined possible, white-hot agony that seemed to erase his very identity.

Through the haze of torment, he saw Varen's men standing in a loose circle around the fire pit. Some watched with horrified fascination; others averted their eyes. None dared intervene.

"Who's next?" Frey managed to gasp when the rotation brought temporary relief. "Which of you... will he cook... tomorrow?"

Varen laughed, the sound almost childlike in its delight. "Clever to the end, trying to sow discord." He cut another piece, this time from Frey's shoulder where the skin had crisped to a golden brown. "But unnecessary. After tonight's ritual, I'll have no need for such... primitive nourishment."

Blood and liquefied fat dripped from Frey's suspended body, sizzling in the flames below. The smell would have turned his stomach if he'd been merely a witness rather than the source. His consciousness began to fragment, shock mercifully dulling the worst edges of the pain.

"Your Majesty," one of the soldiers ventured hesitantly, "the preparations for the ritual—"

"Can wait," Varen interrupted, slicing off another strip of flesh. "This is a rare opportunity. When was the last time any of you tasted a traitor's heart while it still beats?"

Frey's vision dimmed, darkness encroaching from the edges. Death approached, but too slowly. The mechanical spit continued its relentless rotation, his body passing through excruciating heat with each turn.

"Look at me, Sergeant," Varen commanded, moving closer. "I want to see the light leave your eyes."

With monumental effort, Frey raised his head. Instead of giving Varen the satisfaction of seeing his terror, he summoned his last reserves of defiance.

"Helena will... destroy you," he rasped, blood bubbling between cracked lips. "And I'll... laugh... from hell..."

"Bold words from a man being eaten alive," Varen replied, amusement dancing in his eyes. He reached toward Frey's exposed chest where the skin had been burned away, revealing the still-pulsing muscle beneath. "But I think I'll have your heart now, before you're entirely gone."

CHAPTER 18 –

WHAT SIDE OF THE BRIDGE WILL YOU BE ON?

Eldric watched Helena's retreating figure with growing unease, the weight of her words settling like stones in her stomach. The queen's silhouette seemed different now — more predatory, her movements carrying an unsettling grace that reminded her uncomfortably of her absent protector.

As the royal guards fell into step behind their sovereign, whispered conversations ceased abruptly in the corridors. Servants pressed themselves against stone walls, eyes downcast, but Eldric caught the fear flickering across their faces. Word of the queen's transformation — whether literal or merely political — was spreading faster than wildfire through dry wheat.

"Captain Mercer." The voice belonged to Rowan Blackthorn, who materialized from an alcove with his characteristic silent approach. "A moment, if you would."

Eldric's hand instinctively moved to his sword hilt. "Lord Blackthorn. I thought you were attending to matters in the eastern provinces."

"Plans change." Rowan's scarred smile held no warmth. "Tell me, Captain—in your professional opinion, how long do you think our beloved queen can maintain order through fear alone?"

"Careful, my lord. Such words could be construed as treason."

"Could they?" Rowan stepped closer, his voice dropping to barely above a whisper. "Or could they be construed as the concerns of a loyal subject who fears for his kingdom's future? After all, when the people begin to whisper that perhaps Lord Varen's rule might have been... gentler... well, that's when kingdoms fall."

Eldric's jaw tightened. "Varen was a usurper and a murderer."

"Was he? Or was he simply a man who understood that some alliances are too dangerous to forge?" Rowan's eyes glittered in the torchlight.

"Tell me, Captain—when you look at our queen now, do you see the same woman who once showed mercy to captured enemies? Or do you see something else entirely?"

The question hung in the air like smoke from a funeral pyre, and despite himself, Eldric found no ready answer.

"She's changing," Rowan pressed, moving closer to Eldric with predatory grace. "Surely you've noticed. The way she moves, the coldness in her eyes, her newfound... appetites. She's becoming like him."

Eldric's hand tightened on his sword hilt. "Mind your words, Lord Blackthorn. I've sworn an oath."

"To protect Morvain," Rowan finished smoothly. "As have I. But ask yourself this—is Helena still Morvain's protector, or has she become something else? Something that threatens the very kingdom she claims to save?"

Eldric's weathered face betrayed nothing as Rowan circled him like a wolf testing its prey.

"There are those who would support you," Rowan murmured. "Lords and ladies of ancient houses who remember what Morvain was before it welcomed darkness into its heart. The church, the merchant guilds, even common folk who tremble at the thought of a blood-drinker's puppet on the throne."

"A coup," Eldric stated flatly. "That's what you're proposing."

Rowan's smile was thin as a knife's edge. "A restoration. Helena would be... contained. For her own safety, of course. Until proper rituals could cleanse whatever taint now flows in her veins." His voice dropped further. "You've seen enough, Captain. You know what must be done."

Eldric laughed—a harsh, bitter sound that echoed off the stone walls. "You're a fool, Blackthorn."

"Am I?" Rowan's eyes narrowed. "Or are you the fool, serving a queen who may no longer be human?"

"Whether she's human or not doesn't matter," Eldric replied, stepping away from the wall to face Rowan directly. "What matters is what would happen if I followed your suicidal plan."

"Enlighten me."

"You want me to move against Helena? To imprison or depose her?" Eldric shook his head, his scarred face grim in the torchlight. "Even if I believed it necessary — which I don't — there's one factor you've conveniently ignored in your calculations."

"Thornwood," Rowan supplied, his voice hardening.

"Precisely." Eldric's eyes took on a haunted quality. "I was on those walls, my lord. I saw what he did to an army of a thousand men. I watched him tear the very blood from their bodies with a gesture. And that was when they merely threatened Helena's crown."

She stepped closer to Rowan, close enough to see the nobleman's pupils contract with unease. "What do you imagine he would do if he returned to find his queen dead or imprisoned? Do you think these ancient walls would stand? Do you think anyone within them would survive his wrath?"

"We could prepare—"

"Prepare?" Eldric barked a laugh. "Against a creature who's lived for centuries? Who commands powers we barely comprehend? He would level this entire castle to reach her. He would slaughter every man, woman, and child between himself and Helena, and he would do it without hesitation or mercy."

Rowan's confidence faltered visibly. "You sound almost admiring, Captain."

"I respect power," Eldric replied evenly. "And I respect the bond between them, whatever its nature. It's not something to be trifled with by ambitious nobles playing at politics."

"So you'll do nothing?" Rowan's lip curled in disgust. "Watch as our kingdom falls under shadow?"

"I'll do my duty," Eldric corrected him. "I'll protect Morvain and its queen. And right now, the greatest threat to both isn't Thornwood—it's men like you who'd risk everything on schemes born of fear and ambition."

She stepped back, hand still resting on her sword. "This conversation never happened, Lord Blackthorn. For your sake and the sake of your house. But should I hear even a whisper of such talk again..." She left the threat unspoken but clear.

Rowan's face hardened into a mask of cold fury. "You've made your choice, Captain. I hope you don't live to regret it."

"And I hope you live at all," Eldric replied quietly. "Because if Thornwood catches wind of your plotting, I wouldn't wager a copper mark on your chances."

He turned to leave, then paused, looking back over his shoulder. "One more thing, my lord. If you think the queen is changing, becoming more like Thornwood... perhaps you should consider why. When faced with enemies on all sides — enemies like you — who wouldn't seek power by any means necessary?"

Without waiting for a response, Eldric strode down the corridor, her armor gleaming in the torchlight. Behind her, Rowan Blackthorn remained motionless, his pale eyes calculating and cold.

The morning air carried the metallic tang of blood as Eldric made her way toward the outer courtyard. Ravenscrest's wounded heart continued to beat — servants hurried about their duties with downcast eyes, guards stood at rigid attention as he passed, and workers cleared debris from last night's attack with grim efficiency.

"Captain!" Sir Gareth called, waving from where a cluster of knights had gathered near the armory. Their faces were haggard, eyes sunken from lack of sleep, but they straightened as Eldric approached.

"Report," Eldric commanded, scanning their ranks. Five knights where there should have been eight.

"The eastern and northern gates are secure," Sir Gareth began, his voice hoarse. "We've doubled the watch as ordered. Three men lost in the night attack—Sir Willem, Sir Donal, and Sir Ferris."

"Good men," Eldric murmured, bowing her head briefly. "And the southern approach?"

"Quiet, sir," replied Sir Kendrick, the youngest of the knights. Fresh blood stained his bandaged forearm. "Almost too quiet. The forest has gone still—no birds, no movement since dawn."

Eldric nodded, absorbing this information with growing unease. "And our supplies?"

"Sufficient for a fortnight's siege," Sir Gareth answered. "Though I doubt we'll face conventional forces again after yesterday's... demonstration."

The knights exchanged troubled glances, several making subtle warding gestures at the reference to Alaric's slaughter.

"Walk with me," Eldric ordered, gesturing toward the western battlement. The knights fell into step behind him as they climbed the narrow stone stairs to the wall.

From this vantage point, Ravenscrest's true situation became clear. The field beyond the castle walls remained a charnel house — hundreds of bodies in various states of dismemberment stretched toward the tree line where Varen's army had emerged. Carrion birds circled overhead, their harsh cries the only sound breaking the eerie silence.

"The Queen has ordered the bodies burned," Eldric informed them, his gaze sweeping the horizon. "No burial rites, no markers. Salt the ashes and scatter them."

"But sir," Sir Kendrick protested, "some of those men were Morvain's sons. Misguided perhaps, but—"

"Traitors," Eldric cut him off sharply. "And potential vessels for whatever dark magic Varen might attempt." He pointed toward the distant forest edge. "Post archers at twenty-pace intervals along this wall. Anyone approaching from the tree line is to be shot on sight—no challenges, no exceptions."

"Even refugees?" Sir Gareth asked quietly.

"There are no refugees," Eldric replied, her voice hardening. "Only enemies and potential enemies. Those loyal to the crown were instructed to seek shelter within our walls days ago."

The knights absorbed this with grim expressions, but none dared voice further objections. Eldric continued her inspection, walking the full length of the western wall. Her eyes constantly scanned the distant tree line, searching for any sign of movement, any hint of the forces that might still gather against them.

"What of Lord Thornwood?" Sir Kendrick finally asked, the question that had clearly been on all their minds. "Has there been any word?"

"None," Eldric replied curtly. "But he will return."

"And if he doesn't?" Sir Gareth pressed. "If Varen proved too strong?"

Eldric stopped abruptly, turning to face his knights directly. "Then may the gods have mercy on us all," he said quietly. "Because the Queen will not."

The brutal honesty of this assessment silenced them. They

continued their patrol in wordless tension, each man lost in his own thoughts of what might await Morvain should Alaric fail.

At the northernmost tower, Eldric dismissed the knights to their duties, remaining alone on the battlement. The wind carried the scent of woodsmoke from the village below, where life continued despite the shadow hanging over the kingdom.

She gazed out toward the Mistwood, where Alaric had ventured to find Varen and end his centuries-long reign of terror. The forest's ancient canopy revealed nothing, its secrets held tight beneath interlaced branches and morning mist.

"Return to us, monster," Eldric murmured, his words carried away by the wind. "For all our sakes."

Movement at the base of the wall caught his attention—a small procession emerging from the castle's main entrance. Even from this distance, the copper gleam of Helena's hair was unmistakable as she strode toward the chapel, flanked by guards and followed by several nobles.

Eldric watched her queen with a soldier's assessing eye. Her posture remained regal, her movements precise, but there was something different in her gait—a predatory grace that hadn't been there before. She paused at the chapel door, looking up suddenly as if sensing his gaze. Even across the distance, Eldric felt the weight of her stare, cold and knowing.

She raised one hand in acknowledgment—or was it warning?—before disappearing into the chapel's shadowed interior.

Eldric turned away, resuming her vigilant watch of the horizon. The sun climbed higher, casting his shadow long against the stone battlements. No army gathered in the distance, no forces massed against their walls, yet the sense of impending doom hung heavy in the air.

A flash of movement in the courtyard below caught Eldric's eye — a dozen guards moving with synchronized precision toward the chapel where Helena had just entered. Something about their formation struck her as wrong — too coordinated, too purposeful.

"The Queen!" Eldric shouted, already running for the stone stairs. She took them three at a time, sword drawn before he reached the bottom.

The courtyard erupted into chaos as he sprinted toward the chapel. Six royal guards lay dead at the entrance, their throats cut with surgical precision. Before Eldric could cross half the distance, four men in castle uniforms intercepted him.

"Stand down, Captain," one ordered, his accent betraying northern origins.

"Traitors!" Eldric roared, blade already swinging.

She cut down the first man with a diagonal slash across the chest, pivoted to impale the second, but never completed the motion. Three more guards appeared from behind, tackling her with crushing force. Her sword clattered across the cobblestones as they drove him face-first into the ground.

"Hold her!" a familiar voice commanded.

Through the tangle of limbs pinning him down, Eldric saw Rowan Blackthorn stride into the courtyard, no longer bothering to hide his triumphant smile. Behind him marched two dozen more men—not castle guards, but mercenaries in hastily donned Morvain uniforms.

"You snake," Eldric spat, blood filling her mouth as a boot pressed his head against the stones. "You'll die screaming for this."

Rowan approached, crouching beside the immobilized captain. "Oh, I think not." He gestured toward the chapel, where Helena was being dragged out between four burly soldiers. "You see, I'm merely restoring order to a kingdom that has fallen under unholy influence."

The queen fought like a wildcat, her copper hair streaming behind her as she kicked and clawed at her captors. "Unhand me!" she commanded, her voice carrying the full weight of royal authority. "I am your queen!"

"No longer," Rowan called back, rising to his full height. To the courtyard at large, he announced: "Queen Helena has been corrupted by dark powers! She has consorted with demons and brought their taint into the very heart of Morvain!"

From the chapel doors emerged the bodies of Helena's loyal guards, throats slit and still dripping crimson onto the chapel steps. The soldiers who had killed them stood at attention, awaiting Rowan's next command.

"Take the witch and her captain to the dungeons," Rowan ordered, his voice carrying across the now-silent courtyard. "Raise the portcullis and lower the drawbridge. Our true lord returns to reclaim his rightful place."

"You fool," Helena snarled as they dragged her past Rowan. "Do you have any idea what you've done? What he'll do to you when he returns?"

Rowan's smile never wavered. "Lord Thornwood won't be returning, Your Majesty. Our forces intercepted him in the Mistwood. Even monsters can be overwhelmed by sufficient numbers."

Something flashed in Helena's eyes — grief or rage or perhaps both intermingled. "You're lying," she hissed. "Alaric cannot be killed by ordinary men."

"Perhaps not," Rowan conceded. "But he can be contained. Iron spikes through the heart and limbs, silver chains, a lead-lined coffin... He'll spend eternity buried beneath the weight of the mountain, conscious but immobile. A fitting end for a creature of his depravity."

Eldric struggled against her captors, managing to raise her head enough to lock eyes with Helena. "My Queen," he gasped, "I failed you —"

A boot to her ribs silenced her, driving precious air from her lungs. Through watering eyes, she watched as the great gates of Ravenscrest swung open. A lone figure approached on horseback, tall and regal in ornate armor that gleamed like obsidian in the midday sun.

Lord Varen had returned.

The usurper dismounted with fluid grace, his pale features unmarked by age or strain despite the weeks of warfare. He surveyed the courtyard with cold eyes that lingered on Helena's struggling form with something like satisfaction.

"Niece," he greeted her, his voice carrying an unnatural resonance that sent shivers down Eldric's spine. "How kind of you to prepare such a welcome."

"Uncle," Helena spat the word like poison. "Or should I call you by your true name? The one you bore when you murdered your first king centuries ago?"

Varen's smile never reached his eyes. "You know so little, child, despite your vampire pet's tutelage." He approached her, reaching out to grasp her chin with gloved fingers. "But you will learn. Oh yes, you will learn many things in the years to come."

He turned to Rowan, who had dropped to one knee in deference. "You've done well, Lord Blackthorn. Morvain owes you a debt that will be repaid generously."

"Thank you, my lord," Rowan replied, rising. "The castle is yours. The witch-queen's supporters have been identified and will be dealt with accordingly."

"And Thornwood?" Varen asked, his tone casual though his eyes sharpened with interest.

"Contained, as you instructed," Rowan assured him. "The iron maiden was... most effective."

Varen nodded, satisfaction evident in his posture. "Good. I've waited centuries to repay his interference. Let him contemplate eternity from within his metal prison." He gestured toward Helena and Eldric. "Take them below. I'll deal with them personally once I've addressed the court."

As guards dragged them toward the dungeon entrance, Helena locked eyes with Eldric one final time. Despite their dire circumstances, something burned in her gaze—not defeat, but deadly promise.

"Hold fast, Captain," she murmured, her words meant for him alone. "This isn't over."

The dungeon air hit them like a physical blow—damp, cold, and heavy with the stench of despair. Guards threw them into separate cells, iron doors clanging shut with finality. Through the small barred window in her door, Eldric could just make out Helena in the cell across the narrow corridor.

"My Queen," she called softly, once the guards' footsteps had receded up the stone stairs. "Are you injured?"

Helena moved to her door, her face appearing in the small opening. Despite the dirt smudging her cheeks and the blood matting her copper hair, she maintained a regal bearing.

"Nothing serious," she replied, her voice steady. "But Varen will not keep us alive for long. We must escape before nightfall."

"How?" Eldric asked, rattling the solid iron door. "These cells were built to hold the kingdom's most dangerous criminals."

A strange smile curved Helena's lips—a predator's smile that reminded Eldric uncomfortably of Alaric. "They were built to hold humans, Captain." She extended one hand through the bars, and Eldric gasped.

Her nails had lengthened into curved talons, sharp as daggers and gleaming in the dim torchlight.

"What has he done to you?" Eldric whispered, horror and awe mingling in his voice.

"Not done, Captain. Given." Helena flexed her transformed hand, watching the play of shadow across her new appendages. "Alaric's blood flows in my veins now. Not enough to make me like him—not yet—but enough to give me certain... advantages."

Above them, the sounds of Varen addressing the assembled court filtered down through the stone ceiling—promises of restoration, of purging dark influences, of returning Morvain to its former glory. The nobles who had so recently pledged loyalty to Helena now cheered for her usurper, their survival instincts overriding any sense of honor.

"Can you break the lock?" Eldric asked, eyeing her taloned hand with newfound hope.

Helena shook her head. "Not yet. The change is still progressing. By nightfall, perhaps..." She paused, head tilting as if listening to something beyond human hearing. "They're coming."

Heavy footsteps descended the dungeon stairs—multiple men, armor clanking with each step. Eldric pressed against his door, straining to see who approached.

Rowan Blackthorn appeared first, followed by four guards and a fifth figure in hooded robes. They stopped before Helena's cell, Rowan producing a heavy iron key from his belt.

"It seems Lord Varen has special plans for you, Your Former Majesty," Rowan announced, malicious pleasure evident in his tone. "The court has officially recognized him as Morvain's rightful ruler, and your first duty to the new regime begins now."

The cell door swung open with a tortured shriek of hinges. Two guards entered, seizing Helena by the arms. She didn't struggle, her face a mask of cold dignity as they dragged her into the corridor.

"What are you doing?" Eldric demanded, rattling her door. "Where are you taking her?"

Rowan approached Eldric's cell, satisfaction gleaming in his pale eyes.

"Lord Varen requires a vessel for the completion of his immortality ritual," he explained, as if discussing the weather. "Royal blood has... unique properties. Especially blood that has been mingled with that of an ancient vampire."

Horror dawned on Eldric's face. "You can't—she's your queen!"

"She's an abomination," Rowan corrected coldly. "And her sacrifice will ensure Morvain's prosperity for generations to come."

"A vessel?" Helena's voice remained steady despite the guards' bruising grip on her arms. "You think Varen needs my blood for his ritual?"

Rowan smirked. "Not just your blood, my lady. Your essence. Your very life force."

CHAPTER 19 –

THE MONSTERS WE FIGHT

"You're a fool, Blackthorn," Eldric spat through the bars. "Whatever Varen has promised you—"

"Silence her," Rowan ordered sharply.

A guard struck Eldric's cell door with the pommel of his sword, the clang echoing through the dungeon. Rowan gestured, and the hooded figure stepped forward, pulling back their cowl to reveal a face so ordinary it seemed almost deliberately forgettable.

"Lord Varen's personal physician," Rowan explained. "He'll ensure the ritual proceeds... correctly."

The physician said nothing, merely producing a small wooden box from within his robes. He opened it to reveal gleaming surgical tools nestled in velvet.

"Wait," Rowan said suddenly, his eyes narrowing as he studied Helena. "I think our former queen deserves a more... intimate send-off." He turned to the guards. "Bring her too."

Eldric's cell door swung open, and rough hands seized her, forcing iron manacles around her wrists. The guards dragged both prisoners up the narrow stairs, through darkened corridors, and into a chamber Eldric recognized with growing dread — the ritual room beneath the castle's east tower, where ancient kings had conducted blood magic in darker times.

Iron rings jutted from the stone walls at regular intervals. The guards forced Helena against the rough surface, securing her wrists to the highest rings so that she stood spread-eagled, her feet barely touching the floor.

"Chain her there," Rowan ordered, pointing to a spot directly across from Helena. "I want her to see everything."

Eldric fought as they secured her chains to a heavy iron hook embedded in the opposite wall, but the manacles held fast. The guards stepped back, awaiting further orders.

"Leave us," Rowan commanded, his voice dropping to a dangerous purr. "All of you."

The physician hesitated. "Lord Varen instructed me to oversee—"

"And I instruct you to wait outside," Rowan cut him off, his hand moving to his dagger. "The ritual will proceed shortly. First, I have... personal matters to address with our prisoners."

The guards exchanged uncertain glances but obeyed, filing out of the chamber with the reluctant physician following behind. The heavy oak door closed with a dull thud, leaving the three alone in the torchlit room.

"Now," Rowan said, turning to face his captives with undisguised hunger in his eyes, "we can dispense with pretense."

He approached Eldric slowly, drawing a gloved finger down the captain's scarred cheek. "Such loyalty," he murmured. "Such devotion to your queen. I've always wondered what inspired such... passion in you, Captain."

"Touch me and die," Eldric growled, straining against her chains.

Rowan laughed softly. "Oh, I intend to do much more than touch." His hands moved to Eldric's belt, unfastening it with deliberate slowness. "I've watched you for years, you know. Always so righteous, so proper. The noble captain who would never betray her honor."

Helena's voice cut through the chamber like a whip. "He's stalling, Eldric. Trying to break us before Varen arrives." Her eyes burned with cold fury. "Don't give him the satisfaction."

"Clever girl," Rowan acknowledged, turning toward her without removing his hand from Eldric's belt. "But only partly right. Yes, I'm stalling—Varen's ritual requires the midnight hour. But my intentions are entirely sincere."

With unexpected violence, he tore at Eldric's clothing, ripping fabric with savage efficiency. The captain fought against her restraints, metal cutting into her wrists as Rowan stripped her bare from the waist down.

"Stop this!" Helena commanded, her voice carrying the full weight of royal authority despite her captive state.

Rowan ignored her, pressing himself against Eldric's exposed body. "I've imagined this moment," he whispered, his breath hot against the captain's ear. "The great Eldric Mercer, helpless beneath my hands."

"I'll kill you for this," Eldric promised, her voice deadly calm despite the violation. "Slowly."

"Bold words from a bitch in chains," Rowan taunted, unfastening his own breeches. "But I admire your spirit. It makes breaking you all the sweeter."

Helena thrashed against her bonds, the metal cutting into her wrists. "Rowan! This accomplishes nothing!"

"On the contrary," Rowan replied, positioning himself behind the struggling captain. "It accomplishes everything I've desired since I first laid eyes on this man."

With brutal force, he thrust forward, drawing a strangled cry from Eldric that echoed off the stone walls. Helena's face contorted with helpless rage as she watched her loyal captain violated before her eyes.

"Look at her," Rowan commanded, seizing Eldric's hair and forcing her head up. "Look at your precious queen while I take what I want from you."

Eldric's eyes met Helena's across the chamber—pain and humiliation warring with unbroken defiance in his gaze. "My Queen," she managed, voice strained. "Forgive me."

"There is nothing to forgive," Helena replied fiercely. "And much to avenge."

Rowan's rhythm grew more violent, his breathing ragged as he used Eldric's body for his pleasure. "Such touching devotion," he mocked between thrusts. "Perhaps I should take her next, before Varen claims her for his ritual. Would you like to watch that, Captain?"

Eldric's only response was a low growl, her jaw clenched against further sounds of pain.

"No?" Rowan continued, his voice thick with cruel enjoyment. "Then perhaps I'll simply end her now. Varen needs her blood, after all—not necessarily her head attached to her body."

Helena's expression never wavered, her eyes locked with Eldric's in silent communication. Something passed between them—a promise, a plan, a final desperate hope.

Rowan reached his climax with a guttural groan, then withdrew roughly, leaving Eldric sagging against her chains. He fastened his breeches with unhurried movements, then crossed to where his sword leaned against the wall.

"That was... invigorating," he commented, lifting the blade and testing its edge with his thumb. "But now to business. Lord Varen will be displeased if I damage the merchandise too severely, but he said nothing about keeping you intact, Captain."

Helena's lips curved in a cold, calm smile. "We will never be forgotten."

Rowan frowned. "We shall see." He settled the sword's tip at the base of Eldric's throat. "Farewell, Captain."

As the blade pressed forward, Helena screamed — her note of defiance cut short by the final, irreversible decision. The sword fell.

Silence reclaimed the chamber except for the drip of blood on stone. Helena's eyes widened in horror, and she strained against the iron rings, but the bonds held firm.

The heavy oak door opened once more as the physician entered, face impassive. She knelt to extract a vial from Eldric's robes.

"Lord Varen will be pleased," the physician announced.

Helena closed her eyes, a single tear tracing down her cheek. She drew in a steady breath, prepared to face whatever came next—for the memory of a fallen captain who had refused to break would be her guiding light.

The physician wrapped Eldric's head in a cloth, the once-proud features now slack in death, eyes frozen in their final defiance. Blood continued to pool beneath the captain's headless body, spreading across the ancient stone in a crimson tide.

Rowan waved the physician away, snatching the grisly trophy from her hands. "I'll take that," he said, his voice thick with satisfaction. The physician bowed and retreated, closing the heavy oak door behind her.

Alone with Helena once more, Rowan unwrapped the cloth, holding Eldric's severed head by the hair. He approached the chained queen, a cruel smile playing at his lips.

"A gift for you, Your Majesty," he taunted, then hurled the head at Helena's feet. It landed with a sickening thud, rolling slightly before coming to rest facing her, Eldric's empty eyes staring up at the woman she had served so loyally. "Something to contemplate while we prepare for Lord Varen's arrival. Consider your captain's fate a mere appetizer for what awaits you."

Helena stared at Eldric's head, her face unreadable, body rigid against the chains that held her. Then, to Rowan's visible confusion, her shoulders began to shake.

The sound started low—a trembling in her throat that built steadily until it erupted into full, wild laughter that echoed from the stone walls. It was not the laughter of madness or despair, but something darker, more dangerous—a sound that sent an involuntary chill down Rowan's spine despite his victory.

"Have you lost your mind?" he demanded, crossing the chamber in three quick strides. His hand cracked across her face, splitting her lip and leaving a livid mark on her pale cheek. "What could possibly amuse you now, witch?"

Helena's laughter subsided, though her smile remained, blood trickling from the corner of her mouth. "I was just thinking about Alaric's reaction when he sees what you've done here," she replied, her voice eerily calm. "He's quite possessive of what belongs to him, you know. And we both belong to him—Eldric and I."

Rowan's face contorted with fresh rage. He seized her jaw, fingers digging cruelly into her flesh. "Alaric Thornwood is dead," he spat, eyes gleaming with malicious triumph.

"Word reached us this morning. Your vampire lover was ambushed in the Mistwood—iron spikes through his heart, silver chains binding him, his body sealed in a lead coffin and buried beneath a mountain of stone."

For the first time, Helena's composure wavered. Something flickered in her eyes—a momentary flash of uncertainty or grief—before her expression settled once more into that unnerving calm.

"Then you have nothing to fear," she whispered, her words carrying a finality that made Rowan's hand fall away from her face. "Nothing at all."

The torches flickered as if caught in a sudden draft, shadows lengthening across the stone floor. Somewhere far above, the great bell began to toll, signaling midnight—and the beginning of Varen's ritual.

"It's time," Rowan said, straightening his tunic and retrieving his bloodied sword. He cast a final glance at Eldric's severed head, then at Helena's bound form. "Lord Varen awaits his vessel. A pity you won't live to see Morvain's glorious new age."

He turned toward the door, then paused, looking back over his shoulder. "Oh, and Your Majesty? I'll be sure to tell the people how bravely you died — screaming for mercy that never came."

The heavy door closed behind him with the finality of a tomb being sealed. Helena was left alone in the flickering torchlight, Eldric's unseeing eyes fixed upon her face, blood pooling at her feet.

In the silence that followed, Helena closed her eyes, her lips moving in what might have been prayer — or something far older, far darker.

The last torch guttered and died, plunging the chamber into absolute darkness.

CHAPTER 20 –
GONE HUNTING

The evening mist hung heavy over Ashfeld as Alaric rode through its empty streets. His mount's hooves clacked against the cobblestones with unnatural loudness in the deserted town. No smoke rose from chimneys, no light glimmered from windows, no dogs barked in warning at his approach. The village square, normally bustling with traders and townsfolk even at this hour, stood abandoned.

"Strange," Alaric muttered, reining his horse to a stop before the town well. He dismounted, hand resting on his sword hilt as he surveyed the eerie silence. Not even birds called from the eaves of the thatched roofs.

The trail had led him here — unmistakable tracks of a single rider pushing his mount to exhaustion, heading directly for this settlement. Captain Thorne had fled the castle three days prior, escaping the dungeons during the changing of the guard. Helena had been furious, her eyes flashing with that dangerous light that reminded Alaric why he had been drawn to her in the first place.

"Find him," she had commanded, standing before the map table in her war room. "Before he reaches Varen with what he knows."

Now Alaric stood in a ghost town, the scent of recent abandonment hanging in the air alongside something else—fear, sharp and acrid.

He moved methodically through the village, checking houses one by one. Meals sat half-eaten on tables, doors stood ajar, a child's doll lay discarded in the middle of a street. Whatever had happened here had occurred quickly, with little warning.

The inn stood at the far end of the main street, its weathered sign—The Crow's Nest—creaking in the evening breeze. Unlike the other buildings, its doors were firmly shut, windows latched from within.

Alaric approached cautiously, his preternatural senses alert for any sign of danger. A faint heartbeat reached his ears—rapid, frightened, but unmistakably human. Just one, where there should have been dozens.

"Come out, Thorne," Alaric called, his voice carrying through the still air. "We both know you're in there."

Silence answered him.

Alaric sighed, a sound more of annoyance than exertion. "I can hear your heart beating. I can smell your fear. This ends tonight, one way or another."

The inn's door creaked open a fraction, and a haggard face appeared in the gap. Captain Thorne looked nothing like the proud officer who had once commanded the King's Guard. His face was gaunt, bruises mottling his jaw and left eye, his uniform torn and stained with blood both old and new.

"They're all dead," Thorne whispered, his voice cracking. "Everyone. The whole village."

Alaric's eyes narrowed. "Open the door, Captain."

"You don't understand," Thorne insisted, panic rising in his voice. "It wasn't human. What took them—it wasn't human!"

"Neither am I," Alaric reminded him coldly. "Open the door, or I'll remove it."

Thorne hesitated, then stepped back, allowing the door to swing open. Alaric entered, senses immediately assaulted by the metallic tang of blood and the sour stench of fear. The common room was empty save for Thorne, who retreated to the far wall, hands trembling at his sides.

"Where are they?" Alaric demanded, glancing around the deserted inn. "The villagers."

"Gone," Thorne whispered, sinking onto a bench. "Taken. I hid in the cellar when it came. I heard—" His voice broke. "Gods, the screaming."

Alaric moved closer, studying the broken man before him. "When what came, Thorne?"

"I don't know," the captain admitted, burying his face in shaking hands. "Something with too many limbs. Something that spoke without a mouth. It called them by name, Thornwood. It knew them all."

Alaric's expression hardened. "Varen's work."

"No!" Thorne's head snapped up, eyes wild with fear. "Not Varen. Something older. Something he fears."

The vampire circled the room, examining overturned chairs and abandoned drinks. "Tell me why you fled the castle, Captain. What was so important that you betrayed your oath to the crown?"

Thorne laughed — a hollow, broken sound. "My oath? To what crown? The old king is dead. His daughter consorts with the undead.

Varen offers stability, a return to tradition."

"Varen offers death," Alaric corrected sharply. "He's not what you think he is."

"And what are you?" Thorne challenged, a flicker of his former courage returning. "What dark bargain have you struck with the princess? What price will Morvain pay for your protection?"

Alaric moved with inhuman speed, suddenly looming over the seated captain. "Helena is queen now, whether you acknowledge it or not. And my arrangement with her is none of your concern."

Thorne flinched but held his ground. "I saw the texts in the forbidden archives, Thornwood. I know what you are. What she's becoming because of you."

"You know nothing," Alaric growled, his eyes flashing crimson in the dimness.

"I know enough," Thorne insisted. "The blood bond. The transformation. You're turning her into something like yourself—neither living nor dead."

Alaric's hand shot out, gripping Thorne's throat with enough pressure to silence but not kill. "Careful, Captain. You tread on dangerous ground."

Thorne gasped as Alaric released him, rubbing his throat. "Kill me if you must," he wheezed. "But it won't change what's coming. Varen knows about the bond. He knows how to use it against you both."

A flicker of concern crossed Alaric's face before his expression settled back into its habitual mask. "What does Varen know?"

"That you can be controlled through her," Thorne replied, watching Alaric carefully. "That your power, your very will, is bound to hers now. Hurt her, and you're crippled. Kill her..." He trailed off meaningfully.

"And I die with her," Alaric finished, his voice dangerously soft. "Is that what he believes?"

Thorne nodded slowly. "It's why I fled. Not to betray Helena, but to warn her. Varen doesn't want her dead—he wants her captured. He has rituals planned, old magic that will use your bond against you both."

Alaric studied the captain's face, searching for deception. "You expect me to believe you fled to protect her? After you were caught passing information to Varen's spies for months?"

"I was a fool," Thorne admitted, shoulders slumping. "I believed his lies about restoring Morvain to glory. But when I learned what he truly is, what he plans for Helena..." He looked up, meeting Alaric's gaze directly. "I may be a traitor, but I'm not a monster."

Before Alaric could respond, a sound from outside froze them both—the soft, deliberate footfalls of something large moving through the village square. Thorne's eyes widened in terror.

"It's back," he whispered, panic evident in every line of his body. "Gods help us, it's back."

Alaric moved to the window, peering through a gap in the shutters. The mist had thickened, obscuring most of the square, but something massive shifted within it—a darker shadow among shadows, moving with unnatural grace despite its size.

"What is it?" Alaric murmured, more to himself than to Thorne.

"Death," Thorne replied simply, drawing a dagger from his boot—a futile gesture of defiance against the approaching horror.

Alaric turned back to the captain, decision made. "We leave. Now. Through the back."

"It will find us," Thorne protested. "It found everyone else."

"It hasn't met me yet," Alaric replied grimly, drawing his obsidian blade. The sword seemed to drink in what little light remained in the room, its edge gleaming with hungry anticipation.

They moved silently through the kitchen toward the rear door, Alaric leading the way with Thorne close behind. Outside, the mist swirled in patterns that defied the breeze, forming momentary shapes that vanished when looked at directly.

"My horse is at the front," Alaric whispered. "We'll have to circle around."

"We'll never make it," Thorne hissed back, eyes darting to the unnatural fog.

"Then stay here and die," Alaric suggested coldly. "I have a queen to protect."

That silenced the captain, who nodded grimly and followed as Alaric slipped into the narrow alley beside the inn. They hugged the wall, moving as quietly as possible toward the main street. The fog thickened around them, tendrils reaching like searching fingers along the ground.

A low, sonorous hum began to fill the air—not quite a voice, yet somehow conveying meaning. It spoke of hunger, of patience, of centuries spent waiting for this exact moment.

"It knows we're here," Thorne whispered, pressing himself against the rough stone wall.

"Of course it does," Alaric replied calmly. "It's been hunting me all along."

"You?" Thorne's eyes widened. "What would want to—"

His question died as the mist before them solidified into a towering form—vaguely humanoid but wrong in ways that defied description. Too many joints bent in impossible directions, and where a face should have been, only swirling vapor filled the void.

"Alaric Thornwood," it intoned, its voice bypassing their ears to resonate directly within their minds. "The Betrayer returns at last."

Alaric stepped forward, placing himself between the creature and Thorne. "You have me confused with someone else," he said evenly, though his knuckles whitened around his sword hilt.

"No confusion," the entity replied. "We remember. We have waited. The Pact was broken, and the price must be paid."

"What pact?" Thorne demanded from behind Alaric, his voice cracking with fear.

The creature's form rippled, stretching taller until it loomed over the rooftops. "The ancient bargain. Blood for protection. Life for power." Its attention seemed to fix on Alaric. "You took what was offered but failed to fulfill your end. The village remembers. The land remembers."

Understanding dawned in Alaric's eyes. "Ashfeld," he murmured.

"The massacre during the Northern War. Three hundred years ago."

"Three hundred and twelve years, seven months, fourteen days," the entity corrected with terrible precision. "You swore to protect them. You fed on their offerings. And when the raiders came, you were gone."

"I was delayed," Alaric replied, his voice hardening. "By the time I returned, it was too late."

"Excuses," the creature dismissed. "The debt remains unpaid. Blood calls for blood."

Thorne looked between Alaric and the monstrous form, realization dawning. "You lived here? Three centuries ago?"

"Shut the fuck up, Thorne," Alaric snarled, never taking his eyes off the entity. "Your ignorance only makes this worse."

The captain flinched at the vampire's sudden viciousness, pressing himself further against the wall.

Alaric stepped forward, obsidian blade gleaming in the mist-diffused moonlight. "You speak of debts unpaid? Of protection promised?" His voice carried a weight of centuries, of rage long-simmering. "Then know this—I have hunted the one responsible for Ashfeld's slaughter since that blood-soaked dawn. The butcher who intercepted me on the northern road, who ensured I'd arrive too late to save those under my protection."

The entity's formless face swirled faster, something like interest rippling through its massive frame.

"Three centuries I've tracked him," Alaric continued, "through a dozen identities, a score of kingdoms. And now he wears Varen's skin, sitting like a parasite within royal flesh, reaching for Helena's throne."

"Lies," the entity rumbled, though uncertainty tinged its otherworldly voice. "Deception to escape your judgment."

"Search my memories if you doubt me," Alaric challenged, sheathing his sword and spreading his arms wide. "See the truth for yourself. I have never stopped hunting your killer."

The mist surged forward, enveloping Alaric in its cold embrace. Thorne cried out in alarm as the vampire disappeared within the writhing fog, but Alaric made no sound. For long moments, nothing moved except the swirling tendrils that had consumed him.

When the mist finally retreated, Alaric remained standing, though his face had gone deathly pale, veins standing out black against his skin.

"You speak truth," the entity acknowledged, its tone shifting to something ancient and terrible. "The Devourer lives. He wears the noble's flesh."

"Varen," Thorne whispered, comprehension dawning on his battered face. "That's why he wants Helena — not for the throne, but for..."

"For the completion of a ritual centuries in the making," Alaric finished, his strength visibly returning as the mist continued to withdraw. "He needs royal blood with vampire essence — my essence — to achieve perfect immortality."

The entity's form contracted, condensing into something more humanoid, though still towering over them both. "The debt remains, Betrayer. But its collection may be... postponed."

"I offer more than postponement," Alaric countered. "I offer partnership. Help me destroy the Devourer, and your people's souls will finally rest."

"And if we refuse?" The entity's voice resonated through the deserted village.

"Then kill me now," Alaric replied simply. "And watch as Varen completes his ritual, becoming powerful enough to consume even your kind."

Silence fell over the mist-shrouded square as the entity considered. Finally, it extended a vaporous appendage toward Alaric.

"We accept. The hunt will be shared."

Alaric nodded, then turned to Thorne, who stared at the exchange with undisguised horror.

"It seems your warning came too late, Captain," he said coldly. "But not without value."

"What... what is happening?" Thorne managed, his gaze darting between vampire and entity.

"An alliance," Alaric replied, retrieving his sword from its sheath. "One that may yet save your queen—if we move quickly."

"I don't understand," Thorne protested. "This thing slaughtered an entire village!"

"No," the entity corrected, its voice vibrating through their skulls. "We are the village. Three hundred souls bound by shared suffering, by the promise broken, by the blood spilled." Its formless head tilted, studying Thorne with empty malevolence. "This one betrayed his queen. His life would make a suitable offering."

Alaric stepped forward, interposing himself between the entity and the terrified captain. "No. He remains useful for now."

The mist entity writhed in apparent displeasure, tendrils coiling and uncoiling like agitated snakes. "His treachery taints the air around him. His life would feed our hunger."

"His knowledge may save Helena," Alaric countered firmly. "And that is worth more than the momentary satisfaction of his death."

For several heartbeats, the entity remained motionless, its formless mass hovering with unnatural stillness. Then it seemed to sigh—a sound like wind through an abandoned crypt.

"Very well, Betrayer. We shall wait beyond the castle walls while you retrieve your queen. Her blood carries your essence now—we can taste it on the night air." The mist began to thin, its voice growing fainter. "But know this: should you fail to return, should you break faith with us again, no realm of existence will hide you from our vengeance."

As suddenly as it had appeared, the entity dissipated, wisps of fog retreating into the shadows between buildings until only the natural evening mist remained. The oppressive weight of its presence lifted, leaving the village square eerily silent once more.

Thorne slumped against the inn's outer wall, sliding down until he sat on the cold cobblestones. His breath came in ragged gasps, face slick with cold sweat. "What in all the hells was that thing?"

Alaric didn't answer immediately. He staggered to the opposite wall and sank down, his normally graceful movements now heavy and labored. Sweat beaded on his forehead despite the chill night air, and the veins beneath his pale skin had darkened to an unhealthy gray.

"Shit," he muttered, head falling back against the rough stone. The battle at Ravenscrest's eastern gate had cost him dearly—transforming fully, commanding the forest creatures, maintaining his wings for hours. He'd expended far too much energy, and the encounter with the mist entity had drained what little remained.

It would be hours, perhaps days, before he could transform again. Hours that Helena might not have.

"You look terrible," Thorne observed, some of his old boldness returning now that the immediate threat had passed.

Alaric shot him a withering glance. "Your concern is touching."

"Not concern. Observation." Thorne shifted, wincing at his own injuries. "You're weakened. Vulnerable."

"Strong enough to end you," Alaric warned, though they both knew it wasn't entirely true—not in his current state.

Thorne studied him with the calculating gaze of a military man assessing an opponent. "You can't transform again, can you? That's why you didn't just fly us both out of here."

Alaric's silence was confirmation enough.

"How long?" Thorne pressed.

"Too long," Alaric admitted reluctantly. "And every moment we waste here puts Helena in greater danger."

Thorne nodded slowly, an unexpected resolve hardening his features. "Then we ride. My horse died two villages back, but yours looked strong enough to carry double."

Alaric raised an eyebrow. "We?"

"You need me," Thorne stated simply. "I know which nobles have aligned with Varen, which passages remain unguarded, where Helena is likely being held." He met Alaric's suspicious gaze without flinching. "And you're in no condition to storm the castle alone."

"Why the sudden loyalty, Captain?" Alaric's voice dripped with skepticism. "Not long ago, you were Varen's willing spy."

CHAPTER 21 –
IRON MAIDEN

Thorne's jaw tightened. "I was a fool who believed lies about tradition and stability. But I've seen what Varen truly is now — what he does to those who trust him." His hand unconsciously moved to the bruises mottling his face. "And I've seen what awaits Helena if he succeeds."

For a long moment, Alaric studied the broken captain, searching for deception. Finally, he nodded once. "If you betray us again —"

"You'll kill me slowly," Thorne finished wearily. "Yes, I'm well aware."

"No," Alaric corrected, his voice dropping to a deadly whisper. "Death would be mercy. If any harm comes to Helena because of you, I'll ensure you live — for centuries — in agony beyond human comprehension."

The blood drained from Thorne's face at the cold certainty in Alaric's voice. "Understood."

Alaric pushed himself to his feet with visible effort, his movements lacking their usual predatory grace. "We ride within the hour. Find food in the inn if you can — you'll need your strength."

"And you?" Thorne asked, rising more slowly. "What do you need?"

Alaric's lips curved in a humorless smile, revealing the tips of fangs that seemed duller than before. "Something you can't provide, Captain. Not if you wish to reach Ravenscrest alive."

Understanding dawned in Thorne's eyes. "Blood."

"Indeed." Alaric turned toward the inn's entrance. "Now go. Gather supplies while I... recover what strength I can."

As Thorne disappeared into the abandoned building, Alaric gazed toward the distant horizon where Ravenscrest's towers would be visible in daylight. His hand moved unconsciously to his chest, to the hollow ache that had grown there since forming the blood bond with Helena.

He could feel her—faintly, like a candle flame seen through frosted glass. Still alive, but in pain. Afraid.

"Hold fast, my queen," he whispered into the night. "I'm coming."

Behind him, the mist swirled briefly into a vaguely human shape before dissipating once more, a silent reminder of the ancient debt still to be paid.

The night deepened around Ashfeld's empty streets as Alaric contemplated the coming battle. Without his full powers, he would need to rely on cunning rather than strength. On allies rather than raw force.

On a queen whose transformation remained incomplete, caught between humanity and something far darker.

And on a mist entity born of slaughter, bound by vengeance, willing to wait—but not forever.

"Thornwood!" Thorne's voice called from within the inn. "I've found something you should see."

With a final glance toward Ravenscrest's distant silhouette, Alaric turned and walked into the abandoned building, each step measured and deliberate as he conserved what little strength remained.

The inn's common room felt colder now, shadows gathering in corners despite the small fire Thorne had kindled in the hearth. The captain stood before a small table, a collection of items spread across its scarred wooden surface.

"Let's go," Alaric said, gesturing toward the door. "Every moment wasted is another moment Helena remains in danger."

Thorne nodded, shouldering the small pack of supplies he'd gathered. "After you," he said, stepping aside to let Alaric pass.

Alaric moved toward the door, his weakened state making him less attentive than usual. As he stepped through the threshold into the misty night, a flash of movement caught his peripheral vision — too late. Something massive and metallic crashed against his temple with bone-shattering force. The world exploded in white-hot pain as he crumpled to the cobblestones.

"Now!" Thorne bellowed, tossing aside the iron fireplace poker he'd wielded with such devastating effect.

Alaric's hand fumbled for his sword, vision swimming as blood poured down his face. Before his fingers could close around the hilt, armored figures emerged from the shadows, four knights in Varen's colors rushing forward with practiced coordination.

"Grab his arms! His legs!" Thorne shouted, leaping into the fray as the knights descended upon the dazed vampire.

Despite his weakened state, Alaric's survival instincts surged through him. His elbow connected with one knight's throat, crushing his windpipe. A savage kick sent another flying backward, armor clanging as he collapsed in an unconscious heap against the inn's outer wall.

"Damn you!" Thorne cursed, diving onto Alaric's legs as the remaining knights struggled to secure his arms. "He's too strong! The chains! Use the silver chains!"

Alaric bucked and thrashed, his supernatural strength diminished but still formidable. Blood matted his dark hair, running into his eyes as he fought with desperate fury. One of the knights produced silver manacles that glowed with runes similar to those on the dagger.

"You treacherous bastard," Alaric snarled at Thorne, managing to land a punishing blow to the captain's jaw that sent teeth flying. "She'll die because of you!"

"She was already dead," Thorne spat back, blood streaming from his ruined mouth as he and the remaining knights finally secured Alaric's thrashing limbs. "Drag him! Quickly, before the entity returns!"

They hauled Alaric's struggling form around the back of the inn, toward a structure that hadn't been visible from the road. The vampire fought every step, but the silver chains burned where they touched his skin, sapping what little strength remained.

Behind the abandoned stable stood a freshly dug pit, ten feet deep and lined with strange symbols carved into the earth. At its bottom rested a massive iron coffin, its lid open like a waiting maw.

"Varen sends his regards," Thorne gasped, his face a mask of blood and sweat as they reached the edge of the pit. "And thanks you for your service to the queen. Your essence in her blood is the final ingredient he needed."

With a coordinated heave, they pitched Alaric into the darkness. He crashed against the iron coffin with bone-breaking force, momentarily stunned by the impact.

"Close it!" Thorne commanded. One of the knights leapt down, slamming the heavy lid shut before Alaric could recover. The sound of massive locks engaging echoed in the night air.

Alaric's fists pounded against the coffin lid, each impact reverberating through the iron like a funeral bell. "Thorne!" he roared, voice muffled by the thick metal. "I will find you! I will tear your heart from your chest while you still live to see it!"

Above, Thorne's laughter echoed down to him. "Hear that, lads? Our vampire friend thinks he has a future." His voice dropped to a theatrical whisper. "Let's show him otherwise."

The first silver spear pierced the coffin with a shriek of metal, its tip slicing through Alaric's shoulder. His scream of agony filled the confined space as the enchanted silver burned through flesh and muscle like acid. Before he could recover, a second spear punctured the lid, then a third—each finding his flesh with agonizing precision.

"More!" Thorne commanded, his voice thick with savage joy. "Pierce him everywhere! Make sure he can't move!"

The knights worked methodically, driving spear after silver spear through the iron maiden. Inside, Alaric writhed as each new weapon found its mark—thigh, abdomen, chest, arms. Blood pooled beneath him, hot and thick, soaking his clothes and hair. His supernatural healing fought against the silver's corruption, but it was a losing battle. Each wound burned with unholy fire, the metal designed specifically to torture his kind.

"That's it!" Thorne crowed, his boots visible through the small punctures as he danced around the coffin. "The Iron Maiden is complete! A perfect prison for the perfect monster!"

Alaric's struggles weakened as more of his blood leaked from the dozen wounds. His vision blurred, consciousness slipping away despite his desperate attempts to cling to it. Helena's face swam before him—her copper hair, her determined eyes, the way she'd looked at him when he'd first revealed his true nature. Not with fear, but with fascination.

"Helena," he whispered, blood bubbling from his lips. "Forgive me."

Above, the sound of shovels scraping dirt grew louder. "Bury him deep!" Thorne commanded. "Let him rot in darkness for eternity!"

Earth rained down on the coffin, pattering against the metal like distant applause. Alaric felt the weight increasing, pressing down as the pit filled. His fingers, once capable of rending stone, now barely had strength to twitch against the coffin's lining.

Death had never been a possibility before—not in his centuries of existence. Yet now, with silver burning through his veins and his strength ebbing away with each labored heartbeat, Alaric found himself facing true mortality.

"Hades," he murmured, the ancient name feeling strange on his tongue. How long had it been since he'd prayed to any god? "Lord of the Underworld, if you can hear me... I ask passage into your realm."

The weight above increased as more earth filled the pit. The sounds from above grew fainter, more distant. Alaric's body had gone numb, the pain of the silver spears fading as death approached. His eyelids grew heavy, impossibly so.

"I am ready," he whispered to the darkness.

His eyes closed, consciousness slipping away like water through cupped hands. The last of his strength ebbed, and Alaric Thornwood, who had walked the earth for centuries, surrendered to the inevitable.

Time lost meaning in the darkness. Pain receded like a tide pulling back from shore. When awareness returned, it came slowly — a gradual lightening behind his eyelids, a strange warmth where there had been only cold.

CHAPTER 22 –
SO WE MEET

Alaric opened his eyes, expecting nothing but the coffin's metal interior. Instead, he found the spears gone, his wounds healed, and the coffin lid slightly ajar. Warm amber light filtered through the gap, carrying with it the scent of brimstone and ancient stone.

With tentative fingers, he pushed against the lid. It swung open easily, revealing not the earthen pit of his burial, but a vast courtyard paved with obsidian tiles that gleamed like black mirrors. Above, the sky burned crimson without sun or stars, casting everything in bloody light.

Alaric rose from the coffin, his movements fluid and painless. His clothing had changed—his battle-worn armor replaced by flowing robes of midnight blue embroidered with silver constellations. As he stepped onto the obsidian tiles, they rippled like disturbed water beneath his feet.

Before him rose a castle unlike any in the mortal realm. Its towers spiraled impossibly high, disappearing into the crimson sky. Walls of black marble veined with gold stretched in both directions, their surfaces carved with scenes of judgment and damnation. At its center, massive doors of polished bronze stood open in silent invitation.

"The Underworld," Alaric murmured, understanding dawning. His prayer had been answered.

"Not quite what you expected, is it?" a voice asked from behind him.

Alaric turned to find a figure seated on a throne of fused bones that hadn't been there moments before. The man—if man he was—appeared deceptively ordinary: middle-aged, with salt-and-pepper hair and a neatly trimmed beard. Only his eyes betrayed his true nature—bottomless black pools that reflected the suffering of countless souls.

"Hades," Alaric said, recognizing the deity instantly despite never having seen him before.

The god inclined his head slightly. "Alaric Thornwood. Or should I say, Alexandru of Thornwald? You've had so many names over the centuries, it's hard to keep track."

Alaric dropped to one knee, head bowed. "My lord. You heard my prayer."

"I hear all prayers of the dying," Hades replied, rising from his throne. He approached with measured steps, circling Alaric like a collector examining a rare specimen. "Though yours was... unusual. Vampires rarely seek my domain willingly. Your kind typically fears true death above all else."

"I had failed in my duty," Alaric said simply. "I could not protect her."

"Ah yes. The queen." Hades stopped before him, dark eyes studying Alaric's face. "Helena of Morvain. Your latest obsession. Tell me, Alexandru, how many mortal lives have you watched flicker and fade while you remained unchanged? What makes this one worth dying for?"

Alaric met the god's gaze without flinching. "She is different."

"They're all different," Hades countered with a dismissive wave. "Until they're not. Until they age and wither and beg you for what you cannot give them."

"I gave her my blood," Alaric said quietly. "We are bound."

This seemed to genuinely surprise the Lord of the Underworld. His eyebrows rose slightly, and he leaned closer to examine Alaric with renewed interest.

"A blood bond? After all these centuries of solitude?" A slow smile spread across Hades' face, revealing teeth too sharp for a human mouth. "How fascinating. And how inconvenient for you, given your current... situation."

"She will die without my protection," Alaric said, rising to his feet despite the impropriety. "Varen will use her for his ritual and discard her hollow shell."

"And this concerns me how?" Hades asked, returning to his throne with languid grace. "The dead come to me regardless of how they meet their end. Varen's victims are no exception."

"Because Varen seeks to cheat you," Alaric replied, playing his only card. "His ritual of transference — it doesn't just extend life. It bypasses death entirely. Each successful transference removes another soul from your eventual grasp."

Hades went very still, his fingers tightening on the armrests of his bone throne. "Explain."

"The ritual he plans with Helena's blood — my blood in her veins — will grant him true immortality. Not the half-life of a vampire, but eternal existence. His consciousness will transcend the physical, becoming something that can never die, never face judgment." Alaric took a step closer to the throne. "How many souls has he already stolen from your realm through his previous transfers? How many more will he take if he succeeds with Helena?"

The air in the courtyard grew heavy, charged with divine displeasure. The obsidian tiles cracked beneath Hades' throne as his power manifested.

"This... displeases me," the god said, his voice no longer human but a chorus of the damned speaking in unison. "The natural order must be maintained. All souls must eventually come to judgment."

"Then send me back," Alaric urged, pressing his advantage. "Let me stop him. Let me save her."

Hades studied him for what felt like an eternity, those fathomless eyes peering into Alaric's very essence. Finally, he sighed—a sound like wind through a mausoleum.

"You are dead, Alexandru of Thornwald. Your body lies ruined in that iron prison, pierced by silver, your power spent." He rose once more, approaching Alaric with measured steps. "But perhaps... perhaps there is a way."

Hope flared in Alaric's chest. "Name it."

"A bargain," Hades said, circling him again. "I will return you to the mortal realm, restore your body, grant you the strength to save your queen and destroy Varen's abomination of a ritual."

"In exchange for what?" Alaric asked warily, knowing divine bargains always came with steep prices.

Hades smiled—a terrible, beautiful expression. "In exchange for certainty. When Helena's natural life ends—be it in days or decades—you will bring her soul to me personally. No vampire transformation to cheat death. No blood magic to extend her years beyond their allotted span. When her time comes, she dies as a mortal."

The price struck Alaric like a physical blow. To save Helena now, he must surrender any hope of keeping her forever. The very reason he had initiated the blood bond—to gradually transform her, to make her his eternal companion—would be forfeit.

"You ask me to give up eternity with her," he said quietly.

"I ask you to respect the natural order," Hades corrected. "Something you've defied for centuries through your own existence." The god leaned closer, his voice dropping to a whisper. "Consider carefully, vampire. Without my intervention, you remain dead, she becomes Varen's sacrifice, and you spend eternity in my realm knowing you failed her. With my help, you save her, you destroy your ancient enemy, and you enjoy whatever years a mortal queen might have."

Alaric closed his eyes, weighing the choice. Helena's face filled his mind—not as an immortal queen ruling by his side through endless centuries, but as she was now. Brave, determined, brilliant in her fleeting humanity.

"I accept," he said finally, opening his eyes to meet Hades' eternal gaze.

The god extended his hand. "Then let it be sealed in blood."

A dagger materialized in Hades' other hand—a blade of bone and obsidian that seemed to absorb light rather than reflect it. He drew it across his palm, then offered it to Alaric, who did the same without hesitation. Their blood mingled—mortal red and immortal black—as they clasped hands.

Power surged between their joined hands, ancient and terrible. The obsidian tiles cracked beneath their feet as reality itself bent around their pact.

Hades released Alaric's hand and stepped back, studying him with those fathomless eyes. He drew a deep breath, his chest expanding beyond what should have been physically possible.

"There is something you should know before you return," Hades said, his voice suddenly grave. "Time flows differently between realms. For each minute you've spent in my domain, a full day has passed in the world above."

Alaric's expression hardened as he calculated the implications. "How long have I been here?"

"Long enough for Varen to have moved his plans forward considerably," Hades replied with a thin smile. "Does that change your decision?"

"No," Alaric said firmly. "I understand the cost. Send me back."

Hades threw back his head and laughed—a sound like breaking glass and crumbling stone. "Oh, I do love this part," he said, wiping an imaginary tear from his eye. "The noble sacrifice, the determined hero, the—"

Alaric frowned. "What do you mean, this pa—"

The god's fist connected with Alaric's jaw with devastating force. The vampire flew backward, bracing for impact with the obsidian floor. Instead, his back slammed against cold iron as consciousness returned with brutal suddenness.

Darkness. Complete, suffocating darkness. The metallic taste of his own blood filled Alaric's mouth as reality reasserted itself. He was back in the iron coffin, still pierced by silver spears, still buried beneath tons of earth.

But something had changed. Power thrummed through his veins, different from his vampire strength — older, deeper, touched by divinity. The silver spears still burned, but the pain had become distant, manageable.

Alaric flexed his fingers experimentally. They responded, though the movement sent fresh rivulets of blood flowing from his puncture wounds. He reached up, touching the coffin lid that had seemed immovable before his death.

"Thank you, Lord Hades," he whispered, gathering his newfound strength. "I will honor our bargain."

With a roar that shook the very earth around him, Alaric pushed against the coffin lid. Metal groaned in protest as supernatural force bent it upward. Silver spears tore through his flesh as he moved, but he ignored the pain, focusing only on escape.

The lid buckled, then split along its seams. Earth cascaded through the opening, threatening to bury him again, but Alaric continued to push. His muscles strained beyond mortal limits, his wounds reopening as he fought against the crushing weight above.

Inch by excruciating inch, he clawed his way upward through the loosened soil. His lungs burned, though he had no need to breathe. His body screamed for blood to replenish what he'd lost. Still, he pushed on, Hades' power sustaining him where his own strength would have failed.

After what felt like hours, his hand broke through to open air. Moonlight gleamed on his bloodied fingers as he pulled himself from the earthen tomb, emerging like a nightmare into the abandoned village of Ashfeld.

Alaric collapsed beside the ruined pit, his body a mass of puncture wounds and torn flesh. Silver spears still protruded from his chest and limbs, but he was free—and alive, after a fashion.

He lay there for several moments, allowing Hades' borrowed power to begin knitting his wounds. The night air carried scents that told him much— Thorne and the knights were long gone, their trail cold. The mist entity had departed as well, perhaps assuming he'd been destroyed.

And beneath it all, carried on the faintest breeze, the scent of Helena's blood.

With trembling hands, Alaric grasped the first silver spear embedded in his shoulder. The metal sizzled against his palm, but he gritted his teeth and pulled. It slid free with a wet, sickening sound, and he cast it aside. One by one, he removed the remaining spears, each extraction bringing fresh agony but also increasing strength as the silver's influence diminished.

When the last spear clattered to the ground, Alaric forced himself to his feet. His clothing hung in bloody tatters, his body a roadmap of partially healed wounds. He needed blood — desperately — but there was none to be had in this ghost town.

He staggered toward the stable where he'd left his horse, hoping the animal had escaped Thorne's notice. To his surprise, the magnificent black stallion remained, nervously pawing the ground as if sensing its master's approach.

"Good boy, Thanatos," Alaric murmured, leaning against the stable door for support. "Faithful to the end."

The horse whickered softly, pushing its nose against Alaric's outstretched hand. The vampire stroked its muzzle, leaving smears of his own blood on the glossy coat.

"We ride for Ravenscrest," he told the animal, pulling himself painfully into the saddle. "And pray we're not too late."

As Thanatos carried him from the abandoned village, Alaric's mind calculated rapidly. If Hades spoke truth—and gods rarely lied outright, preferring half-truths and omissions— then for every minute he'd spent in the Underworld, a day had passed here. How long had his audience with the Lord of the Dead lasted? An hour? Two? That would mean weeks had passed in the mortal realm.

Weeks during which Varen had held Helena captive. Weeks during which the blood bond between them had been stretched to its breaking point. Weeks during which the ritual preparations had surely advanced.

The thought sent fresh determination coursing through him. He urged Thanatos to greater speed, the landscape blurring around them as the horse's hooves barely seemed to touch the ground.

"Hold on, my queen," Alaric whispered into the night wind. "I'm coming."

Behind him, unseen in the darkness, the first houses of Ashfeld began to crumble, stone and wood collapsing inward as if crushed by invisible hands. The mist rose once more, swirling around the ruins as the entity reclaimed what remained of its domain.

And somewhere ahead, in Ravenscrest's highest tower, Helena waited — changed, as he was changed, by forces beyond mortal comprehension.

The pact with Hades had been sealed in blood. Now it would be fulfilled in vengeance.

The night stretched endlessly before Alaric as Thanatos thundered across the countryside. Each mile brought fresh pain as his wounds reopened, the divine strength from Hades warring with his body's supernatural healing. Without blood to replenish what he'd lost, the process was agonizingly slow.

Villages flashed by, dark and silent in the midnight hour. Alaric avoided them, knowing he couldn't trust himself around mortals in his current state. The hunger clawed at him, a primal need that threatened to overwhelm rational thought.

As dawn approached, he felt its coming like a physical weight. Normally, daylight merely weakened him, but in his current condition, direct sunlight would be devastating. He guided Thanatos toward a dense copse of trees beside a small stream, dismounting with painful slowness.

"Rest," he told the exhausted horse, removing its saddle. "We continue at nightfall."

Alaric dragged himself beneath the thickest part of the canopy, where interlaced branches would block most of the sun's rays. He lay on the cool earth, feeling his body's desperate attempts to heal. Without blood, the process had nearly stalled, leaving him caught in a limbo of partial recovery.

As the first golden rays pierced the horizon, Alaric closed his eyes and reached out through the blood bond. Somewhere, miles away, Helena's presence flickered like a distant candle—alive, but altered. Changed in ways he couldn't fully comprehend through their attenuated connection.

"Helena," he whispered, pouring what little strength he had into the bond. "I'm coming. Hold fast."

Whether she could sense him, he didn't know. The bond had weakened during his death and rebirth, stretched thin by distance and divine intervention. But it remained—a fragile thread connecting them across the miles.

As the sun climbed higher, Alaric fell into a state between consciousness and oblivion. Not true sleep—his kind never truly slept—but a suspended animation that conserved what little energy remained.

In this twilight state, fragments of the past and present swirled together. Helena as he'd first seen her, standing defiant before her father's council. The blood bond, initiated in desperation as Varen's forces closed in. The mist entity of Ashfeld, born from his ancient failure. Hades on his bone throne, offering a bargain with terrible consequences.

And through it all, the certainty that time was running out. That for every moment he lay healing beneath these trees, Varen moved one step closer to completing his unholy ritual.

When consciousness returned fully, the sun was setting, painting the western sky in shades of crimson and gold. Alaric rose, his movements still stiff but stronger than before. The worst of his wounds had closed, though angry red scars remained where silver had pierced his flesh.

CHAPTER 23 –
JOURNEY TO THE END

Thanatos grazed nearby, raising his head as Alaric approached. The vampire mounted, his resolve hardening as night fell once more.

"To Ravenscrest," he commanded, and the great horse leapt forward, hooves thundering against the packed earth.

They rode through the night, covering ground at a pace no mortal steed could match. Thanatos seemed to draw strength from the darkness itself, never flagging despite the punishing pace.

As they crested a hill just before dawn, Ravenscrest came into view at last. The castle rose from the mist-shrouded valley, its towers silhouetted against the pre-dawn sky. Even from this distance, Alaric could sense something wrong—a malevolent energy that hung over the fortress like a shroud.

Varen's banners flew from the highest towers, the usurper's symbol—a crowned serpent devouring its own tail—snapping in the morning breeze. Guards patrolled the walls, their armor glinting in the first light of dawn.

Alaric dismounted, studying the castle with narrowed eyes. In his weakened state, a frontal assault would be suicide. He needed to infiltrate unseen, find Helena, and escape before Varen realized he still lived.

"Wait here," he told Thanatos, patting the horse's flank. "I'll return with our queen."

As Alaric turned to move toward the castle, the air around him thickened, coalescing into tendrils of silvery vapor that twisted and writhed with unnatural purpose. The mist entity had found him once more.

"Betrayer," its voice resonated directly in his mind, bypassing his ears entirely. "You still live. How... unexpected."

Alaric stood his ground, though every instinct screamed to retreat from the ancient presence. "I am not so easily killed."

The mist swirled faster, forming a vaguely humanoid shape that towered over him. "Yet you are diminished. Broken. A shadow of what you were when last we spoke."

"I have enough strength to fulfill my promise," Alaric countered, his hand instinctively moving to his sword hilt.

"Your promise?" The entity's laughter felt like ice water trickling down his spine. "You have been absent for a week, vampire. The world has changed in your absence."

Alaric's face hardened. "A week? Impossible. I was buried for—"

"Time matters not to the dead," the entity interrupted. "Or to those who walk with death's touch upon them." Its formless face leaned closer. "You reek of the Underworld, Betrayer. What bargain have you struck?"

"That is between me and Hades," Alaric replied coldly. "Tell me what has happened at Ravenscrest."

The mist entity rippled with what might have been amusement. "You demand knowledge from us? After your failure? Your absence?"

"I demand nothing," Alaric corrected, forcing his voice to remain steady. "I ask."

The entity considered this, its massive form shifting and reforming as it deliberated. Finally, it reached out with a tendril of fog that stopped just short of touching Alaric's forehead.

"We will show you," it intoned. "We have watched. We have waited. We have seen."

Before Alaric could react, the tendril pressed against his skin. Cold beyond imagining shot through his body as his consciousness was torn from its moorings and hurled into a maelstrom of images and sensations.

He stood in Ravenscrest's great hall, invisible and incorporeal as the scene unfolded before him. Varen sat upon Helena's throne, resplendent in robes of crimson and black. Before him knelt Captain Thorne, presenting something wrapped in bloodied cloth.

"Your Majesty," Thorne announced, his voice carrying across the silent hall. "I present the head of Captain Eldric Mercer, loyal to the false queen until her last breath."

Varen smiled, a cruel twist of lips that never reached his eyes. "Unwrap it. Let all see the price of defiance."

Thorne obeyed, revealing Eldric's severed head, her features frozen in a final expression of defiance despite the agony that must have preceded her death. Her eyes, once so alert and watchful, stared sightlessly at the vaulted ceiling.

The vision shifted, dissolving into mist before reforming in the castle dungeons. Helena hung suspended by silver chains, her once-vibrant copper hair now lank and dull. Blood crusted around manacles that bit into her wrists and ankles. Yet despite her obvious suffering, her eyes burned with the same fierce determination Alaric had always admired.

Varen circled her like a predator, his fingers trailing along her cheek in a mockery of tenderness. "The ritual is almost ready, niece. Your blood—infused with your vampire lover's essence—is the final key."

"He will come for me," Helena replied, her voice hoarse but unwavering. "And when he does, your centuries of stolen life will end in seconds."

Varen laughed, the sound echoing off the stone walls. "Thornwood is dead, child. Buried beneath tons of earth, his body pierced by silver, his power broken." He leaned closer, his lips nearly touching her ear. "No one is coming to save you."

The vision blurred again, fragments of other scenes flashing before Alaric's consciousness — Varen's men slaughtering those loyal to Helena, the ritual chamber being prepared with arcane symbols painted in blood, Thorne receiving lands and titles as reward for his treachery.

With brutal suddenness, Alaric found himself back in his own body, gasping as the mist entity withdrew its tendril. He staggered, nearly falling as the weight of what he'd witnessed crashed over him.

"Eldric," he whispered, genuine grief tightening his throat. The captain had been a worthy adversary, then a reluctant ally, and finally a loyal defender of her queen. Her death would not go unavenged.

"Now you see," the entity said, its voice almost gentle despite its inhuman nature. "The Devourer prepares his ritual. The queen suffers. And you..." It gestured at Alaric's wounded body. "You are broken."

Alaric straightened, pushing aside his grief to focus on what mattered most. "Helena lives. That is enough."

The mist entity studied him with its formless gaze. "Perhaps. But for how long? The ritual begins at midnight. You have mere hours, and the castle is heavily guarded."

"I've faced worse odds," Alaric replied, though even he heard the hollow note in his voice.

The entity seemed to sigh—a sound like wind through a forgotten graveyard. "We have fulfilled our part of our bargain, Betrayer. We showed you the truth. We guided you here." Its massive form began to thin, dissipating at the edges. "Consider your ancient debt paid. We do not believe you will survive this night, but we acknowledge your attempt."

"Wait," Alaric called, stepping forward. "Will you not help me? Together, we could—"

"Our vengeance is satisfied," the entity interrupted, continuing to fade. "Yours may yet go unfulfilled. Such is the way of mortal endeavors." Its voice grew fainter as its form retreated toward the distant forests. "We return to our village, to the ruins of what was. Farewell, Betrayer."

Within moments, the entity had vanished completely, leaving only wisps of ordinary morning mist that burned away in the strengthening sunlight. Alaric stood alone on the hilltop, the enormity of his task looming before him like the castle's imposing silhouette.

He was wounded, weakened, without allies. Varen held every advantage—numbers, position, and Helena herself as hostage. The ritual would begin at midnight, leaving precious little time to infiltrate a fortress designed to repel armies.

And yet...

Alaric's hand closed around the hilt of his obsidian blade, drawing comfort from its familiar weight. He had died and returned. He had bargained with Hades himself. He had survived centuries of hunting and being hunted.

Most importantly, he had promised Helena he would return. And in all his long existence, he had never broken a promise to those he loved.

With renewed determination, Alaric studied Ravenscrest's defenses, searching for weaknesses. There would be no frontal assault, no dramatic battle with wings unfurled. This would require subtlety, cunning, and the element of surprise.

Fortunately, those who believed him dead would not be looking for ghosts.

The sun climbed higher as Alaric formulated his plan. He would need to conserve what little strength remained, striking only when absolutely necessary.

He would need to move unseen through a castle where every loyal face had been removed.

And he would need blood. Soon.

As if in answer to his unspoken need, a rider appeared on the road below, bearing Varen's colors and moving at speed toward Ravenscrest. A messenger, perhaps, or a scout.

Alaric's eyes narrowed, tracking the lone figure's progress. The first piece of his plan had just presented itself.

"Forgive me, Helena," he murmured, drawing his blade as he moved down the hillside with predatory grace. "But mercy is a luxury I can no longer afford."

The messenger never saw the shadow that detached itself from the trees beside the road. Never heard the whisper of steel through air. Never felt the blade that severed his spine before he could cry out.

Alaric caught the body before it hit the ground, dragging it and the horse into the concealing underbrush. As he lowered his mouth to the dying man's throat, he silently renewed his vow to Helena.

Tonight, Varen would learn the true meaning of immortal vengeance.

The messenger's blood coursed through Alaric's veins, strength flooding back into his limbs with each powerful heartbeat. He flexed his fingers, feeling the divine power granted by Hades mingling with his restored vampire abilities. His wounds closed completely, leaving only silver-white scars where the spears had pierced him.

Dressed in the dead messenger's uniform, Alaric led his horse deeper into the Mistwood that bordered Ravenscrest's western approach. The ancient trees loomed overhead, their massive trunks disappearing into a canopy so thick it turned midday to dusk.

"I know you're watching," Alaric called into the shadowed undergrowth.

"Show yourselves. I haven't come to hunt you."

Silence answered him at first. Then, a rustling of leaves as something massive shifted in the darkness. Yellow eyes blinked open among the ferns — dozens of pairs, at different heights, surrounding him completely.

A low, rumbling growl emanated from the largest set of eyes. "Blood-drinker returns," the creature said, its voice like stones grinding together. "We thought you dead."

"I was," Alaric replied simply. "Death didn't agree with me."

A different creature slithered forward, its serpentine body covered in iridescent scales that caught what little light filtered through the canopy. "Your offering before was... magnificent," it hissed, forked tongue tasting the air. "Varen's soldiers screamed so sweetly as we feasted."

"I need your help again," Alaric said, getting straight to the point. "Varen holds the castle. He holds my queen. Tonight at midnight, he performs a ritual that will make him truly immortal—beyond my power to kill."

The yellow eyes blinked, considering. The serpent creature coiled around a fallen log, its massive head swaying hypnotically.

"Why should we care about human kingdoms?" asked a third voice, this one female and eerily melodic despite coming from a creature with too many limbs that clung to a nearby trunk. "Varen or queen, they all fear us. Hunt us."

"Because Varen won't stop with humans," Alaric countered. "His power grows with each life he consumes. If his ritual succeeds, he'll turn his attention to the Mistwood next. To you."

A heavy thud shook the forest floor as something massive dropped from the rocky outcropping above. Alaric spun, hand on his sword hilt, as a cave troll straightened to its full twelve-foot height.

"Truth," the troll rumbled, its craggy face twisting into what might have been a smile. "Varen already hunts us. Uses us."

Alaric tensed, memories of the troll attack on Ravenscrest's gates flashing through his mind. "Your kind attacked the castle not long ago," he said cautiously. "They fought under Varen's banner."

The troll's massive fist pounded against its chest, leaving a dusty imprint. "Not by choice! Varen took minds of brothers. Made them puppets." Its beady eyes narrowed with unmistakable hatred. "Iron collar here." It pointed to a raw wound circling its thick neck. "Broke free when you killed master's men."

Alaric studied the troll, recognizing genuine rage in its posture. "And now?"

"Now we want blood," the troll growled, spittle flying from its tusked mouth. "Troll blood was spilled. Troll minds were stolen. We pay back in kind."

The forest creatures had gone silent, watching the exchange with predatory intensity. The serpent's coils tightened around the log until the wood splintered with a sharp crack.

"If trolls fight," it hissed, "we fight too."

The many-limbed female creature dropped from her perch, landing beside Alaric with unsettling grace. "What is your plan, blood-drinker? The castle walls are high. The guards are many."

Alaric smiled, revealing fangs that gleamed in the dim forest light. "They expect an attack from without. They won't be looking within."

He outlined his strategy quickly — the secret tunnel beneath the east wall, the timing of guard rotations, the location of the ritual chamber in the highest tower. The creatures listened, occasionally interrupting with questions or suggestions.

"The tunnel will be too small for you," Alaric told the troll, who grunted in acknowledgment. "You'll need to create a distraction at the main gate. Something loud. Something terrifying."

"Trolls good at terrifying," the massive creature agreed, its laugh like boulders tumbling down a mountainside.

"Once inside, I'll locate Helena and disrupt the ritual," Alaric continued. "When you hear the bell tower ring three times, that's your signal to breach the walls. Show no mercy to anyone wearing Varen's colors."

The serpent's tongue flicked out excitedly. "And the others? The servants? The nobles who bent knee to the usurper?"

"No innocents," Alaric said firmly. "Varen's willing followers only. I'll know who they are."

The forest erupted with sounds of agreement—growls, hisses, chittering calls that echoed through the ancient trees. The troll stamped its feet in anticipation, sending small creatures scurrying from the undergrowth.

"Blood for blood," it declared, raising a fist the size of a war hammer. "Varen dies tonight!"

Alaric nodded, satisfaction coursing through him as he surveyed his makeshift army. "Spread the word to your kin. Gather at the forest edge by nightfall. And bring your hunger—there will be plenty to feast upon before dawn."

As the creatures melted back into the shadows, Alaric turned to face Ravenscrest once more. The castle's silhouette seemed to mock him, its towers reaching toward the sky like accusing fingers. Within those walls, Helena waited—changed, perhaps, but still his queen. Still the woman for whom he'd bargained with Hades himself.

"Soon, my love," he whispered, the promise carrying on the wind. "Hold fast just a little longer."

Behind him, the forest stirred with preparation as creatures long feared by humanity readied themselves for war. The troll's heavy footsteps retreated toward the mountains where its brethren dwelled. The serpent slithered away to rally its nest-mates. The many-limbed female and her kin spread through the canopy, their movements barely disturbing the leaves.

By sunset, an army unlike any Morvain had ever seen would gather at the Mistwood's edge. By midnight, Varen would learn that some enemies could not be buried, some vengeance could not be thwarted, and some bonds could not be broken—even by death itself.

Alaric mounted his stolen horse, guiding it back toward the road. There was one more ally to secure before night fell—one whose aid might prove most crucial of all.

The mist entity of Ashfeld had declared their ancient debt settled. But Alaric hoped that vengeance might prove motivation enough for one final alliance.

CHAPTER 24 –
VAREN'S PREPARATIONS

As twilight descended over Ravenscrest, the first howls echoed from the Mistwood—hungry, eager, and promising blood. Guards on the battlements shifted nervously, crossbows ready as they peered into the gathering darkness.

Within the highest tower, Varen looked up from his preparations, a frown creasing his ageless features as the inhuman cries reached his ears.

"Double the guard," he ordered the captain at his side. "Something stirs in the forest tonight."

"Yes, my lord," the man replied, bowing deeply before hurrying away.

Varen returned his attention to the ritual circle, where Helena hung suspended by silver chains, her eyes closed but her breathing steady. The ancient symbols painted around her in blood and quicksilver would ensure his final transformation—his ultimate victory over death itself.

"Just a few more hours, niece," he murmured, tracing a cold finger down her cheek. "A pity your vampire lover isn't here to witness your sacrifice. He would have appreciated the artistry, if nothing else."

Helena's eyes snapped open, startling Varen with their intensity. Though weakened by days of captivity, something burned in their depths that gave even the ancient usurper pause.

"He's coming," she whispered, her cracked lips curving into a smile that held no warmth. "And all your guards, all your magic, all your centuries of stolen life won't save you when he does."

Varen recovered quickly, his own smile matching hers in coldness if not conviction. "Brave words from a woman about to die. Your faith in the dead is touching, if futile."

Another howl rose from the forest, closer this time, joined by a second, then a third—a chorus of predators calling to one another in the darkness. Varen's smile faltered slightly as he moved to the window, gazing out at the impenetrable blackness of the Mistwood.

"Just wolves," he told himself, though the hairs on the back of his neck rose at the unnatural harmony of their cries. "Nothing more."

Behind him, Helena's chains clinked softly as she shifted position. Her smile widened, revealing teeth that seemed sharper than they had been days before.

"Nothing more," she echoed, her voice carrying a certainty that sent an involuntary chill down Varen's spine. "Nothing more than the end of everything you've built."

The usurper turned away from the window, forcing confidence back into his posture. "Prepare the final elements," he ordered the robed acolytes who hovered at the chamber's edges.

"The ritual begins at midnight, precisely."

As they scurried to obey, Varen cast one final glance toward the Mistwood, where shadows seemed to move with purpose beneath the ancient trees. For the first time in centuries, he felt something akin to unease stir in his chest—a sensation so long forgotten he almost didn't recognize it.

Fear.

Varen paused at the chamber door, glancing back at Helena with a cruel smile. "I'll return at midnight. Say your farewells to your faithful captain." With that final mockery, he descended the winding staircase, his footsteps fading into silence.

Helena strained against her silver chains, tears welling in her eyes as she stared at Eldric's headless corpse. Blood still pooled beneath the captain's body, spreading across ancient stone like a crimson map of all they'd lost.

"I'm sorry," she whispered, voice breaking. "You deserved better than this."

The silver chains bit deeper into her wrists as she struggled, but something was changing within her. The blood bond with Alaric—stretched thin but not broken—pulsed with renewed strength. She could feel him now, closer than before, his presence burning at the edges of her consciousness like a dark star rising.

CHAPTER 25 –
I'VE COME FOR YOU

At the forest's edge, hidden within the shadows of ancient trees, Alaric surveyed Ravenscrest's imposing silhouette. Beside him gathered his unholy alliance — trolls with skin like weathered stone, serpents with scales that drank the moonlight, creatures with too many limbs and too many teeth. Their breathing filled the night air with a symphony of hunger and anticipation.

"The queen is there," Alaric pointed to the highest tower where a single window glowed with eerie blue light. "Remember our agreement. Varen's soldiers die. Innocents live."

The troll chieftain — twelve feet of muscle and primal rage — grunted dismissively. Its beady eyes fixed on the castle with undisguised hatred. The raw wound around its neck where Varen's control collar had been still oozed black blood.

"Too long wait," it growled, massive hands clenching into fists the size of anvils. "Troll brothers dead. Troll blood spilled."

Before Alaric could respond, the troll lurched toward a boulder half-buried in the forest floor. With a roar that shook leaves from nearby trees, it wrenched the massive stone free, tendons standing out like steel cables along its arms.

"No!" Alaric shouted, but it was too late.

The troll spun once, twice, building momentum before releasing the boulder with devastating force. The stone whistled through the night air, its trajectory a perfect arc toward the ritual tower.

Inside the chamber, Helena's head snapped up, some primal instinct screaming danger. The air seemed to vibrate with approaching violence.

The boulder smashed into the tower wall with a thunderous impact, shattering centuries-old stone as if it were glass. The entire structure shuddered, massive blocks raining down into the courtyard below. The wall beside Helena disintegrated, chains still binding her wrists as the floor beneath her tilted precariously.

Alaric's heart seized with terror as he watched the tower partially collapse. "Helena!" he roared, his voice carrying across the valley.

Without conscious thought, his transformation began — bones cracking and reforming, muscles swelling with supernatural power. Massive wings erupted from his back, leathery membranes unfurling like dark sails as his skin hardened into obsidian scales.

He launched himself skyward with a powerful thrust, the wind of his passage flattening the grass beneath. Behind him, the forest erupted as his monstrous army surged forward, abandoning stealth for savage speed.

Castle guards barely had time to sound the alarm before the trolls reached the outer wall. Stone crumbled beneath their massive fists as they tore through fortifications built to withstand armies. The serpents slithered through gaps in the defenses, their massive bodies crushing soldiers foolish enough to stand their ground.

Alaric soared toward the crumbling tower, his enhanced vision picking out Helena's copper hair amid the ruins. She hung suspended over a dizzying drop, silver chains still binding her to what remained of the wall. Their eyes met across the distance — hers widening with recognition and desperate hope.

"Alaric!" she cried, her voice nearly lost in the cacophony of battle below.

He tucked his wings and dove, the air screaming around him as he plummeted toward the ruined tower. Below, the courtyard had become a slaughterhouse. Creatures from nightmare legends descended upon Varen's soldiers with centuries of pent-up hatred. Men screamed as many-limbed horrors peeled armor and flesh with equal ease, their entrails becoming gruesome feasts for the chittering masses.

The trolls moved through the lower town with terrible purpose, reducing stone houses to rubble with casual swings of their massive arms. Those who fled were allowed to escape; those who fought died screaming beneath fists that pulverized bone and flesh into unrecognizable paste.

Alaric reached the tower, wings flaring to slow his descent as he landed on the precarious edge of the ruined floor. Helena stared at him with wonder and relief, her eyes drinking in his transformed appearance.

"You came back," she whispered, tears streaking through the grime on her face. "He said you were dead."

"I was," Alaric replied, his voice deeper and resonant in this form. With careful precision, he snapped the silver chains binding her wrists, catching her as she collapsed forward. "Death is not the barrier it once was."

He gathered her against his chest, her body feeling frighteningly fragile after days of captivity. The blood bond between them pulsed with renewed strength at their contact, and he could feel the changes in her—subtle transformations that mirrored his own nature.

"Eldric," Helena gasped, looking back at the headless corpse still visible in the partial ruins. "They killed her. Rowan and Varen—they made me watch."

"I know," Alaric growled, rage building behind his crimson eyes. "And they will pay. But first, we must get you to safety."

Below them, the battle intensified as Varen's elite guard emerged from the inner keep. Unlike the regular soldiers, these men moved with supernatural speed and strength—evidence of

Varen's blood in their veins. They engaged the forest creatures with grim efficiency, blades flashing in the torchlight.

"No," Helena said, surprising Alaric with her firmness. She pushed against his chest, standing on her own despite her weakened state. "No more running. No more hiding. Varen ends tonight."

Something had changed in her beyond the physical alterations from their blood bond. Steel had replaced the compassion in her eyes, vengeance overshadowing mercy.

"The ritual chamber," she continued, pointing toward the intact section of the tower. "He's preparing it now. If we strike before midnight—"

A terrible roar from below cut her off. One of the trolls had fallen, multiple spears protruding from its massive chest. Its brothers bellowed in rage, redoubling their assault on the castle walls. Stone crumbled like sand beneath their fists as they tore through centuries-old fortifications.

"Time grows short," Alaric agreed, his wings mantling protectively around Helena. "Can you fight?"

In answer, Helena flexed her fingers, revealing talons where human nails had been. Her smile held no warmth, only predatory anticipation. "I've been waiting for this moment since they dragged me from my chambers. Since they murdered Eldric before my eyes."

Alaric nodded, pride mingling with concern at her transformation. What price would she pay for embracing the darkness within her? What would remain of the woman he'd fallen in love with when vengeance had been sated?

Questions for another time. Now, there was only the hunt.

"Then let us end this," he said, extending his hand. "Together."

Helena took it without hesitation, her fingers intertwining with his scaled ones. "Together."

As they turned toward the ritual chamber, a shadow appeared in the doorway — Varen, his ageless features contorted with rage as he surveyed the destruction of his fortress.

"You," he hissed, eyes fixing on Alaric with hatred that spanned centuries. "Death itself rejects you, it seems."

"Not rejected," Alaric corrected, stepping forward with Helena at his side. "Merely delayed. I made a bargain with Hades himself to return for this moment."

Varen's eyes widened fractionally, genuine fear flickering across his face before his mask of cold arrogance reasserted itself. "No matter. The ritual is nearly complete. Even without your precious queen, I have alternatives."

He gestured, and from the shadows behind him emerged Rowan Blackthorn, dragging a struggling figure—a young woman with Helena's copper hair and similar features.

"My cousin," Helena gasped, recognition and horror washing over her face. "Elise. You wouldn't—"

"Royal blood is royal blood," Varen shrugged. "Less potent without your vampire essence, but serviceable. The question is—" his lips curved in a cruel smile "—can you save her before my men tear her apart?"

Behind them, the sounds of battle intensified. A section of the castle's eastern wall collapsed entirely, crushing defenders beneath tons of stone. Trolls roared in triumph as they poured through the breach, their massive forms silhouetted against fires now burning throughout the lower town.

Human screams mingled with inhuman howls as the forest creatures exacted centuries of vengeance upon those who had hunted and feared them. Blood ran in rivers across the cobblestones, feeding ancient hatreds that would not be easily quenched.

Helena stepped forward, her face hardening into something barely recognizable as human. "No more innocents die for your ambition, Uncle. This ends now."

"Indeed it does," Varen agreed, drawing a ritual dagger from his robes. "But not as you imagine."

With blinding speed, he slashed the blade across Rowan's throat. The nobleman's eyes widened in shock as his lifeblood sprayed across the chamber floor, completing a symbol that had been partially drawn in preparation for the midnight ritual.

"Blood freely given is best," Varen intoned, his voice taking on an otherworldly resonance. "But blood spilled in betrayal has its own power."

The symbol began to glow with sickly green light, illuminating the chamber with its unholy radiance. Power crackled through the air, raising the hairs on Helena's arms and causing even Alaric to step back instinctively.

"You think your forest pets can stop me?" Varen laughed, spreading his arms wide as energy coursed visibly through his body. "I've consumed the life force of dozens of royal bloodlines. I've bathed in the blood of creatures older than your vampire lover. I am beyond death, beyond judgment!"

The floor beneath them trembled as the ritual gained momentum, feeding on Rowan's still-pumping heart. Elise cowered against the far wall, forgotten in Varen's moment of triumph.

Alaric's wings flared wide, his transformation deepening as he called upon the power granted by Hades. "Helena," he said urgently, "get your cousin. This chamber won't stand much longer."

Helena hesitated, torn between concern for her kin and the desire to see Varen destroyed. "What about you?"

"I made a promise to a god," Alaric replied, his eyes never leaving Varen's glowing form. "And I intend to keep it."

Helena lunged across the room, talons extended as she seized Elise's trembling hand. "Run!" she commanded, yanking her cousin toward the chamber door.

The castle shuddered around them as another troll's fist connected with the foundation stones. Dust and mortar rained from the ceiling as the two women fled, leaving Alaric facing Varen alone in the collapsing ritual chamber.

"What's happening?" Elise sobbed, stumbling as Helena dragged her down the winding staircase. "Who was that creature? What's happened to your hands?"

"Later," Helena snapped, her heightened senses guiding them through the darkened passage. "If we survive this night, I'll explain everything."

They burst into the main corridor, dodging falling debris as they sprinted toward the courtyard. Behind them, the tower trembled as supernatural power clashed above — Varen's centuries of stolen life force against Alaric's divine bargain.

The courtyard had become a battlefield of nightmares. Forest creatures tore through Varen's soldiers with savage efficiency, their inhuman forms moving with terrible purpose amid the chaos. Blood slicked the cobblestones, making footing treacherous as Helena pulled Elise toward the castle gates.

"Stay close!" Helena shouted over the cacophony of screams and bestial roars.

A soldier in Varen's colors lunged from an alcove, blade slashing toward Helena's exposed back. She spun with inhuman speed, her talons ripping through his throat before he could complete his attack. Blood sprayed across her face as the man collapsed, gurgling his last breath.

Elise stared in horror at her cousin, witnessing the transformation that had overtaken her. "Helena, your eyes—"

"Keep moving!" Helena interrupted, seizing Elise's wrist once more. Three more soldiers blocked their path to freedom, weapons raised.

They darted left, racing between burning buildings as the remaining guards gave chase. The main gate loomed ahead, its massive doors hanging broken from their hinges where trolls had torn through.

Freedom was within reach when a soldier's gauntleted hand caught Elise by her copper hair, wrenching her backward with brutal force. She screamed as he yanked her head back, exposing her pale throat to his raised blade.

"For Lord Varen!" the soldier cried, sword glinting in the firelight as it began its killing arc.

The blow never fell.

A massive shadow blotted out the moon as a troll — twelve feet of primal rage — appeared behind the soldier. Its fist connected with the man's armored body, the impact sounding like a blacksmith's hammer striking an anvil. The soldier's scream cut short as his body sailed over the castle wall, disappearing into the darkness beyond.

Elise stood frozen, staring up at her monstrous savior. The troll met her gaze, its beady eyes reflecting the fires burning throughout the courtyard. It threw back its head and unleashed a roar that shook the very foundations of Ravenscrest, spittle flying from its tusked mouth.

With methodical fury, it turned its attention to the surrounding structures. Stone walls crumbled beneath its massive fists as it pounded building after building, generations of royal architecture reduced to rubble in moments of unleashed vengeance.

"Come on!" Helena grabbed Elise again, pulling her through the shattered gate as the troll continued its rampage behind them.

They stumbled down the road leading from the castle, lungs burning with exertion. Other refugees fled alongside them—servants, stable hands, kitchen staff—all escaping the horror that Ravenscrest had become.

Helena glanced back over her shoulder. The castle blazed against the night sky, sections collapsing inward as trolls systematically demolished the fortress that had stood for centuries. At the highest point of the remaining tower, flashes of unnatural light illuminated two silhouettes locked in combat—one winged and massive, the other surrounded by a nimbus of sickly green energy.

"Alaric," she whispered, torn between the need to protect her cousin and the desire to return to her lover's side.

"Who is he?" Elise asked, following Helena's gaze. "What is he?"

"He's mine," Helena answered simply, her voice carrying a possessive note that made Elise shiver. "And he's fighting to save us all."

A deafening crack split the night as the remaining tower began to collapse. Stone and timber plummeted toward the courtyard below, crushing everything in their path. The magical energies contained within the ritual chamber exploded outward in a shockwave that flattened the surrounding trees.

"No!" Helena cried, starting back toward the castle.

Elise caught her arm. "You can't go back! It's suicide!"

"I have to," Helena insisted, eyes fixed on the destruction. "He needs me. I can feel it through our bond."

"Bond? What bond?" Elise's face crumpled with confusion and fear. "Helena, please, I don't understand any of this!"

Before Helena could respond, the ground beneath their feet trembled. The remaining walls of Ravenscrest began to glow with the same sickly light that had surrounded Varen, the stones themselves seeming to melt and reform into something grotesque and unnatural.

The ground lurched beneath their feet as Helena pulled Elise back from the collapsing castle.

"Stay here!" Helena commanded, shoving her cousin behind a fallen section of wall.

In the ruined ritual chamber, Alaric's obsidian blade flashed in the firelight as he charged Varen with inhuman speed. The usurper barely had time to raise his own weapon before Alaric crashed into him with the force of a battering ram.

"You should have stayed dead," Varen snarled, parrying a blow that would have separated his head from his shoulders.

Alaric's lips pulled back in a feral grin, revealing fangs that gleamed in the magical light still pulsing from the ritual circle. "Death and I have an understanding."

Their blades met again with a sound like thunder, sparks cascading around them as they traded blows too fast for mortal eyes to follow. Alaric's wings spread wide, knocking over ancient artifacts that shattered against the stone floor.

"You've lost, Varen," Alaric growled, seizing the usurper by his ornate robes and hurling him through a bookcase. Ancient tomes and scrolls scattered as Varen crashed through the wooden structure, rolling to his feet with supernatural agility.

"Lost?" Varen laughed, blood trickling from a cut above his eye. "The ritual has already begun. Can't you feel it, vampire? The walls themselves answer to me now."

As if in response, the stones around them shuddered, bulging inward like living flesh before reshaping into grotesque, reaching appendages.

Alaric dodged a stone tendril that would have impaled him, his sword severing it with a single stroke. "Then I'll tear down every last stone of this cursed place!"

He launched himself at Varen again, wings propelling him across the chamber with devastating force. They crashed through the remains of the ritual altar, tumbling across the floor in a blur of talons and blades.

Outside, Helena watched in horror as the castle continued its unnatural transformation. Beside her, Elise clutched at her arm, tears streaming down her dirt-smudged face.

"We need to run," Elise pleaded. "Please, Helena!"

"I can't leave him," Helena whispered, her enhanced vision allowing her to glimpse the battle raging within the ruined tower.

Inside the chamber, Varen struck with serpentine quickness, his enchanted blade slicing across Alaric's scaled forearm. Black blood hissed where the edge cut, but Alaric barely seemed to notice. He seized Varen by the throat, massive wings beating once to lift them both from the floor before slamming the usurper through a stone column.

Marble shattered beneath the impact, dust and debris raining down as Varen gasped for breath. Before he could recover, Alaric was on him again, talons ripping through expensive robes to the flesh beneath.

"Centuries I've hunted you," Alaric snarled, his voice barely human as rage consumed him. "Centuries watching you slither from one stolen body to the next."

Varen's hand shot out, fingers curling in an arcane gesture. Invisible force slammed into Alaric, sending him crashing across the room. His sword skittered away, coming to rest near Rowan's cooling corpse.

"You never understood the gift I offered," Varen said, rising to his feet with unnatural grace. "Immortality without the thirst. Power without the weaknesses of your kind."

Alaric lunged for his weapon, but Varen was faster. A blast of sickly green energy struck the sword, sending it spinning over the edge of the ruined chamber to the courtyard below.

"Now what, monster?" Varen taunted, advancing with his own blade raised. "Will you die again for your precious queen?"

Alaric's crimson gaze shifted to Rowan's corpse, then back to Varen. Without warning, he seized the dead nobleman's arm, wrenching it from the socket with a wet, tearing sound.

"What—" Varen began, momentarily stunned by the savage display.

He never finished the question. Alaric swung Rowan's severed arm like a club, the impact shattering Varen's jaw with a sickening crack. Before the usurper could recover, Alaric tore off Rowan's other arm, wielding both limbs with brutal efficiency.

"You wanted his loyalty," Alaric growled, striking again and again as Varen stumbled backward. "Now you have it."

Blood sprayed across the chamber as Alaric continued his relentless assault. He ripped Rowan's head from his shoulders, fingers tangled in the nobleman's hair as he slammed the grisly weapon into Varen's face.

In the courtyard below, Helena held Elise tightly as her cousin retched at the sounds emanating from the tower—wet, tearing noises punctuated by impacts that shook the remaining structure.

"We can't stay here," Helena said, finally accepting what her instincts had been screaming. "The castle is coming down."

As if to confirm her words, the foundation stones groaned beneath them, the very earth seeming to reject Ravenscrest's corrupted presence. Cracks spread across the courtyard, widening into fissures that glowed with the same unhealthy light as Varen's magic.

"But Alaric—" Helena began, looking back toward the tower.

"He made his choice," Elise said, surprising Helena with her sudden firmness. "Now make yours. Live to fight another day, or die here for nothing."

The tower shuddered as another deafening impact echoed from above. Something massive crashed through what remained of the wall — Varen's body, bloodied and broken but still moving as it hit the courtyard stones thirty feet away.

Alaric appeared in the ragged opening, his massive wings spread wide, Rowan's severed torso clutched in one taloned hand. His face was barely recognizable, transformed by rage into something ancient and terrible.

"Run," Helena whispered to her cousin, eyes fixed on the scene unfolding before them. "Get to the village. I'll follow."

"You promised!" Elise protested, but Helena silenced her with a look that brooked no argument.

"Go. Now."

As Elise fled toward the shattered gates, Helena pressed herself against the fallen wall, watching as Alaric descended toward Varen's crumpled form. The usurper was trying to rise, his shattered body already beginning to heal as he drew power from the corrupted stones beneath him.

"It's not enough," Varen laughed, blood bubbling from his ruined mouth as Alaric landed beside him. "Kill this body, and I'll simply take another. I've done it for centuries."

Alaric cast aside Rowan's torso, advancing on Varen with predatory focus. "Not this time," he promised, voice resonating with power beyond mortal comprehension. "Hades sends his regards."

Helena felt a chill run through her at those words. What bargain had Alaric struck to return from death? What price would he pay?

The ground bucked beneath her feet, nearly sending her sprawling as more fissures opened across the courtyard. The castle walls were fully transforming now, stone flowing like wax into shapes that defied natural law — reaching arms, gaping maws, writhing tentacles that groped blindly for anything living.

Elise cast one final glance at Helena before fleeing down the road, her copper hair streaming behind her as she raced toward the distant village. Forest creatures emerged from the shadows, their misshapen forms dragging fallen soldiers into the darkness. Wet, tearing sounds followed as they began their grisly feast, celebrating victory with blood and flesh.

The trolls retreated to the edges of the courtyard, massive forms silhouetted against the burning buildings as they gathered to witness the final confrontation. Their beady eyes reflected the firelight, ancient hatred giving way to something like reverence as they watched the vampire lord face his centuries-old enemy.

Helena pressed against the crumbled wall, her enhanced vision capturing every detail of the battle unfolding before her. Her breath caught in her throat as Varen scrambled backward, desperation evident in his movements.

"You cannot end me," Varen snarled, seizing a fallen sword and swinging it wildly. "I am eternal!"

Alaric dodged the blade with contemptuous ease, his wings creating gusts that scattered ash and embers across the ruined courtyard. "Nothing is eternal," he replied, voice resonating with otherworldly power. "Not even gods."

Varen's hand shot out, fingers curling as he tore a stone column from a nearby archway, hurling it at Alaric with supernatural strength. The vampire batted it aside, talons scoring deep gouges in the ancient marble.

"Is that the best you can offer?" Alaric taunted, advancing inexorably. "After all these centuries?"

With a roar of frustration, Varen ripped a fallen soldier's shield from beneath rubble, flinging it like a discus. It whistled through the air, slicing across Alaric's shoulder before embedding itself in a distant wall.

Black blood oozed from the wound, but Alaric showed no sign of pain. His taloned hand shot out, seizing Varen by the throat. Wings beat once, powerful enough to send dust swirling in miniature cyclones as they lifted both combatants into the night air.

"Look upon your kingdom," Alaric commanded, forcing Varen to witness the devastation below. "Look upon your legacy of blood and lies."

Then he plummeted, driving Varen into the courtyard stones with bone-shattering force. The impact created a crater, cobblestones shattering beneath the usurper's body. Before Varen could recover, Alaric seized two fallen swords, driving them through the usurper's shoulders, pinning him to the ground like an insect to a collector's board.

Varen screamed, the sound more rage than pain as he thrashed against his impalement. "You think this will hold me?" he spat, blood flecking his lips. "This body means nothing! I'll simply—"

His words cut off as Alaric produced something from within his tattered clothing—a ring of dull metal that seemed to absorb the surrounding light. With preternatural speed, he forced it onto Varen's finger.

The effect was immediate. Varen's eyes widened in genuine fear as the ring began to glow with sickly amber light. "No," he whispered, recognition dawning. "Where did you get that? What have you done?"

"A gift from Hades," Alaric replied, satisfaction evident in his voice. "You're bound to this flesh now. No more transfers. No more stolen bodies." He leaned closer, his breath hot against Varen's ear. "When this body dies, your soul goes directly to the Underworld for judgment."

Varen's struggles intensified, panic replacing his earlier confidence. The ring burned against his skin, searing flesh but refusing to be removed. "I'll kill you for this," he snarled, fingers clawing at the enchanted band. "I'll destroy everything you love!"

With unexpected strength born of desperation, Varen tore one arm free, the sword ripping through muscle and bone as he wrenched himself upward. Blood fountained from the wound, but the usurper seemed beyond caring about physical pain. His hand shot out, fingers curling around a fallen axe half-buried in debris.

Before Alaric could react, Varen swung the weapon with devastating force. The blade connected with Alaric's chest, sending him staggering backward. The vampire recovered quickly, but Varen was already on his feet, the remaining sword still protruding from his other shoulder.

"You should have killed me when you had the chance," Varen taunted, advancing with the axe raised. His movements were jerky, uncoordinated, but driven by a frenzied strength that made him dangerous still.

Helena watched in horror as Varen gained momentum, each swing forcing Alaric further back. The vampire lord was tiring, his earlier wounds and the divine energy he'd expended taking their toll.

A particularly vicious blow caught Alaric across the ribs, sending him crashing to the ground. Varen stood over him, axe raised for a killing stroke, triumph blazing in his inhuman eyes.

"Die knowing you failed," Varen hissed, muscles tensing for the final blow.

Helena moved without conscious thought. She darted from her hiding place, seizing a woodsman's axe from a fallen soldier. Her feet barely seemed to touch the ground as she raced across the courtyard, talons extended, eyes blazing with crimson fire.

Alaric saw her coming, realization and horror dawning on his face. "Helena, no!" he shouted, struggling to rise.

Too late. Varen sensed her approach, spinning with inhuman speed to face this new threat. Time seemed to slow as Helena closed the final distance, axe raised, determination etched into every line of her face.

Varen's hand shot forward—not to block her attack, but to punch straight through her chest. Bone splintered, flesh tore, and blood sprayed in a crimson arc as his fingers closed around Helena's heart.

Her momentum carried her forward even as life fled her body. The axe slipped from nerveless fingers, clattering to the stones as Varen ripped her heart from her chest with a wet, tearing sound.

Helena's eyes found Alaric's in that final moment—shock, pain, and something like apology passing between them before the light faded from her gaze. She collapsed at Varen's feet, copper hair spreading around her like a pool of blood.

The courtyard went utterly silent. Every creature, every troll, every living thing witnessing the scene froze in horrified recognition of what had just occurred. Their eyes moved as one to Alaric, still prone on the ground, staring at Helena's lifeless body.

Something broke in the vampire lord's expression—something fundamental and irreparable. His face contorted into a mask of such primal anguish that even the trolls took involuntary steps backward.

The first creature fled—a many-limbed horror that scuttled up the ruined wall with frantic speed. Others followed, abandoning their feast, their victory, their vengeance in the face of what was coming. The trolls exchanged glances of ancient understanding before turning as one, massive forms moving with surprising speed as they retreated into the night.

Within moments, the courtyard stood empty save for the three figures at its center—Varen, still holding Helena's dripping heart; Helena herself, sprawled lifelessly on the stones; and Alaric, whose transformation was only beginning.

Darkness gathered around the vampire lord as he rose to his feet. Not the physical darkness of night, but something older, deeper—a primordial absence that seemed to devour light itself. His wings expanded, doubling in size as scales spread across his body like liquid obsidian, covering every inch of exposed skin.

"You shouldn't have done that," Alaric whispered, his voice no longer recognizable as human or even vampire. It resonated with power beyond mortal comprehension, carrying echoes of the Underworld itself.

Varen took an involuntary step back, Helena's heart still clutched in his bloody fist. For the first time in centuries, genuine fear showed on his ageless features as he beheld what his actions had unleashed.

"What are you?" he breathed, the question barely audible.

Alaric's transformed face split in a smile that promised only suffering. "I am her vengeance."

He surged forward, darkness trailing from his wings like living shadow. Varen hurled Helena's heart at him in desperation, but Alaric caught it midair, cradling the still-warm organ with terrible gentleness.

"This belongs to me," he said, tucking it within his transformed body. "As does your soul."

Varen turned to flee, but Alaric was already upon him. Talons ripped through flesh and bone, not killing but dismembering with surgical precision. First the legs, separated at the knees with wet, tearing sounds. Then the arms, removed joint by joint as Varen screamed in agony.

Alaric's talons sank deep into Varen's chest, ripping outward with a savage force that shattered ribs like brittle twigs. The usurper's scream died in his throat as Alaric plunged his hand deeper, fingers closing around Varen's still-beating heart.

"Feel it," Alaric hissed, his voice no longer anything human. "Feel death coming for you — as she felt it."

With a grotesque twist, he extracted Varen's heart, holding it before the usurper's widening eyes. Unlike Helena's quick death, Alaric kept Varen conscious, kept him alive to witness his own dismemberment.

"Please," Varen gasped, blood bubbling from his lips as his body struggled to heal wounds beyond repair. "Mercy—"

"Mercy?" The word emerged as a sound between laughter and rage. Alaric's massive jaws unhinged, revealing rows of obsidian teeth. With deliberate slowness, he bit into Varen's heart, tearing away a chunk of the still-pulsing organ.

Blood cascaded down Alaric's scaled chest as he chewed, swallowed, then tore another piece. Varen's eyes rolled back, his body convulsing as he felt each bite through their unholy connection.

"Watch," Alaric commanded, his voice compelling obedience even as Varen's consciousness tried to flee into merciful darkness. "Watch as I consume everything you are."

When the heart was gone, Alaric moved to Varen's face. Talons pierced the usurper's cheeks, peeling skin from bone with methodical precision. Varen's screams became wet, gurgling sounds as his jaw was torn away, then his nose, his ears, until only bulging eyes remained in a ruined skull.

"Still alive?" Alaric whispered, leaning close to what remained of Varen's face. "Good."

His massive hand closed around Varen's throat, crushing the windpipe but leaving enough passage for ragged, tortured breaths. With his other hand, he reached lower, talons slicing through Varen's abdomen with surgical precision.

Intestines spilled onto the cobblestones, steaming in the night air. Alaric gathered them in his massive fist, pulling slowly, inexorably, unwinding them from Varen's body while the usurper watched his own evisceration with bulging, unblinking eyes.

"Your ambition," Alaric growled, tearing away organ after organ, "your greed, your betrayal—all for nothing."

The ruined courtyard filled with the stench of blood and viscera as Alaric continued his grisly work. Bones cracked beneath his hands as he systematically disassembled what remained of Varen's torso, each break precise and calculated to maximize suffering without granting the release of death.

Throughout it all, Hades' ring glowed on what remained of Varen's hand, binding his soul to his disintegrating flesh, preventing the escape he so desperately sought.

Only when Varen had been reduced to barely recognizable pieces did Alaric finally pause, his crimson gaze settling on the usurper's remaining eye—the last window to a consciousness trapped in unspeakable agony.

"Helena awaits you in the Underworld," Alaric whispered, leaning close to the ruined head. "But she will not be alone."

With terrible finality, he crushed Varen's skull between his massive hands. The sound — like overripe fruit being pulverized — echoed across the silent courtyard as the last spark of life finally fled the usurper's broken form.

The ring on Varen's severed finger flared with blinding amber light, then crumbled to ash. Alaric felt the moment Varen's soul was dragged screaming to Hades' realm, the bargain fulfilled at last.

Only then did he turn to Helena's body, still lying where she had fallen. The transformation that had overtaken him began to recede, scales melting back into skin, wings folding into his body as grief replaced rage. He gathered her in his arms, cradling her against his chest as he had done so many times before.

"I'm sorry," he whispered, pressing his forehead to hers. "I failed you."

Around them, Ravenscrest continued its slow collapse, stone

grinding against stone as centuries of history crumbled into dust. The magical corruption that Varen had unleashed ate through the foundations, ensuring nothing would remain by dawn's light.

Alaric barely noticed. His world had narrowed to the woman in his arms, her copper hair spilling across his bloodied forearms, her eyes staring sightlessly at the star-filled sky.

"My Queen," he murmured, voice breaking. "My love."

He closed her eyes with gentle fingers, then lifted her, turning away from the carnage he had wrought. There was nothing left for him here—nothing but death and memory and the weight of a bargain he could no longer fulfill.

As he carried Helena from the ruins, a shadow detached itself from a crumbled wall. The mist entity of Ashfeld stood before him, its formless presence somehow conveying both satisfaction and sorrow.

"The debt is paid," it intoned, tendrils swirling around its vaporous form. "Blood has answered blood."

Alaric nodded once, unable to speak past the grief lodged in his throat. He moved to step around the entity, Helena's body light in his arms despite the leaden weight in his chest.

"Wait," the entity commanded, its voice gentler than before. "There is something you should know."

Alaric paused, crimson eyes lifting to meet the entity's formless gaze.

"The bargain with Hades," the entity continued. "We heard its terms. Her natural life, then judgment."

"It no longer matters," Alaric replied, voice hollow. "She is dead. My bargain is broken."

The entity's form rippled, almost like laughter. "Is she?"

Alaric's brow furrowed in confusion, then shock as he felt movement against his chest. He looked down to see Helena's fingers twitching, her chest rising with a shallow breath.

"Impossible," he whispered, hope warring with disbelief. "Varen tore out her heart."

"And you took it back," the entity reminded him. "Placed it within yourself, where your essence could preserve it." Tendrils of mist brushed against Helena's pale cheek. "Her natural life was always meant to end tonight. What follows... is something else entirely."

Understanding dawned in Alaric's eyes as Helena stirred again, stronger this time. The blood bond between them pulsed with renewed vigor, darkness calling to darkness across the threshold of death itself.

"The transformation," he breathed. "It's completing itself."

The entity's form began to disperse, fading into the night mist. "We have witnessed enough death for one age. Perhaps it is fitting to witness rebirth as well."

As the last of the mist entity vanished, Helena's eyes fluttered open. They were no longer the warm brown he remembered, but crimson—the same shade as his own. She gasped, hand flying to her chest where a wound was already closing, new flesh knitting together with supernatural speed.

"Alaric?" she whispered, voice ragged but unmistakably hers. "What happened? I saw... darkness. A throne of bones. A bargain."

He held her tighter, wonder replacing grief as her strength visibly returned. "You died," he said simply. "But death, it seems, has rejected us both."

Helena's gaze moved past him to the ruins of Ravenscrest, to the scattered remains of what had once been Varen. Understanding dawned in her transformed eyes.

"The blood bond," she said, fingers tracing the closing wound in her chest. "It completed itself."

Alaric nodded, helping her to stand on unsteady feet. "You're something new now. Neither human nor quite vampire. Something... in between."

Helena looked down at her hands, at the talons that had replaced her nails, feeling the new strength flowing through her limbs. "And your bargain with Hades? What becomes of it now?"

"I don't know," Alaric admitted, glancing toward the eastern horizon where the first hints of dawn were appearing. "But we'll face it together — whatever comes."

He extended his hand, and Helena took it without hesitation, their fingers intertwining as they turned away from the ruins of Ravenscrest. Behind them, the last tower collapsed with a thunderous roar, sending dust and debris billowing into the night sky.

"Where will we go?" Helena asked as they walked toward the forest's edge.

Alaric's lips curved in a smile that held equal parts tenderness and danger. "Anywhere. Everywhere. We have time now—more than either of us imagined possible."

As they reached the tree line, Helena paused, looking back one final time at the destruction they left behind. "And Elise? My people?"

"They'll rebuild," Alaric assured her. "Morvain has survived worse than Varen. And when they're ready—when you're ready—we can return."

CHAPTER 26 –

THE END.

Of Book 1.

Helena nodded, decision made. She turned away from her former kingdom, from the life that had ended with Varen's hand through her chest. What awaited her now was unknown, uncharted—a darkness to explore with the one being who truly understood what she had become.

"Together, then," she said, squeezing his hand as they disappeared into the shadows of the ancient forest.

The forest swallowed them whole, ancient trees towering above like silent sentinels. They'd walked for hours, leaving the burning ruins of Ravenscrest far behind. Helena's newfound strength surged through her limbs, each step more confident than the last as her body adjusted to its transformation.

Suddenly, Alaric stopped. His shoulders tensed, head tilting as though listening to something beyond human hearing.

"What is it?" Helena asked, moving closer.

A strange smile spread across Alaric's face—one she'd never seen before. Cold. Calculating. Wrong.

"Do you know," he said, voice unnervingly casual, "how tedious it is to maintain appearances for so long?"

Before she could respond, he spun around and shoved her violently. Helena crashed into the forest floor, dead leaves cushioning her fall as she stared up at him in confusion.

Alaric threw back his head and laughed—a sound utterly devoid of warmth that echoed through the trees, sending night birds scattering in panic.

"The look on your face," he said between bursts of laughter. "Priceless. Absolutely priceless."

"Alaric?" Helena pushed herself up on her elbows. "What are you doing?"

He wiped an imaginary tear from his eye. "I can't believe I had to keep up this bullshit charade for so long. Protecting you, professing love, making that ridiculous bargain with Hades — all to finally kill Varen."

"Charade?" The word felt like ice in her veins. "I don't understand."

Alaric crouched beside her; head tilted in mock sympathy. "Of course you don't, my queen." He spat the title like a curse. "You never questioned why I appeared in your kingdom just as Varen made his move, did you? Never wondered about my convenient hatred for your uncle?"

"You said he killed your family centuries ago—"

"I said many things." His smile widened. "Most of them lies."

Helena scrambled backward, the full horror of his betrayal dawning on her. "The blood bond—"

"A means to an end." Alaric shrugged, following her retreat with predatory grace. "I needed you transformed enough to help destroy him, but not enough to threaten me afterward."

"Why?" The single word carried the weight of her shattered heart.

Alaric sighed, his expression almost regretful. "I must apologize for wasting your time. Old habits die hard—I've always had a flair for the dramatic." He rose to his full height, shadows gathering around him. "The truth is embarrassingly simple: I wanted Varen dead because he controlled the creatures of night. Bound them with his ritual magic, restricted our hunting grounds, our feeding."

"Our?" Helena whispered.

"The ancient ones. The nightmares men fear." His eyes gleamed crimson in the darkness. "With him gone, we're free again. No more boundaries, no more rules." His hand shot out, fingers closing around her throat as he lifted her effortlessly. "No more need for human kingdoms at all."

Helena clawed at his hand, her newfound strength nothing compared to his ancient power. "You... loved me," she gasped.

"I loved what you represented — the key to Varen's destruction." His grip tightened. "Nothing more."

Realization struck her with devastating clarity. "The transformation... you never meant for me to survive it."

"Clever girl." Alaric's smile was almost fond. "You would have made a formidable vampire, given time. Unfortunately, that would complicate things considerably."

Helena's mind raced, searching desperately for some way to reach him. "Alaric, please — "

"Enough talking." His features hardened as he lifted her higher. "The night calls, and I've indulged this farewell long enough."

With terrifying speed, his hands moved to either side of her head.

Helena's scream died in her throat as Alaric wrenched with inhuman strength. The sound—like wet wood splintering—echoed through the silent forest as her head separated from her body.

Blood fountained from the severed neck as her body collapsed, twitching grotesquely before going still. Alaric held her head aloft, studying her face—eyes wide with final betrayal, mouth frozen in an unfinished plea.

"You really should have run when you had the chance," he told her lifeless eyes. Then, with casual disregard, he tossed her head aside into the underbrush.

Alaric straightened his tattered clothing, brushing forest debris from his sleeves with fastidious care. The night creatures were stirring now, drawn by the scent of royal blood. Shadows moved between distant trees as ancient beings long confined to legend emerged to investigate.

"Come," he called to them, arms spread wide in welcome. "The age of men wanes. Our time returns."

As he walked deeper into the Mistwood, leaving Helena's broken body behind, something moved in the darkness. A tendril of mist curled around her severed head, then her lifeless torso. More tendrils joined the first, weaving together into a familiar form—the mist entity of Ashfeld.

"Poor queen," it whispered, formless face hovering over her remains. "Betrayed twice in one night."

The mist thickened, enveloping Helena completely as Alaric's footsteps faded into the distance. The entity's voice resonated through the ancient trees, carrying a promise as old as death itself.

"But bargains cut both ways. And Hades... Hades remembers."

Deep in the Underworld, seated upon his throne of bones, the Lord of the Dead smiled.

The game was only beginning.

The bargain with Hades remained, its terms altered but not forgotten. In the Underworld, the Lord of the Dead smiled upon his bone throne, patient as only immortals can be.

After all, eternity was a very long time, and debts always came due in the end.

www.ingramcontent.com/pod-product-compliance
Lightning Source LLC
Chambersburg PA
CBHW070729120726
47910CB00001B/28